THE FOLK TALES OF SCOTLAND

EX LIBRIS

(Your name)

First published by the Bodley Head in 1975
This edition (with illustrations by Norah Montgomerie from
the 1956 Hogarth Press edition) published in 2005 by Mercat
Press, reprinted in 2008 by Birlinn Ltd, West Newington
House, 10 Newington Road, Edinburgh EH9 1QS
www.birlinn.co.uk

ISBN: 978-1-84158-694-6

'I have told you all the tales I can
remember, and I am glad that they have
been written. I hope they shorten the
night for those who read them or hear
them being read, and let them not forget
me in their prayers, nor the old people
from whom I myself learned them.'

Sean O Conaill, the great storyteller, to J. H. Delargy

Set in Adobe Jenson and Silvus at Mercat Press
Printed and bound in Great Britain by
Bell & Bain Ltd., Glasgow

THE FOLK TALES OF SCOTLAND

NORAH AND WILLIAM MONTGOMERIE

THE WELL AT THE WORLD'S END AND OTHER STORIES

BIRLINN

ACKNOWLEDGMENTS TO THE 1975 EDITION

ALL modern collections of folk tales rely on the work of a small band of nineteenth-century folklorists who, without typewriters, tape recorders or any other modern aids, listened to traditional storytellers and patiently wrote down, word for word, the stories they told and the songs they sang, with no thought of personal fame or reward. In Scotland, we all owe a special debt to such enthusiasts as J. F. Campbell, Lord Archibald Campbell and the Reverend J. Macdougall, who collected and translated folk tales from the Gaelic into English, and also to Robert Chambers who collected rhymes as well as stories in Lowland Scots. Their work might have been confined to the archives of the Scottish National Library, were it not for the farsighted publishers of the day, like Alexander Gardner of Paisley, David Nutt of London and Robert Chambers of Edinburgh. We are indebted to them all. We would have liked to thank by name all the kind folk and children who have encouraged us in one way and another. The first friend to reassure us was the poet, Edwin Muir, and the most recent encouragement has come from our friend, Kathleen Lines, who has edited so many fine children's books. Again, we too have been lucky enough to find discerning and helpful publishers, The Hogarth Press (who issued the earlier edition of *The Well at the World's End* in 1956) and now The Bodley Head. We thank them all.

Contents

INTRODUCTION TO THE 1975 EDITION

ONCE, walking in Wester Ross, we came to Loch Maree, one of the grandest of Scottish lochs, dominated by Ben Sleoch. It has twenty-seven islands, most of them in the middle where the water is more than two miles broad. That evening we heard of a holy well on one of the islands and next morning, borrowing the forester's boat, we rowed out into the loch. On the second day we found a round island with many oaks—trees famous in mythology and legend—but there was no well, only a small dead tree scaled with copper coins knocked into the wood with stones. We paid our tribute to the spirit of the place and rowed back to the shore.

Many years later we read the legend of the Princess Thyra of Ulster (see *The Legend of Loch Maree*, p. 224), written down by the Reverend J. G. Campbell of Tiree at the end of last century from the lips of an anonymous storyteller. The tree he describes, beside a well, with a hollow in its side into which gifts were dropped, may have been the mother of the little tree we saw. There were no ruins of monastery or chapel, but this well and another are in the title of this book.

We have sat with the travellers, once called tinkers, listening till long after midnight to their Lowland tales, driving home in the dark through an Angus mist so thick the trees by the roadside were invisible. We have listened to, and recorded, Jeannie Robertson in Aberdeen singing the traditional ballads and songs which had come to her from her mother, and not from books.

The stories in this book, all of them, came originally out of that world of storytellers and singers. For many years they were passed on from one storyteller to another. For a very long time they were not written down, nor printed, but there are a few references to some of them. James IV of Scotland (1488-1513) encouraged tale-tellers, minstrels, stage-players, singers, fools or privileged buffoons, and jesters, who might contribute to the amusement of the court.' Sir David Lindsay, Scottish poet and tutor to the King's son, tells us some of the things he taught the young Prince (later James V):

> The Propheceis of Rymour, Beid and Marlyng,
> And of mony uther plesand starye,
> Of the Reid Etin, and the Gyir Carlyng,
> Confortand thee, quhen that I saw thee sorye.

The Red Etin (p. 206) is one of the stories in this book.

Some of these stories have appeared over and over again. Childe Rowland to the Dark Tower Came (p. 231) was used by George Peele, the Elizabethan dramatist, in his Old Wives' Tale (1595); Shakespeare quoted the title in King Lear (III, iv, 197), and Robert Browning based a poem on the title.

The song of Pippety Pew (p. 42) also has many variants. A woman in Forfar told us her mother had composed it, but Goethe adapted the same song—Margarete sings it in prison at the end of the first part of Faust. The Juniper Tree, in Grimm, is a variant of the Pippety Pew story.

What we now call Scotland was Celtic in language and culture before the Scots from Ireland invaded from the west, bringing with them their Gaelic songs and stories. This happened around 500 A.D., and many of their tales are still told in the Hebrides and Highlands. Some of them, translated into English, are in this book.

About the same time, Teutonic Angles from the south penetrated into what is now Scotland. They spoke a form of English, which became the Scottish language, and has now broken up into the Lowland dialects of the southern Uplands, the central Lowlands and the north-east, ringing the Highlands and pressing in on the Gaelic speakers of the West Highlands and Islands. Most of the tales told in Scots are retold in this book in English. We have included one story, *Robin Reidbreist and the Wran*, in the original Scots, to give some idea of the folk qualities of the Scottish version.

Orkney and Shetland tales are a small third group. They have some Scandinavian overtones.

The Gaelic tales posed particular problems of adaptation. Professor Delargy, in his fascinating Rhys Memorial Lecture of 1945, said: 'To read these tales is for many of us today a dreary duty, as we strip apart the story imprisoned in the tangled net of this beloved verbiage.' To ourselves we described the process of adaptation to modern taste as chipping away the barnacles and sea-tangle, aiming at conciseness and clarification of obscurities where necessary; but we have tried not to lose the oral flavour of the original.

The Hogarth Press, who published our collections of Scottish nursery rhymes, first issued *The Well at the World's End* in 1956. The publication of this new edition by the Bodley Head has given us the opportunity to add twenty new tales. There are, of course, many more in the great nineteenth-century collections, and more are being collected and published even now. The list of sources at the back of this book will be a guide for those who wish to read further.

The Well at the World's End

ONCE upon a time there was a King and a Queen. The King had a daughter and the Queen had a daughter. The King's daughter was good-natured and everybody liked her. The Queen's daughter was bad-tempered and nobody liked her. Now, the Queen was jealous of the King's daughter, and wished her away. So she sent her to the Well at the World's End to fetch a bottle of water, thinking she would never return.

The King's daughter took a bottle, and away she went. Far and far she went, till she came to a pony tethered to a tree, and the pony said to her:

'Free me, free me,
My bonny maiden,
For I've not been free
Seven years and a day!'

'Yes, I'll free you,' said the King's daughter, and she did.

'Jump on my back,' said the pony, 'and I'll carry you over the moor of sharp thorns.'

So she jumped on his back, and the pony carried her over the moor of sharp thorns, then they parted. The King's daughter went on far, and far, and farther than I can tell, till she came to the Well at the World's End.

She found the Well was very deep and she couldn't dip her bottle. As she was looking down into the dark Well, wondering what to do, she saw three scaly men's heads. They looked up at her and said:

'Wash me, wash me,
My bonny maiden,
And dry me with
Your clean linen apron!'

'Yes, I'll wash you,' said the King's daughter.

She washed the three scaly heads, and dried them with her clean linen apron. They took her bottle, dipped it and filled it with well water.

Then the three scaly men's heads said one to the other:

'Wish, Brother, wish! What will you wish?'

'I wish if she was bonny before, she'll be ten times bonnier now,' said the first.

'I wish that every time she speaks there will drop a ruby, a diamond and a pearl from her mouth,' said the second.

'I wish that every time she combs her hair she'll comb a peck of gold and a peck of silver from it,' said the third.

The King's daughter went home, and if she was bonny before, she was ten times bonnier now. Each time she spoke, a ruby, a diamond, and a pearl dropped from her mouth. Each time she combed her hair she combed a peck of gold and a peck of silver out of it.

The Queen was so angry she didn't know what to do. She thought she would send her own daughter to the Well at the World's End to see if she would have the same luck. She gave her a bottle and sent her to fill it with water from the Well.

The Queen's daughter went, and went, till she came to the tethered pony, and the pony said:

'Free me, free me,
My bonny maiden,
For I've not been free
Seven years and a day!'

'Oh, you stupid creature, do you think I'll free you?' said she. 'I am the Queen's daughter.'

'Then I'll not carry you over the moor of sharp thorns,' said the pony.

So the Queen's daughter had to go on her bare feet, and the thorns cut them. She could scarcely walk at all.

She went far, and far, and farther than I can tell, till she came to the Well at the World's End. But the Well was so deep that she couldn't reach the water to fill her bottle. As she sat there, wondering what to do, three scaly men's heads looked up at her, and said:

> 'Wash me, wash me,
> My bonny maiden,
> And dry me with
> Your clean linen apron!'

'Oh, you horrid creatures, do you think I am going to wash you?' she said. 'I am the Queen's daughter.'

She did not wash their heads and so they did not dip her bottle and fill it for her. They said one to the other:

'Wish, brother, wish! What will you wish?'

'I wish that if she was ugly before, she'll be ten times uglier now,' said the first.

'I wish that every time she speaks there will drop a frog and a toad from her mouth,' said the second.

'I wish that every time she combs her hair she'll comb a peck of lice and a peck of fleas out of it,' said the third.

So the Queen's daughter went home with an empty bottle. The Queen was mad with rage, for if her daughter had been ugly before, she was ten times uglier now, and each time she spoke a frog and a toad dropped from her mouth. Each time she combed her hair, she combed a peck of lice and fleas out of it. So they had to send her away from the Court.

A young Prince came and married the King's daughter, but the Queen's daughter had to put up with an ill-natured cobbler, who beat her every day.

RASHIE COAT

RASHIE Coat was a King's daughter, and her father wanted her to marry, but she did not like the man he had chosen. Her father said she must marry this man, so she went to a hen-wife to ask her advice.

'Say you won't take him,' said the hen-wife, 'unless you're given a coat of beaten gold.'

Her father gave her a coat of beaten gold, but she didn't want the man for all that. So she went to the hen-wife again.

'Say you won't take the man unless you are given a coat made of feathers from all the birds of the air,' said the hen-wife.

So the King sent a man with a large basket of oats, who called to the birds of the air:

'Each bird take up a grain and put down a feather! Each bird take up a grain and put down a feather!'

So each bird took up a grain and put down a feather, and all the feathers were made into a coat and given to Rashie Coat. But she didn't want the man for all that.

She went to the hen-wife and asked her what she should do.

'Say you won't take him unless you're given a coat and slippers made of rushes,' said the hen-wife.

The King gave her a coat and slippers made of rushes, but she did not like the man for all that. So she went to the hen-wife again.

'I can't help you any more,' said the hen-wife.

So Rashie Coat left her father's house and went far, and far, and farther than I can tell, till she came to another King's house.

'What do you want?' said the servants, when she went to the door.

'I would like to work in this house,' said Rashie Coat.

So they put her in the kitchen to wash the dishes, and take out the ashes.

When the Sabbath Day came, everyone went to the Kirk, but Rashie Coat was left at home to cook the dinner. While she was alone a fairy came to her, and told her to put on the coat of beaten gold, and go to the Kirk.

'I can't do that,' she said. 'I have to cook the dinner.' The fairy told her to go and she would cook the dinner. So Rashie Coat said:

'One peat make another peat burn,
One spit make another spit turn,
One pot make another pot play,
Let Rashie Coat go to the Kirk today.'

Then she put on her coat of beaten gold, and went to the Kirk. There the King's son saw her and fell in love with her, but she left before everyone else, and he couldn't find out who she was. When she reached home, she found the dinner cooked, and nobody knew she had been out of the house.

The next Sabbath Day the fairy came again, and told her to put on the coat of feathers from all the birds of the air, and go to the Kirk, for she would cook the dinner for her. So Rashie Coat said:

'One peat make another peat burn,
One spit make another spit turn,
One pot make another pot play,
Let Rashie Coat go to the Kirk today.'

Then she put on her coat of feathers, and went to the Kirk. Again she left before anyone else, and when the King's son saw her go out, he followed her. But she had already vanished, and he could not find out who she was. When she reached the kitchen, she took off the coat of feathers, and found the dinner cooked. Nobody knew she had been out at all.

The next Sabbath Day the fairy came once more, and told her to put on her coat of rushes and the slippers, and go to the Kirk while the dinner was being cooked. So Rashie Coat said:

> 'One peat make another peat burn,
> One spit make another spit turn,
> One pot make another pot play,
> Let Rashie Coat go to the Kirk today.'

Then she put on her coat of rushes and the pair of slippers and went to the Kirk.

This time the King's son sat near the door. When he saw Rashie Coat slipping out before everyone else, he followed her at once, but again she was too quick for him, and was nowhere to be seen.

She ran home, but in her haste she lost one of her slippers. The Prince found the slipper, and sent a Royal Proclamation through all the country, announcing that he would marry whosoever could put on the slipper.

All the ladies of the Court, and their ladies-in-waiting, tried to put on the slipper, but it wouldn't fit any of them, nor the daughters of merchants, farmers and tradesmen who came from far and wide to try their luck. Then the old hen-wife brought her ugly daughter to try it on. She nipped her foot and clipped her foot, and squeezed it on that way. So the King's son said he would marry her.

He was riding away with her on horseback, and she behind him, when they came to a wood, and there was a bird sitting on a tree. As they rode by, the bird sang:

> 'Nipped foot and clipped foot
> Behind the King's son rides;
> But bonny foot and true foot
> Behind the cauldron hides.'

When the King's son heard this, he flung the hen-wife's daughter off the horse, and rode home. He looked behind the cauldron in the royal kitchen and there he found Rashie Coat. He tried the slipper on her foot and it went on easily. So he married her and they lived happily ever after.

Prince Iain

ONCE upon a time there was a King and a Queen, and they had one son. But the Queen died, and the King married another wife. The name of the first Queen's son was Iain. He was handsome and a good hunter. No bird could escape his arrow, and he could bring venison home any day he went out hunting.

But one day he was unlucky for the first time. He saw no deer, and when he shot an arrow at a Blue Falcon, he knocked a feather out of her wing. Putting the feather into his bag, he went home.

'What did you kill today?' said his stepmother.

Iain took the Blue Falcon's feather from his bag and gave it to her.

'I'm putting a spell on you,' said his stepmother. 'The water will run into your shoes and out again, and your feet will be cold and wet with brown bog-water, till you bring me the bird this feather is from.'

'I'm putting a spell on YOU,' said Prince Iain to the Queen, his stepmother. 'Till I come back, you will stand with one foot on that house, and your other foot on that castle and suffer every tempest and every wind that blows.'

Prince Iain went off as fast as he could, leaving his stepmother with one foot on the house and her other foot on the castle. (She was much colder than he was with his wet feet.)

Prince Iain walked all day over waste land, looking for the Blue Falcon. As night fell, the little birds flew off to roost in the trees and bushes. When it was dark, Iain sheltered under a briar bush, when who should pass but Gillie Martin the Fox.

'No wonder you're down in the mouth, Prince Iain,' said he. 'You've come on a bad night. All I've got to eat is a sheep's leg and cheek. We'll have to do with that.'

So they lit a fire and roasted the scraps of mutton. After their scanty supper, they slept side by side under the briar bush till morning.

'Prince Iain,' said the Fox, 'the Blue Falcon you're looking for belongs to the Big Giant with Five Heads. I'll show you where his house is, and my advice to you is this, become his servant. Tell him you can feed birds and swine, or look after cows, goats and sheep. Be quick to do everything he asks you, and be very good to his birds. In time he may trust you to feed his Blue Falcon. When this happens, be very kind to the bird and when the Giant is not at home, carry her off. But, take care that not one feather touches anything in the Giant's house. If this happens, you'll be in trouble.'

'I'll be careful,' said Prince Iain.

He went to the Giant's house and knocked on the door.

'Who's there?' shouted the Giant.

'It's me,' said Iain. 'I've come to see if you need a servant.'

'What are you good at?' asked the Giant.

'I can feed birds and swine. I can feed and milk a cow, or goats or sheep.'

'It's a lad like you I want,' said the Giant, coming out of his house.

They came to an agreement about Iain's wages, and the lad began to feed the Giant's birds and animals. He was kind to the hens and the ducks. The Giant saw how well Iain was doing, and compared his food now with what it had been before Iain came. The hens and the ducks tasted better, and the Giant said he would rather have one now than two he had had before.

'This lad's so good, I think I can trust him to feed my Blue Falcon,' said the Giant. So he gave Iain the Blue Falcon to look after, and the lad took great care of the bird, such care that the Giant thought Iain could be trusted to look after the Blue Falcon when its master was away from home.

So the Giant left his house one day in Iain's care. 'Now's my chance,' said Iain. He seized the Falcon and opened the door, but when the Falcon saw the daylight she spread her wings to fly, and one feather of one wing touched the doorpost. The doorpost screamed, and the Giant came running home. He took the Blue Falcon from Iain.

'I'll not give you my Falcon,' said the Giant, 'unless you bring me the White Sword of Light from the Big Women of Jura.'

Prince Iain had to leave the Giant's house at once, and he wandered through the waste land. As it was growing dark, Gillie Martin the Fox met him.

'You're down in the mouth,' said the Fox, 'because you'll not do as I tell you. This is another bad night like the last. All I've got to eat is a sheep's leg and cheek. We'll have to do with that.'

They lit a fire and cooked the mutton in the white flame of the dripping fat. After supper they went to sleep on the ground until morning.

'We'll go to the edge of the ocean,' said Gillie Martin. So Iain went with the Fox to the shore.

'I'll shape-shift myself into a boat,' said the Fox. 'Go on board and I'll take you over to Jura. Go to the Seven Big Women of Jura and be their servant. When they ask you what you can do, say you're good at polishing steel and iron, gold and silver. Take care you do everything well, till they trust you with the White Sword of Light. When you have a chance, run off with it, but take care the sheath does not touch anything in the house, or you'll be in trouble.'

Gillie Martin the Fox changed into a boat, and Iain went on board. When the boat reached land to the north of Jura, Iain jumped ashore and went off to take service with the Seven Big Women of Jura. He reached their house and knocked on the door.

'What are you looking for?' they asked him.

'I'm looking for work,' said Iain. 'I can polish gold and silver, steel and iron.'

'We need a lad like you,' they said.

They agreed about his wages, and for six weeks Iain worked very hard. The Big Women were watching him.

'This is the best lad we've had,' they said. 'Now we may trust him with the White Sword of Light.'

They gave him the White Sword of Light to look after, and he took great care of it, till one day the Big Women were out of the house. Iain thought this was his chance. He put the White Sword of Light into its sheath and put it over his shoulder, but going out of the door the sheath touched the lintel of the door, and the lintel screamed. The Seven Big Women came running home and took the Sword from him.

'We'll not give you our White Sword of Light, unless you give us in return the Yellow Filly of the King of Erin.'

Iain went to the shore of the ocean, where Gillie Martin met him.

'You're down in the mouth, Iain,' said the Fox, 'because you'll not do as I tell you. This is another bad night like the last. All I've got to eat is a sheep's leg and cheek. We'll have to do with that.'

They lit a fire, cooked the mutton and satisfied their hunger.

'I'll shape-shift myself and become a barque,' said Gillie Martin the Fox. 'Go aboard and I'll take you to Erin. When we reach Erin, go to the house of the King and ask service as a stable-lad. When he asks what you can do, tell him you can groom and feed horses, polish the silver-work and the steel-work on their harness. Be willing to do everything necessary and keep the horses and their harness in good order, till the King trusts you with the Yellow Filly. This will give you a chance to run away with her. But take care when you're leading her out that no bit of her, except her shoes, touches anything within the stable gate, or there'll be trouble.'

Everything happened as the Fox said, till they reached the King's house.

'Where are you going?' asked the gate-keeper,

'To see if the King has need of a stable-lad,' said Iain.

So he was taken to the King, who said: 'What are you looking for here?'

'I came to see if you needed a stable-lad.'

'What can you do?'

'I can groom and feed the horses, polish the silver-work and the steel-work on their harness.'

So the King gave him the job at good wages. Soon the King noticed that his horses had never looked so well, so he gave Iain the Yellow Filly to care for. The Yellow Filly improved so much in appearance and speed that she could leave the wind behind her and overtake the wind ahead.

One day the King went out hunting, leaving the Yellow Filly in her stable. Iain saw that this was his chance, so he saddled and bridled her and took her out of the stable. But at the gate the Yellow Filly flicked her tail and touched the gate-post. The gate-post screamed, and the King came galloping back from the hunt.

'I'll not give you the Yellow Filly, unless you fetch me the daughter of the King of France,' he said. So Iain went down to the seashore, where he met Gillie Martin.

'You're down in the mouth,' said the Fox, 'because you'll not do as I tell you. But I'll turn myself into a ship and take you to France in no time.'

The Fox changed himself into a ship, and Iain went on board. Soon they came to France, where the ship ran herself aground on a rock. Then Iain climbed down on to the shore and walked up to the King's house.

'Where have you come from, and what are you doing here?' asked the King of France.

'A great storm came on, and we lost our captain at sea. Our ship is aground on a rock, and I don't know if we'll get her off again,' said Iain.

The King and Queen and their family went down to the shore to see the ship. As they were looking at it, wonderful music sounded on board, and the King of France's daughter went with Iain on board to find out where the music came from. But the music was always in another part of the ship, till at last it came from the upper deck. The Princess and Iain climbed to the upper deck to find that the ship was, by that time, far out at sea, out of sight of land.

'That's a bad trick you played on me,' said the Princess. 'Where are you taking me?'

'To Erin,' said Iain, 'to give you to the King of Erin in return for the Yellow Filly, which I'll give to the Seven Big Women of Jura in return for their Sword of Light, which I'll give to the Giant with the Five Heads in return for his Blue Falcon, which I'll take home to my stepmother so that she'll free me from her spells. But you'll be safe with the King of Erin, who wishes to make you his wife.'

'I'd rather be your wife,' said the King of France's daughter.

When the ship came to the shores of Erin, Gillie Martin changed himself into a woman as beautiful as the King of France's daughter.

'Leave the King of France's daughter here till we come back,' said the Fox. 'I'll go with you to the King of Erin, and give him enough of a wife!'

So the Fox, in the form of a beautiful young woman, took Iain's arm. The King of Erin came to meet them, and gave Iain the Yellow Filly with a golden saddle on her back, and a silver bridle. Iain galloped back to the King of France's daughter who was still waiting by the seashore.

Meanwhile, the King of Erin and his new wife went to bed. But in the night, Gillie Martin changed back from a beautiful young woman and became the Fox again. He tore the flesh from the King, from his neck to his waist, and left him a cripple. Then the Fox ran down to the shore where Iain and the Princess of France were waiting.

'Leave the Princess and the Yellow Filly here,' said the Fox. 'I'll go with you to the Seven Big Women of Jura, and give them enough of fillies!'

Then the Fox changed himself into a yellow filly. Iain saddled him with a golden saddle, and bridled him with a silver bridle, and rode on the filly's back to the Seven Big Women of Jura, who gave him the White Sword of Light in exchange for the filly. Iain took the golden saddle and the silver bridle off the yellow filly, and carried them, with the White Sword of Light, back to the shore. Here the Princess of France was waiting with the real Yellow Filly.

Meanwhile the Seven Big Women of Jura, very eager to ride on the back of the Yellow Filly, put a saddle on the Fox's back. The first Big Woman climbed into the saddle. The second Big Woman climbed on to the back of the first Big Woman; and the third Big Woman climbed on to the back of the second Big Woman; and the fourth Big Woman climbed on to the back of the third Big Woman; and the fifth Big Woman climbed on to the back of the fourth Big Woman; and the sixth Big Woman climbed on to the back of the fifth Big Woman; and the seventh Big Woman climbed on to the back of the sixth Big Woman.

The first Big Woman hit the filly with a stick. The filly ran backward and forward with the Seven Big Women of Jura on her back. Then she ran across moors, and then she ran up a mountain to the very top. She stopped with her forefeet on the edge of a precipice, kicked up her hind legs, and threw the Seven Big Women of Jura over the cliff. Then the filly changed back into the Fox, and ran laughing down to the seashore where Iain and the Princess of France, and the real Yellow Filly, and the White Sword of Light, were all waiting for him.

Gillie Martin the Fox became a boat and Iain helped the Princess of France into the boat, with the Yellow Filly, and carried the Sword of

Light on board. Then the boat took them across the water to the mainland, where it changed back into Gillie Martin the Fox.

'Leave the Princess here,' said the Fox, 'and the Yellow Filly, and the Sword of Light. I'll change into a white sword, which you will give to the Giant with Five Heads. In return he'll give you the Blue Falcon. I'll see that he has enough of swords!'

When the Giant with Five Heads saw Iain coming with the sword, he thought it was the White Sword of Light, and he put the Blue Falcon into a basket and gave it to Iain, who carried the Blue Falcon back to the seashore where he had left the Princess waiting with the Yellow Filly and the real Sword of Light.

Meanwhile, the Giant with the Five Heads began fencing with the white sword, and swinging it round his head. Suddenly the sword bent itself and, before the Giant realised what was happening, he cut off his own heads, all five of them. Then the sword changed back into Gillie Martin the Fox, who ran down to the seashore where he had left Iain and the Princess.

'Now, listen carefully,' he said to Iain. 'Put the gold saddle on the Yellow Filly, and the silver bridle. Let the Princess of France, with the Blue Falcon in its basket, sit behind you on the back of the Yellow Filly. You, Iain, will hold the White Sword of Light with the back of the blade against your nose, and the edge of the sword toward your stepmother, the Queen. If you make any mistake, your stepmother will change you into a faggot of firewood. But do as I tell you, with the sword held exactly as I have said. When she tries to bewitch you she will fall down as a bundle of sticks.'

Iain was specially careful this time, and did exactly as Gillie Martin the Fox told him. He held the Sword of Light with the back of its blade against his nose, and the edge of the sword towards his stepmother, the Queen, and when she fell down as a bundle of firewood, Prince Iain burned her to wood ash.

Now he had the best wife in Scotland; and the Yellow Filly, that could leave one wind behind her and catch the wind in front; and the Blue Falcon which kept him supplied with plenty of game; and the White Sword of Light to defend him from his enemies.

'You're welcome,' said Prince Iain to Gillie Martin the Fox, 'to hunt over my ground, and take any beast you want. I'll forbid my servants to fire a single arrow at you, no matter what you do, even if you take a lamb from my flocks.'

'Keep your herd of sheep!' said the Fox. 'There's plenty of sheep in Scotland without troubling you!'

With that, Gillie Martin the Fox blessed Prince Iain and his Princess, wished them well and went on his way.

THE FLEA AND THE LOUSE

The Flea and the Louse lived together in a house:
  And as they shook their sheets,
The Flea she stumbled and fell in the fire,
  And now the Louse she weeps.

The Pot-hook he saw the Louse weeping.

'Louse! Louse! Why are you weeping?'

'Oh! The Flea and I were shaking our sheets:
The Flea she fell and she fell in the fire,
So what can I do but weep?'

'Oh, then,' said the Hook,
'I'll wig-wag back and forward!'

So the Hook wig-wagged, and Louse she wept.

The Chair saw the Hook wig-wagging.

'Hook! Hook! Why are you wig-wagging?'

'Oh! The Flea and the Louse were shaking their sheets:
The Flea she fell in the fire and burned,
So the Louse she weeps, and I wig-wag.'

'Oh, then,' said the Chair,
'I'll jump over the floor.'

So the Chair he jumped; and the Hook wig-wagged; and the Louse she wept.

The Door he saw the Chair jumping.

'Chair! Chair! Why are you jumping on the floor?'

'Oh! The Flea and the Louse were shaking their sheets;
The Flea she falls in the fire, and the Louse she weeps;
The Hook wig-wags, and so I jump.'

'Oh, then,' said the Door,
I'll jingle-jangle on my hinges.'

So the Door jingle-jangled; the Chair he jumped; the Hook wig-wagged; and the Louse she wept.

The Midden he saw the Door jingle-jangling.

'Door! Door! Why are you jingle-jangling on your hinges?'

'Oh! The Flea and the Louse were shaking their sheets;
The Flea she fell in the fire, and the Louse she weeps;
The Hook wig-wags; the Chair he jumps,
And I jingle-jangle on my hinges.'

'Oh, then,' said the Midden,
I'll swarm over with maggots.'

So the Midden he swarmed; the Door jingle-jangled; the Chair he jumped; the Hook wig-wagged; and the Louse she wept.

The Burn he saw the Midden swarming.

'Midden! Midden! Why are you swarming over with maggots?'

'Oh! The Flea and the Louse were shaking their sheets;
The Flea she fell in the fire, and the Louse she weeps;
The Hook wig-wags; the Chair he jumps;
The Door jingle-jangles; and I swarm over with maggots.'

'Oh, then,' said the Burn,
'I'll run wimple-wample.'

So the Burn ran wimple-wample; the Midden he swarmed; the Door jingle-jangled; the Chair he jumped; the Hook wig-wagged; and the Louse she wept.

The Loch he saw the Burn running wimple-wample.

'Burn! Burn! Why are you running wimple-wample?'

'Oh! The Flea and the Louse were shaking their sheets;
The Flea she fell in the fire, and the Louse she weeps;
The Hook wig-wags; the Chair he jumps;
The Door jingle-jangles; the Midden swarms over with maggots,
And I run wimple-wample.'

'Oh, then,' said the Loch,
I'll swell over my brim.'

So the Loch he swelled and he swelled; the Burn ran wimple-wample; the Midden he swarmed; the Door jingle-jangled; the Chair he jumped; the Hook wig-wagged; and the Louse she wept.

Then down came the flood and swept away the house and the Louse, the Hook and the Chair, the Door and the Midden with the maggots— all down the meadow where the Burn ran wimple-wample.

So ends the story of the Flea and the Louse.

WHUPPITY STOORIE

THE Goodman of Kittlerumpit was a bit of a vagabond. He went to the fair one day and was never heard of again.

When the Goodman had gone, the Goodwife was left with little to live on. Few belongings she had, and a wee son. Everybody was sorry for her, but nobody helped her. However she had a sow, that was her consolation, for the sow was soon to farrow, and she hoped for a fine litter of piglets.

But one day, when the Wife went to the sty to fill the sow's trough, what did she find but the sow lying on her back, grunting and groaning, and ready to die.

This was a blow to the Goodwife, so she sat down on the flat knocking stone, with her bairn on her knee, and wept more sorely than she did for the loss of her Goodman.

Now, the cottage of Kittlerumpit was built on a brae, with a fir-wood behind it. So, as the Goodwife was wiping her eyes, what did she see but a strange little old woman coming up the brae. She was dressed in green, all but a white apron, a black velvet hood, and a steeple-crowned hat on her head. She had a walking-stick as long as herself in her hand. As the Green Lady drew near, the Goodwife rose and made a curtsey.

'Madam,' said she, 'I'm the most unlucky woman alive.'

'I don't want to hear piper's news and fiddler's tales,' said the Green Lady. 'I know you've lost your Goodman, and your sow is sick. Now, what will you give me if I cure her?'

'Any thing you like,' said the stupid Goodwife, not guessing who she had to deal with.

'Let's wet thumbs on that bargain,' said the Green Lady.

So thumbs were wet, and into the sty she marched.

The Green Lady looked at the sow with a frown, and then began to mutter to herself words the Goodwife couldn't understand. They sounded like:

> 'Pitter patter,
> Haly watter.'

Then she took out of her pocket a wee bottle with some kind of oil in it, and rubbed the sow with it above the snout, behind the ears and on top of the tail.

'Get up, beast,' said the Green Lady. Up got the sow with a grunt, and away to her trough for her dinner.

The Goodwife of Kittlerumpit was overjoyed when she saw that,

'Now that I've cured your sick beast, let us carry out our bargain,' said the Green Lady. 'You'll not find me unreasonable. I always like to

do a turn for small reward. All I ask, and *will* have, is that wee son in your arms.'

The Goodwife gave a shriek like a stuck pig, for she now knew that the Green Lady was a fairy. So she wept, and she begged, but it was no use.

'You can spare your row,' said the fairy, 'shrieking as if I was as deaf as a door nail; but I can't, by the law we live by, take your bairn till the third day after this; and not then, if you can tell me my name.'

With that the fairy went away down the brae and out of sight.

The Goodwife of Kittlerumpit could not sleep that night for weeping, holding her bairn so tight that she nearly squeezed the breath out of him.

The next day she went for a walk in the wood behind her cottage. Her bairn in her arms, she went far among the trees till she came to an old quarry overgrown with grass, and a bonny spring well in the middle of it. As she drew near, she heard the whirring of a spinning-wheel, and a voice singing a song. So the Wife crept quietly among the bushes, and peeped over the side of the quarry. And what did she see but the Green Lady at her spinning-wheel singing:

> *'Little kens our goodwife at hame*
> *That* WHUPPITY STOORIE *is my name!'*

'Ah, ah!' thought the Goodwife, 'I've got the secret word at last!'

So she went home with a lighter heart than when she came out, and she laughed at the thought of tricking the fairy.

Now, this Goodwife was a merry woman, so she decided to have some sport with the fairy. At the appointed time she put her bairn behind the knocking stone, and sat down on it herself. She pulled her bonnet over her left ear, twisted her mouth on the other side as if she were weeping. She looked the picture of misery. Well, she hadn't long to wait, for up the brae came the fairy, neither lame nor lazy, and long before she reached the knocking stone, she skirled out:

'Goodwife of Kittlerumpit! You well know what I have come for!'

The Goodwife pretended to weep more bitterly than before, wringing her hands and falling on her knees.

'Och, dear mistress,' said she, 'spare my only bairn and take my sow!'

'The deil take the sow for my share,' said the fairy. 'I didn't come here for swine's flesh. Don't be contrary, Goodwife, but give me your child instantly!'

'Ochon, dear lady,' said the weeping Goodwife, 'leave my bairn and take me!'

'The deil's in the daft woman,' said the fairy, looking like the far end of a fiddle. 'I'm sure she's clean demented. Who in all the earthly world, with half an eye in their head, would be bothered with the likes of you?'

This made the Goodwife of Kittlerumpit bristle, for though she had two bleary eyes, and a long red nose besides, she thought herself as bonny as the best of them. She soon got up off her knees, set her bonnet straight, and with her hands folded before her, made a curtsey to the ground.

'I might have known,' said she, 'that the likes of me isn't fit to tie the shoe-strings of the high and mighty fairy WHUPPITY STOORIE!'

The name made the fairy leap high. Down she came again, dump on her heels, and whirling round, she ran down the hill like an owlet chased by witches.

The Goodwife of Kittlerumpit laughed till she nearly burst. Then she took up her bairn and went into her house, singing to him all the way:

> 'Coo and gurgle, my bonny wee tyke,
> You'll now have your four-houries
> Since we've gien Nick a bone to pick,
> With his wheels and his WHUPPITY STOORIES.'

The Fairy-Wife and the Cooking-Pot

CROFTER'S wife had a black iron cooking-pot, and every day a fairy-wife borrowed it. The fairy said nothing, just seized the pot. Each time she made off with it, the goodwife of the croft called after her:

> 'A smith can make cold iron hot with coal.
> A cooking-pot needs meat and bones,
> So bring it back well-filled and whole!'

The fairy always returned the pot filled with meat and bones.

Now, one day, the goodwife had to go by ferry to the town on the mainland, and before she went, she said to her husband:

'Promise you'll say my rhyme to the fairy-wife when she comes for the pot today, then I'll go to town with a quiet mind.'

'I'll do that,' said he. 'I'll do whatever you tell me.'

So the goodwife left her husband busy twisting heather ropes. But when he saw the fairy-wife coming up the hill, he noticed she had no shadow and glided over the ground, unlike any mortal. Terrified, he fled into the house and slammed the door.

The fairy-wife came to the door but the goodman didn't open it. He was too frightened and forgot what his wife had told him to say. So the fairy climbed on to the thatched roof of the croft and stood beside the smoke-hole. The cooking-pot was on the fire, underneath the smoke-hole, and suddenly it gave a leap right through the smoke-hole. The fairy-wife caught it and carried it off, and the goodman was pleased to see the back of her.

Night came but the fairy-wife did not. Only the goodwife came home, and the first thing she looked for was her cooking-pot. She looked high and low but it was nowhere to be seen.

'Where's my cooking-pot?' she cried.

'I don't know,' said her husband, 'and I don't care. When I saw that fairy-wife, I was so scared I shut the door tight. The fairy climbed on to the roof and stood by the smoke-hole. Then the cooking-pot leapt up right through the smoke-hole. She seized it, took it away, and didn't bring it back.'

'You good-for-nothing wretch, what have you done? There'll be no supper for us this night.'

'She'll bring it back tomorrow, you'll see.'

'She will not.'

Next day, the goodwife climbed the hill behind the cottage. At the top was an entrance to the fairies' cave. The goodwife went in, and there, asleep either side of the fire, were two little old men with long white beards, dressed in green. On the hearth was the cooking-pot, half-filled with food. The fairies had eaten their supper and gone off to sleep.

The goodwife crept over to the pot. Very quietly, she took hold of the handle and carried it off, without a word or a blessing for the two old fairy-men, still asleep by the fire.

The pot was very awkward and heavy to carry, and as the goodwife was going out, it knocked against the entrance. There was a terrible shriek. The two old men woke up, sprang to their feet and, when they saw the goodwife carrying off the pot, they screamed:

> 'Silent wife! Silent wife!
> Who came here from the land of chase.
> You, man who guards the fairy hill,
> Let loose the Black Hound, slip the Fierce!'

The goodwife ran so fast the old men couldn't catch her, but the two great dogs were faster. She heard them getting nearer and nearer, so she threw them pieces of food from the pot. The dogs stopped to eat, but soon they had finished and were close at her heels again. She threw them another piece from the pot and ran on, knowing that the hounds were not far behind. She wondered how much meat was left in the pot and if it would last till she reached home.

It was getting dark, but the goodwife could see the lamp shining in the cottage window. She knew she hadn't far to go, but the fairy hounds were closing in on her and she could hear them panting. Then she turned the pot upside-down, threw them every scrap of meat that was left, and reached home safely.

The farm dogs came running to meet her. When they heard the bark of the fairy hounds, they barked even louder. The black hounds stopped in their tracks, stared at the farm dogs and were too frightened to go any nearer. Then they turned and ran off up the hill.

The crofter was very pleased to see his wife and she was glad to be home. The fairy-wife never came to borrow the cooking-pot again and it was never empty.

The Maiden Fair and the Fountain Fairy

Long, long ago a drover courted and married the Miller of Cuthilldorie's only daughter. The drover learned how to grind the corn, and so he set up with his young wife as the Miller of Cuthilldorie when the old miller died. They did not have very much money to begin with, but an old Highlander lent them some silver, and soon they did well.

By and by the young miller and his wife had a daughter, but on the very night she was born the fairies stole her away. The wee thing was carried far away from the house into the wood of Cuthilldorie, where she was found on the very lip of the Black Well. In the air was heard a lilting:

> 'O we'll come back again, my honey, my hert,
> We'll come back again, my ain kind dearie;
> And you will mind upon a time
> When we met in the wood at the Well so wearie!'

The lassie grew up to be by far the bonniest lass in all the country-side. Everything went well at the mill.

One dark night there came a woodcock with a glowing tinder in its beak, and set fire to the mill. Everything was burnt and the miller and his wife were left without a thing in the world. To make matters worse, who should come along next day but the old Highlander who had lent them the silver, demanding payment.

Now, there was a wee old man in the wood of Cuthilldorie beside the Black Well, who would never stay in a house if he could help it. In the winter he went away, nobody knew where. He was an ugly bogle, not more than two and a half feet high.

He had been seen only three times in fifteen years since he came to the place, for he always flew up out of sight when anybody came near him. But if you crept cannily through the wood after dark, you might have heard him playing with the water, and singing the same song:

> 'O when will you come, my honey, my hert,
> O when will you come, my ain kind dearie;
> For don't you mind upon the time
> We met in the wood at the Well so wearie?'

Well, the night after the firing of the mill, the miller's daughter wandered into the wood alone, and wandered and wandered till she came to the Black Well. Then the wee bogle gripped her and jumped about singing:

> 'O come with me, my honey, my hert,
> O come with me, my ain kind dearie;
> For don't you mind upon the time
> We met in the wood at the Well so wearie?'

With that he made her drink three double handfuls of witched water, and away they flew on a flash of lightning. When the poor lass opened her eyes, she was in a palace, all gold and silver and diamonds, and full of fairies.

The King and Queen of the Fairies invited her to stay, and said she would be well looked after. But if she wanted to go home again, she must never tell anybody where she had been or what she had seen.

She said she wanted to go home, and promised to do as she was told. Then the King said:

'The first stranger you meet, give him brose.'

'Give him bannocks,' said the Queen.

'Give him butter,' said her King.

'Give him a drink of the Black Well water,' they both said.

Then they gave her twelve drops of liquid in a wee green bottle, three drops for the brose, three for the bannocks, three for the butter and three for the Black Well water.

She took the green bottle in her hand, and suddenly it was dark. She was flying through the air, and when she opened her eyes she was at her own doorstep. She slipped away to bed, glad to be home again, and said nothing about where she had been or what she had seen.

Next morning, before the sun was up, there came a rap, rap, rap, three times at the door. The sleepy lass looked out and saw an old beggar-man, who began to sing:

> 'O open, the door, my honey, my hert,
> O open the door, my ain kind dearie;
> For don't you mind upon the time
> We met in the wood at the Well so wearie?'

When she heard that, she said nothing, and opened the door. The old beggar came in singing:

'O gie me my brose, my honey, my hert,
O gie me my brose, my ain kind dearie;
For don't you mind upon the time
We met in the wood at the Well so wearie?'

The lassie made a bicker of brose for the beggar, not forgetting the three drops of water from the green bottle. As he was supping the brose the old beggar vanished, and there in his place was the big Highlander who had lent silver to her father, the miller, and he was singing:

'O gie me my bannocks, my honey, my hert,
O gie me my bannocks, my ain kind dearie;
For don't you mind upon the time
We met in the wood at the Well so wearie?'

She baked him some fresh bannocks, not forgetting the three drops from the wee green bottle. He had just finished eating the bannocks when he vanished, and there in his place was the woodcock that had fired the mill, singing:

'O gie me my butter, my honey, my hert,
O gie me my butter, my ain kind dearie;
For don't you mind upon the time
We met in the wood by the Well so wearie?'

She gave him butter as fast as she could, not forgetting the three drops of water from the green bottle. He had only eaten a bite, when he flapped his wings and vanished, and there was the ugly wee bogle that had gripped her at the Black Well the night before, and he was singing:

'O gie me my water, my honey, my hert,
O gie me my water, my ain kind dearie;

For don't you mind upon the time
We met in the wood by the Well so wearie?'

She knew there were only three other drops of water left in the green bottle and she was afraid. She ran fast as she could to the Black Well, but who should be there before her but the wee ugly bogle himself, singing:

'*O gie me my water, my honey, my hert,*
O gie me my water, my ain kind dearie;
For don't you mind upon the time
We met in the wood by the Well so wearie?'

She gave him the water, not forgetting the three drops from the green bottle. But he had scarcely drunk the witched water when he vanished, and there was a fine young Prince, who spoke to her as if he had known her all her days.

They sat down beside the Black Well.

'I was born the same night as you,' he said, 'and I was carried away by the fairies the same night as you were found on the lip of the Well. I was a bogle for so many years because the fairies were scared away. They made me play many tricks before they would let me go and return to my father, the King of France, and make the bonniest lass in all the world my bride.'

'Who is she?' asked the maiden.

'The Miller of Cuthilldorie's daughter,' said the young Prince.

Then they went home and told their stories over again, and that very night they were married. A coach-and-four came for them, and the miller and his wife, and the Prince and the Princess, drove away singing:

'*O but we're happy, my honey, my hert,*
O but we're happy, my ain kind dearie;
For don't you mind upon the time
We met in the wood at the Well so wearie?'

THE TALE OF THE SOLDIER

NCE there was an old soldier who had deserted from the army. He climbed a hill at the top end of the town, and said:

'May the Mischief carry me away on his back the next time I come within sight of this town!'

He walked and walked till he came to a gentleman's house.

'May I stay in your house tonight?' he asked.

'You're an old soldier with the look of a brave man,' said the gentleman. 'You can't stay here, but you may stay in the castle beside that wood yonder till morning. You'll get a pipe and tobacco, a cogie of whisky, and a Bible.'

After supper, the soldier, whose name was John, went to the castle and lit a big fire. When part of the night had gone, two strange brown women came in carrying a chest. They put it by the fireside and went out. With the heel of his boot John stove in the end of it, as he couldn't open the lid, and he pulled out an old grey man. He sat the man in the big chair, gave him a pipe and tobacco, a cogie of whisky and a Bible, but the old grey man let them fall on the floor.

'Poor man,' said John, 'you're cold!'

John stretched himself on the bed, and left the old grey man to warm himself at the fire, and there the grey man stayed till the cock crew, then he took himself off.

The gentleman came in the morning early.

'Did you sleep well?' he asked.

'I did,' said John. 'Your father wasn't the kind of man to frighten me!'

'I'll give you two hundred pounds if you stay in the castle tonight.'

'I'll do that,' said John.

Well, the same thing happened again that night. Three brown women came in carrying a chest. They put it by the fireside and went out. John could not open it, so with the heel of his boot he stove in the end of it, and pulled out the old grey man. As he had done the night before, he sat the old grey man in the big chair and gave him a pipe and tobacco. But the old grey man let them fall.

'Poor man,' said John, 'you're cold!'

So he gave him a cogie of whisky, but the old man let it fall. John slept soundly all night, while the old man stayed awake by the fire till cock crow. Then he went away, as he had the night before.

'If I stay here tonight, and you come,' said John, 'you'll pay for my pipe and tobacco, and my cogie of whisky!'

The gentleman came in the morning early.

'Did you sleep well last night, John?' said he.

'I did,' said John. 'Your old father wasn't the kind of man to frighten me.'

'If you stay in the castle tonight, you shall have three hundred pounds.'

'That's a bargain,' said the soldier.

Well, when part of the night had gone, four strange brown women came carrying a chest, and put it down beside John. He stove in the end of the chest with his boot, pulled out the old grey man, and sat him in the big chair. He gave him the pipe and tobacco, the cogie and the whisky, but the old grey man dropped them, and broke the pipe and the cogie,

'Before you go tonight, you'll pay me for all you've broken,' said John.

The old grey man said nothing. John took the strap of his haversack, tied the old grey man to his side, and took him to bed with him. When the cock crew, the old man begged him to let him go.

'Pay for what you've broken first,' said John.

'I'll tell you then,' said the old grey man. 'There's a wine cellar down there, and in it there's plenty of drink, tobacco and pipes. There's another little room beside the cellar, and in it there's a pot full of gold. Under the threshold of the big door there's a crock full of silver. Did you see the women that brought me last night?'

'I did,' said John.

'They're the four poor women from whom I stole some cows. They carry me every night this way to punish me. Go and tell my son how I am being tired out. Let him pay for the cows, and not be hard on the poor. You and he can divide my gold and silver between you, and you can marry my old widow. But remember, give plenty of what's left to the poor, I was too hard on them. Then I may rest in peace.'

The gentleman came in the morning and John told him all that had happened. But John refused to marry the widow of the old grey man.

After a day or two, John would stay no longer. He filled his pockets with gold, and asked the gentleman to give what was left of his share to the poor.

He went home, but he soon wearied there, and would rather have been back with the regiment. One day he left home and marched on and on till he came to the hill that he had climbed before. He climbed to the top and who should he meet there but the Mischief!

'You've come back, John?'

'I've come back right enough, but who are you?'

'I'm the Mischief. You gave yourself to me when you were last here, remember?'

'I've heard tell of you,' said John, 'but I've never seen you before. My eyes are deceiving me. I don't believe it's you at all, but make yourself into a snake and I'll believe you.'

The Mischief did so.

'Now make yourself into a roaring lion.'

The Mischief did so.

'Well,' said John, 'if I'm to be your servant, go into my haversack and I'll carry you. But you mustn't come out till I tell you, or the bargain's broken.'

The Mischief promised, and did as he was told.

'I'm going to see my brother in the regiment,' said John to the Mischief in his haversack, 'but you must keep quiet.'

John went into the town, and one man here and another man there cried out: 'There's John, the deserter!'

John was arrested and tried in court. He was sentenced to be hanged next day, at noon. John said he'd rather be shot.

'Since you're an old soldier, and have been a long time in the army, you shall have your wish,' said the Colonel.

Next day, John was about to be shot, and the soldiers were all round him, and the firing squad was getting into line, when the Mischief called from inside the haversack:

'What's going on? What's that they're saying? Let me out of here, and I'll not be long in scattering them!'

'Hush, hush,' said John to the Mischief.

'Who's that speaking to you?' said the Colonel.

'Oh, it's only a white mouse,' said John.

'Black or white,' said the Colonel, 'don't let it out of the haversack, and you shall have your discharge from the army. And let us see no more of you!'

John was glad to go and off he went. At dusk he went into a barn where twelve men were threshing.

'Here's my old haversack for you, lads. Thresh it for a while. It's so hard, it's taking the skin off my back.'

For two hours they threshed the haversack with twelve flails. At last every blow they gave it made it jump to the roof of the barn. Now and then it would throw a thresher on his back, so they told John to be out of that, he and his haversack. They said the Mischief was in it.

So John went on his way till he came to a smiddy, where twelve blacksmiths were using their big hammers.

'Here's an old haversack for you, lads. I'll give you half a crown to hammer it for a while with your twelve big hammers. It's so hard, it's taking the skin off my back.'

The soldier's haversack seemed good sport for the blacksmiths, but every blow it got, it jumped to the roof of the smiddy.

'Get out of here, yourself and your haversack,' they said to John. 'You've got the Mischief in it!'

So John went on, and the Mischief on his back, till he reached a great furnace.

'What are you going to do now, John?' said the Mischief.

'A little patience, and you'll see,' said John.

'Let me out,' said the Mischief, 'and I'll never trouble you again in this world.'

'Nor in the next?' said John.

'I agree,' said the Mischief.

John threw the haversack and the Mischief into the furnace, and the Mischief and the furnace went up in a green flame to the sky.

THE FECKLESS ONES

HERE was once a young farmer who married his neighbour's only daughter.

One day he and his young wife, her father and her mother, all went to the peat-hag to cut peat for the winter. When they were hungry, the young wife went to fetch the dinner.

When she got home, she saw the speckled filly's pack-saddle hanging above her head. She looked at the filly, then she sat on the ground and wept.

'If the pack-saddle should fall on to *my* head, whatever would I do?' she wailed. 'It might kill me!' And she sat there, rocking to and fro, weeping bitterly.

The family at the peat-hag wondered why the young wife was so long fetching the dinner.

'I'll go and see what's happened,' said her mother.

She found the young wife sitting on the ground, rocking to and fro, weeping bitterly.

'Oh, if it happened to me!' she cried.

'What has happened?' asked her mother.

'Well, when I came in, I saw the speckled filly's pack-saddle over-head,' she wailed. 'What should I do if it had fallen and killed me?'

'Good gracious me!' cried her mother, 'if that should happen, what should I do without you, my only child, to help me?' And she too sat on the ground and wept.

'Whatever can be keeping those women,' said the father. 'I'd better go and see what has happened to our dinner.'

He found his wife and his daughter sitting on the ground at home, rocking to and fro, and crying their hearts out.

'What's come over you both?' he cried.

'When our daughter came home,' sobbed his wife, 'she saw the pack-saddle over her head. Whatever would I do if it fell and killed her, and I'd have no one to help me?'

'If that should happen we'd all be in a bad way,' said the old man, and he too sat down and wept.

The young farmer grew tired of waiting for his dinner. He went to see what had happened to his wife and her parents.

'What's wrong with you all?' he said, when he saw them, sitting on the ground, crying their eyes out.

'Our daughter came home, saw the speckled filly's pack-saddle above her head and thought she'd be killed if it fell on her,' said the old man. 'If that should happen what would become of us? She's our only child!'

'But the pack-saddle *didn't* fall,' said the young man.

His young wife, her mother and her father didn't reply, they just cried louder than before. So the young man sat at the table, helped himself to the dinner and ate it. He took no notice of them and they took no notice of him. Then he went to bed.

Next morning, the three were still weeping, so he pulled on his boots, shouldered his gun and left.

'I'll not stop,' said he as he left, 'till I see three others as silly as you!'

On and on he went till he came to a house where three women were spinning.

'Are there any silly folk in these parts?' said he.

'There are,' said the women. 'The men here are so stupid, they'll believe anything we tell them.'

'Is that so?' said the young man. 'Well, I'll give a gold coin to the woman whose husband believes her absolutely.'

When the first man came home, his wife said to him: 'You are sick.' 'Am I?' said he.

'Indeed you are. Take off your clothes and go to bed.' So he did as he was told and, as soon as he was under the bed-clothes, his wife said:

'Good gracious me, you're dead!'

'Am I?' said he.

'Indeed you are. Now close your eyes and don't move.'

So her husband closed his eyes and died.

Now, when the second man came home, his wife looked at him, and said: 'You're not *you*!'

'Am I not?' said he. 'Then this can't be my home.' And he went away out of the house.

The third man came home, and his wife welcomed him. She gave him supper and they went to bed. But next morning, when he had to go to his neighbour's funeral, he couldn't find his clothes.

'What are you looking for?' said his wife.

'My clothes.'

'You've got them on, and you'd better hurry or you'll miss the funeral. They've just passed, carrying the coffin. You'll have to run if you want to catch them up!'

So the goodman ran out of his house and after the funeral party, stark naked. When they saw him, the mourners left the coffin on the ground, and fled. The naked man stood at the foot of the coffin and was wondering what to do, when along came the second husband.

'You look lost, Thomas,' said the naked one.

'I'm *not* Thomas,' said he, 'if I was, my wife would know me, and she said I was not me. Why are you going about naked?'

'I'm not, my wife told me I had my clothes on!'

'My wife told me I am dead,' said the corpse in the coffin.

When the other two heard the dead man speak, they ran off as fast as their legs could take them, and were not seen again.

'Which of us has the silliest husband?' the three wives asked the young farmer. 'Which of us has won the gold coin?'

The young man decided that the wife of the dead man deserved the gold coin, for her husband was certainly the silliest he had ever heard of. Along with the two other husbands, all three were even sillier than his wife, her father and her mother.

So he went back home and told them the story. Whether this cured their stupidity, we'll never know.

PIPPETY PEW

THERE was once a man who worked in the fields, and he had a wife, a son and a daughter. One day he caught a hare, took it home to his wife and told her to make it ready for his dinner.

While it was on the fire cooking, the goodwife kept on tasting it till she had tasted it all away, and she didn't know what to do for her husband's dinner. So she called Johnnie, her son, to come and have his hair combed. When she was combing his head, she slew him, and put him into the pot.

The goodman came home for his dinner, and his wife set down Johnnie to him well boiled. When he was eating, he took up a foot.

'Surely that's my Johnnie's foot,' said he.

'Nonsense. It is one of the hare's,' said she.

Then he took up a hand.

'That's surely my Johnnie's hand,' said he.

'You're talking nonsense, goodman,' said she. 'That's another of the hare's feet.'

When the goodman had eaten his dinner, his daughter Katy gathered all the bones and put them below a stone at the cheek of the door.

> *Where they grew, and they grew,*
> *To a milk-white doo,*
> *That took to its wings,*
> *And away it flew.*

The dove flew till it came to a burn where two women were washing clothes. It sat down on a stone, and cried:

> 'Pippety pew!
> My mammy me slew,
> My daddy me ate,
> My sister Kate
> Gathered all my banes,
> And laid them between
> Two milk-white stanes.
> So a bird I grew,
> And away I flew,
> Sing Pippety Pew!'

'Say that again, my pretty bird, and we'll give you all these clothes,' said one of the women.

> 'Pippety Pew!
> My mammy me slew,
> My daddy me ate,
> My sister Kate
> Gathered all my banes,
> And laid them between

Two milk-white stanes.
So a bird I grew,
And away I flew,
Sing Pippety Pew!'

The bird took the clothes, and away it flew till it came to a man counting a great heap of silver. It sat down beside him and cried:

'Pippety Pew!
My mammy me slew,
My daddy me ate,
My sister Kate
Gathered all my banes,
And laid them between
Two milk-white stanes.
So a bird I grew,
And away I flew,
Sing Pippety Pew!'

'Say that again, my bonny bird, and I'll give you all this silver,' said the man.

'Pippety Pew!
My mammy me slew.
My daddy me ate,
My sister Kate
Gathered all my banes,
And laid them between
Two milk-white stanes.
So a bird I grew,
And away I flew,
Sing Pippety Pew!'

The man gave the bird all the silver. It flew till it came to a miller grinding corn, and cried:

'Pippety Pew!
My mammy me slew,
My daddy me ate,
My sister Kate
Qathered all my banes,
And laid them between
Two milk-white stanes.
So a bird I grew,
And away I flew,
Sing Pippety Pew!'

'Say that again, my bonny bird, and I'll give you this millstone,' said the miller.

'Pippety Pew!
My mammy me slew,
My daddy me ate,
My sister Kate
Qathered all my banes,
And laid them between
Two milk'white stanes.
So a bird I grew,
And away I flew,
Sing Pippety Pew!'

The miller gave the millstone to the bird, and away it flew till it lighted on its father's housetop. It threw small stones down the chimney, and Katy came out to see what was the matter. The dove threw all the clothes down to her. Then the father came out, and the dove threw all the silver down to him. Then the mother came out. The dove threw the millstone down on her and killed her.

Then the dove flew away, and after that the goodman and his daughter lived happy and died happy.

THE BLACK BULL OF NORROWAY

IN Norroway, long ago, there lived a lady, and she had three daughters. The eldest of them said to her mother:

'Mother, bake me an oatcake, and roast me a collop, for I'm going away to seek my fortune.'

Her mother did so, while her daughter went to an old spey-wife and asked her what she should do. The spey-wife told her to look out of the back door to see what she could see.

She saw nothing the first day, and she saw nothing the second day. But on the third day she looked out again and saw a coach-and-six coming along the road. She ran in and told the spey-wife.

'Well,' said the old wife, 'that's for you.'

So she stepped into the coach, and off she went.

The second daughter then said to her mother:

'Mother, bake me an oatcake, and roast me a collop, for I'm going away to seek my fortune.'

Her mother did so, and away she went to the old spey-wife, just as her sister had done. The spey-wife told her to look out of the back door to see what she could see. She saw nothing the first day, and she saw nothing the second day, but on the third day she looked out and saw a coach-and-four coming along the road.

'That's for you,' said the old wife.

The lass was taken into the coach and off they went.

Then the third daughter went to her mother, and said:

'Mother, bake me an oatcake, and roast me a collop, for I'm going away to seek my fortune.'

Her mother did so, and away she went to the old spey-wife, who told her to look out of the back door to see what she could see.

She saw nothing the first day, and she saw nothing the second day. But on the third day she looked again, and came back and told the old wife she could see nothing but a great Black Bull coming roaring along the road.

'Well,' said the old wife, 'that's for you.'

When she heard this the poor lass was almost out of her mind with grief and terror. But she was lifted up, set on the Black Bull's back, and away they went.

Long they travelled, and on they travelled, till the lass grew faint with hunger.

'Eat out of my right ear,' said the Black Bull, 'drink out of my left ear, and set aside your leavings.'

She did as he said, and was refreshed.

Long they travelled, and hard they travelled, till they came in sight of a castle.

'That is where we must be this night,' said the Bull, 'for my brother lives there.'

Soon they reached the castle. Servants lifted the lass off the Bull's back, took her in, and sent him into a field for the night.

In the morning, when they brought the Bull to the castle, they took the lass into a fine room and gave her an apple. They told her not to break it open till she was in the greatest strait a mortal could be in, then it would help her.

Again she was lifted on to the Bull's back, and after they had ridden far, and far, and farther than I can tell, they came in sight of another castle, farther away than the last.

'That is where we must be this night,' said the Bull, 'for my second brother lives there.'

Soon they readied the castle. Servants lifted her down, took her in, and sent the Bull to a field for the night.

In the morning, the lass was taken into a fine rich room and given a pear. They told her not to break open the pear until she was in the greatest difficulty a mortal could be in, and then it would help her.

Once more she was lifted up and set on the Bull's back, and away they went. Long they rode, and hard they rode, till they came in sight of the grandest castle they had yet seen.

'That is where we must be tonight,' said the Bull, 'for my youngest brother lives there.'

They were there directly. Servants lifted her down, took her in and sent the Bull to a field for the night.

In the morning the lass was taken into the finest room of all, and given a plum. She was told not to break it open until she was in the greatest strait a mortal could be in, and then it would help her. After that, she was set on the Bull's back, and away they went.

Long they rode, and on they rode, till they came to a dark and ugly glen. There they stopped and she alighted. At that moment she noticed a pin sticking in the hide of the Bull. She pulled it out and at once the Bull changed into the most handsome young knight she had ever seen. He thanked her for breaking his cruel enchantment.

'But alas,' said he, 'you must stick the pin back into my skin, for before I can be finally released from this cruel spell, I must go and fight the devil. While I'm away, you must sit here on this stone and never move either your hands or your feet till I return. If everything about you changes to blue, I'll have won and this spell will be broken for ever, but if everything turns red, the devil will have conquered me and we'll never meet again.'

So the maiden did as the knight had told her, and stuck the pin into his skin. At once he changed back into the Black Bull and galloped off. She sat on the stone, and by and by everything around her turned blue. Overcome with joy, she lifted one foot and crossed it over the other.

The Black Bull returned and looked for the lass, but he could not find her.

Long she sat, and wept, until she was wearied. At last she got up and sadly went away, not knowing where she was going. On she wandered till she came to a great hill of glass that she tried to climb, but could not. Round the bottom of the hill she went, looking for a path over the hill, till at last she came to a smiddy. The blacksmith promised, if she would serve him for seven years, to make her a pair of iron shoes, and with these she would be able to climb over the glass mountain.

At the end of seven years she was given the iron shoes. She climbed the glass hill, and came to an old washerwoman's cottage. The washerwoman told of a gallant young knight who had given her some bloodstained shirts to be washed. He said that she who washed his shirts clean would be his bride.

The old wife had washed and washed until she was tired, and then she had set her daughter to it. They had both washed, and washed, and washed, in hope of winning the young knight: but do what they might, they had not been able to take out a single stain.

So they set the stranger lass to work and, as soon as she began, the stains came out, leaving the shirts clean and white. But the old wife told the knight that her daughter had washed the shirts.

So the young knight and the washerwife's daughter were to be married. The stranger lass was distracted by the thought of it, for she had recognized the knight at once. It was he she had known as the Black Bull. Then she remembered her apple, and breaking it open, she found it full of precious gold and precious jewellery, the richest she had ever seen.

'All these,' she said to the washerwife's daughter, 'I will give you, if you put off your marriage for one day, and allow me to go into his room alone tonight.'

The daughter agreed but told her mother, who prepared a sleeping draught and gave it to the knight. He drank it, and slept until the next morning. All night long the poor lass wept and sang at his bedside:

> 'Seven long years I served for you,
> The glassy hill I climbed for you,
> The blood-stained shirts I washed for you,
> Will you not waken and turn to me?'

But the knight did not waken, and next day she did not know what to do. Then she remembered the pear, so she broke it, and she found it filled with jewellery richer than before. With these she bargained with the washerwife's daughter to be a second night in the young knight's room. But the old wife gave him another sleeping draught, and he slept till morning. He did not hear the lass as she sat by his side all night and sang:

> 'Seven long years I served for you,
> The glassy hill I climbed for you,
> The blood-stained shirts I washed for you,
> Will you not waken and turn to me?'

Still he slept, and she nearly lost hope. But that day, when he was out hunting, someone asked him what sad singing and moaning it was they had heard all night in his room. He had not heard a sound himself, but he made up his mind to keep awake this night.

The poor lass, between hope and despair, broke open her plum and it held the richest jewels of the three. She bargained with the washerwife's daughter as before, and the old wife took the sleeping draught to the knight. But this time he said he wouldn't drink it without sweetening. While she went to fetch the honey, he poured out the drink, and then pretended he had already drunk it.

That night, when everyone was in bed, the young lass went to the knight's room and sat by his bed and sang:

> 'Seven long years I served for you,
> The glassy hill I dimbed for you,
> The blood-stained shirts I washed for you,
> Will you not waken and turn to me?'

The knight heard and turned to her. She told him all that had happened to her, and he told her all that had happened to him. After the washerwife and her daughter had been punished, the knight and the lass were married and lived happily ever after.

ROBIN REIDBREIST AND THE WRAN

THERE was an auld grey Poussie Baudrons, and she gaed awa doon by a waterside. There she saw a wee Robin Reidbreist happin on a brier, and Poussie Baudrons says:

'Whaur's tu gaun, wee Robin?'

And wee Robin says:

'I'm gaun awa tae the King tae sing him a sang this guid Yule mornin.'

Poussie Baudrons says:

'Come here, wee Robin, and I'll let ye see a bonny white ring roond my neck.'

But wee Robin says:

'Na, na, grey Poussie Baudrons, na, na! Ye worrit the wee mousie, but ye'se no worry me.'

Sae, wee Robin flew awa till he cam tae a fail fauld-dyke. There he saw a grey Greedy Gled sittin, and grey Greedy Gled says:

'Whaur's tu gaun, wee Robin?'

And wee Robin says:

'I'm gaun awa tae the King tae sing him a sang this guid Yule mornin.'

Grey Greedy Gled says:

'Come here, wee Robin, and I'll let ye see a bonny feather in my wing.'

But wee Robin says:

'Na, na, grey Greedy Gled, na, na! Ye pookit a' the wee lintie, but ye'se no pook me.'

Sae, wee Robin flew awa till he cam tae the cleuch o' the craig. There he saw slee Tod Lowrie sittin, and slee Tod Lowrie says:

'Whaur's tu gaun, wee Robin?'

And wee Robin says:

'I'm gaun awa tae the King tae sing him a sang this guid Yule mornin.'

Slee Tod Lowrie says:

'Come here, wee Robin, and I'll let ye see a bonny spot on the tap o' my tail.'

'Na, na, slee Tod Lowrie, na, na! Ye worrit the wee lammie, but ye'se no worry me.'

Sae, wee Robin flew awa till he cam tae a bonny burn-side. There he saw a wee callant sittin, and the wee callant says:

'Whaur's tu gaun, wee Robin?'

And wee Robin says:

'I'm gaun awa tae the King tae sing him a sang this guid Yule mornin.'

The wee callant says:

'Come here, wee Robin, and I'll gie ye a wheen grand moolins oot o' my pooch.'

But wee Robin says:

'Na, na, wee callant, na, na! Ye speldert the gowdspink, but ye'se no spelder me.'

Sae, wee Robin flew awa till he cam tae the King. There he sat on a winnock sole, and sang the King a bonny sang. And the King says tae the Queen:

'What'll we gie tae wee Robin for singin us this bonny sang?'

The Queen says tae the King:

'I think we'll gie him the wee Wran tae be his wife.'

Sae, wee Robin and the wee Wran were merriet. The King and the Queen, and a' the coort danced at the waddin. Syne he flew awa hame tae his ain water-side, and happit on a brier.

ROBIN REDBREAST AND THE WREN

THERE was an old grey Cat, and she went away down by a water's edge. There she saw a wee Robin Redbreast sheltering on a briar, and Pussie Cat says:

'Where are you going, wee Robin?'

'I'm going away to the King to sing him a song this good Yule morning.'

Pussie Cat says:

'Come here, wee Robin, and I'll let you see a bonny white ring round my neck.'

But wee Robin says:

'No, no, grey Pussie Cat, no, no! You worried the wee Mousie, but you'll not worry me.'

So, wee Robin flew away till he came to the turf wall of a sheep-fold. There he saw grey Greedy Kite sitting, and grey Greedy Kite says:

'Where are you going, wee Robin?'

And Wee Robin says:

'I'm going away to the King to sing him a song this good Yule morning.'

Grey Greedy Kite says:

'Come here, wee Robin, and I'll let you see a bonny feather in my wing.'

But wee Robin says:

'No, no, grey Greedy Kite, no, no! You plucked the wee Linnet, but you'll not pluck me.'

So Wee Robin flew away till he came to the steep crag. There he saw sly Fox Lowrie sitting, and sly Fox Lowrie says:

'Where are you going, wee Robin?'

And wee Robin says:

'I'm going away to the King to sing him a song this good Yule morning.'

Sly Fox Lowrie says:

'Come here, wee Robin, and I'll let you see a bonny spot on the top of my tail.'

'Na, na, sly Fox Lowrie, no, no! You worried the wee Lamb, but you'll not worry me.'

So, wee Robin flew away till he came to a bonny stream. There he saw a wee Lad sitting, and the wee Lad says:

'Where are you going, wee Robin?'

And wee Robin says:

'I'm going away to the King to sing him a song this good Yule morning.'

The wee Lad says:

'Come here, wee Robin, and I'll give you a few fine crumbs out of my pocket.'

But wee Robin says:

'Na, na, wee Lad, na, na! You cut up the Goldfinch, but you'll not cut me up.'

So, wee Robin flew away till he came to the King. There he sat on a window sill, and sang the King a bonny song. And the King says to the Queen:

'What'll we give wee Robin for singing us the bonny song?'

The Queen says to the King:

'I think we'll give him the wee Wren to be his wife.'

So wee Robin and wee Wren were married. The King and the Queen and all the Court danced at the wedding.

Then wee Robin flew away home to his own river-bank, and sheltered on a briar.

THE BATTLE OF THE BIRDS

ONCE upon a time all the animals and birds were at war. The King's son went to see the battle. He saw one fight between a black raven and a snake, and to help the raven he cut the snake's head off.

'For your kindness to me,' said the raven, 'I'll let you see something. Come up between my two wings.'

The King's son mounted the raven's back, and was carried over seven bens, seven glens and seven mountain moors.

'Now,' said the raven, 'you see that house there? Go there and tell my sister you saw me at the battle of the birds. But be sure to meet me here tomorrow morning.'

'I'll do that,' said the King's son.

He was well treated that night, with the best meat and drink, and warm water for his feet, and a soft bed to lie on.

Next day the raven took him over seven bens, seven glens and seven mountain moors. They came to a house belonging to the raven's second sister, and there the Prince was well treated, with plenty of meat and drink, warm water for his feet, and a soft bed to lie on.

Next morning he was again met by the raven, and taken over seven bens, seven glens and seven mountain moors. He was well treated by the raven's third sister, but next morning, instead of the raven, there was a young man with a bundle in his hand waiting for him.

'Have you seen a raven, young man?' said the Prince.

'I am that raven,' said the young man. 'You loosed me from a spell, and for that I give you this bundle. Retrace your steps, stay a night at each house as before, but do not open this bundle till you are at the place you would most like to live.'

The Prince retraced his steps. He stayed with the raven's sisters as before. But as he was going through a deep wood the bundle grew heavy, and he looked to see what was in it.

In an instant, a great castle sprang up, with orchards filled with every kind of fruit, and gardens with every kind of herb and flower. The castle was in the wrong place, but the King's son could not put it back into the bundle.

Looking round, he saw a giant coming towards him.

'You've built your castle in a stupid place, Prince,' said the giant.

'I don't want it here,' said the Prince. 'It came here by accident.'

'What reward will you give me for putting it back in the bundle?' asked the giant.

'What reward do you want?'

'Give me your first son, when he is seven years old,' replied the giant.

'Yes, I'll do that, if I have a son,' said the Prince, who couldn't imagine himself having a son.

In an instant, the giant put the castle, orchards and gardens back into the bundle as before.

'Now go your way,' said the giant, 'and I'll go mine. But remember your promise. If you forget, I'll remember.'

The Prince set off, and after several days reached his favourite place. He opened the bundle in a fresh green hollow and there was his castle, with its orchards and gardens.

When he opened the castle door he saw a beautiful maiden.

'Everything is ready,' she said, 'if you are willing to marry me tonight.'

'I am willing,' said the Prince. And they were married that night.

When nine months had passed a fine son was born to them. In the years that followed, the old King died and the young Prince became King in his place.

At the end of seven years and a day, the giant came to the castle. The young King remembered his promise.

'Do not worry,' said the Queen, 'just leave it to me. I know what to do.'

Now, the giant grew impatient.

'Bring out your son,' said he. 'Remember your promise.'

'You can have him,' said the King, 'when his mother has made him ready for the journey.'

The Queen dressed the cook's son, brought him out, and put his hand into the giant's hand. The giant led him away, but he had not gone far before he handed the boy a rod.

'If your father had that rod,' said the giant, 'what would he do with it?'

'He would beat the dogs and the cats if they went near the King's meat,' said the lad.

'You're the cook's son!' said the giant, and returned to the castle with the lad.

'If you do not hand over your true son to me,' he roared, 'the highest stone of your castle will be the lowest.'

'We'll try again,' said the Queen to her husband. 'The butler's son is the same age as ours.'

She dressed the butler's son in the young prince's clothes, brought him out, and put his hand into the giant's hand. The giant led him away. They had not gone far before the giant handed the boy a rod.

'If your father had that rod, what would he do with it?'

'He'd beat the cats and the dogs if they came near the King's wine-cellar.'

'You are the butler's son,' said the giant, and returned to the castle. The earth trembled under his feet, the castle shook and everything in it.

'Bring your son out here,' he shouted, 'or in a flash the highest stone in your castle will be the lowest.'

So the King brought his son and gave him to the giant, who led him away. They had not gone far before the giant handed the boy a rod.

'If your father had that rod,' said the giant, 'what would he do with it?'

'He'd use it as a sceptre and rule the land with it,' said the young Prince.

'Come with me,' said the giant. 'You're the King's own son, right enough.' And he took the young Prince home and brought him up as his own son.

One day, years later, when the giant was out, the lad heard music coming from a window at the top of the giant's house, and looking up he saw the giant's youngest daughter. She told him to come again at midnight.

He did so and the giant's daughter climbed down beside him.

'Tomorrow you will be given the choice of my two sisters in marriage,' said she. 'Say you will take no one but me. My father wants me to marry the son of the King of the Green City, but I don't love him.'

Next day the giant brought out his three daughters.

'Now, King's son,' said he, 'you've lost nothing by living with me so long. Now you'll marry one of my daughters.'

'If you give me your youngest daughter,' said the King's son, 'I'll agree.'

'Before you have her,' said the giant, 'you must do three things.'

The giant took him to the byre.

'A hundred cattle have been in the byre, and it hasn't been cleaned for seven years,' said the giant. 'If, before night, the byre is not so clean that a golden apple will run from one end to the other, you'll not marry my youngest daughter, and I'll kill you.'

The Prince began to clean the byre, but he might as well have tried to bale out the ocean. After midday, when his sweat was blinding him, the giant's youngest daughter came to him.

'You are being punished, King's son,' said she.

'I am that,' said he.

'Come here,' said she, 'and lay down your weariness.'

'I'll do that,' said he, 'there's only death awaiting me.'

He sat down beside her and was so tired that he fell asleep. When he awoke, the giant's daughter was gone, and the byre was so clean that a golden apple would run from one end to the other.

'You've cleaned the byre, King's son,' said the giant, as he came in.

'I have,' said the Prince.

'Someone has cleaned it,' said the giant. 'Now you must thatch the byre with feathers by this time tomorrow, and no two feathers are to be the same colour.'

The Prince was up before the sun. He took his bow and a quiver of arrows to shoot the birds. He ran after them till the sweat blinded him, but he missed all but two. Then the youngest daughter came to him.

'You are tiring yourself, King's son,' said she.

'Only two blackbirds fell, and they're both the same colour.'

'Come here, and lay down your weariness,' she said.

He lay down beside her and soon fell asleep. When he awoke she had gone, but the byre was thatched with feathers, and no two were the same colour.

'You've thatched the byre, King's son,' said the giant as he came in.

'I have,' said the Prince.

'Someone has thatched it,' said the giant. 'Well now, there's a fir tree by the loch, and on its branches a magpie's nest with five eggs in it. Bring them to me by this time tomorrow.'

The Prince was up before the sun. He went round and round the fir tree, trying to find a foothold, till he was blinded by sweat. Then the giant's youngest daughter came to him.

'You're losing the skin off your hands,' she said.

'I'm no sooner up than I'm down,' said he.

'There's no time to lose,' she said, putting her fingers, like nails, one after the other into the tree, making footholds up to the magpie's nest. He climbed the tree and took the eggs.

'Make haste!' she cried. 'I feel my father's breath burning my neck.' In her hurry she left the little finger of her right hand in the tree.

'Take the eggs to my father,' she said. 'Tonight he'll give you the choice of his three daughters. We'll be dressed alike, but choose the one whose little finger is missing.'

So the Prince gave the eggs to the giant.

'Now you can choose your wife,' the giant said.

The giant presented his three daughters, dressed exactly alike, and the Prince chose the one whose little finger was missing. They were married, but when night came, she said:

'We must fly, or my father will kill you. Go saddle the grey filly while I play a trick on him.'

She took nine apples. She put two at the head of her bed, two at the foot of her bed, two at the bedroom door, two at the house door and one in the garden. Then they mounted the grey filly, and rode away.

The giant woke up.

'Are you asleep?' he called.

'Not yet,' said the apples at the head of the bed.

'Are you asleep?' he called, after a while.

'Not yet,' said the apples at the foot of the bed.

'Are you asleep?' he called again.

'Not yet,' said the apples at the bedroom door.

'Are you asleep?' the giant called later.

'Not yet,' said the apples at the house door.

'You are going away,' said the giant.

'Not yet,' said the apple in the garden.

At that, the giant jumped out of bed and, finding the Prince and his bride had gone, ran after them.

In the mouth of the day, the giant's daughter said her father's breath was burning her neck.

'Quickly, put your hand in the grey filly's ear!' said she.

'There's a twig of blackthorn,' said he.

'Throw it behind you!' said she.

No sooner had he done this than there sprang up twenty miles of blackthorn wood, so thick that a weasel could not go through.

The giant came striding headlong, and fleeced his head and neck in the thorns.

'More of my daughter's tricks!' said he. 'If I had my big axe and wood knife, I wouldn't be long making my way through this.'

He went home for his big axe and wood knife. He was not long returning, and soon made his way through the blackthorn.

'I'll leave the axe and wood knife here till I return,' said he.

'If you leave them, we'll steal them,' said a hoodie in a tree.

'Then I'll take them home,' said the giant, took them back to his house, and left them there.

In the heat of the day, the giant's daughter said:

'I feel my father's breath burning my neck. Put your hand in the filly's ear, and whatever you find there, throw it behind you!'

He found a splinter of grey stone, and threw it behind him. At once there sprang up twenty miles of grey rock, high and broad as a range of mountains. The giant came full pelt after them, but past the rock he could not go.

'My daughter's tricks are hard to bear,' said he, 'but if I had my lever and my big mattock, I'd make my way through this rock in no time.'

There was no help for it. He had to return for his lever and mattock. But he was not long returning, and was through the rock in no time.

'I'll just leave the tools here,' said he.

'If you do, we'll steal them,' said a hoodie perched on the rock.

'Steal them if you want to,' said the giant. 'There's no time to go back with them.'

Meanwhile, the Prince and the giant's daughter rode on.

'I feel my father's breath burning my neck,' said she. 'Put your hand in the filly's ear, King's son, and whatever you find there, throw behind you!'

This time he found a thimble of water. He threw it behind him, and at once there was a fresh-water loch, twenty miles in length and breadth.

The giant came on, but was running so quickly he did not stop till he was in the middle of the loch, where he sank and did not come up.

Next day the Prince and his wife came in sight of his father's house.

'Before we go farther, go in to your father and tell him about me. But don't let any man or creature kiss you. If you do, you'll forget me.'

He was given a warm welcome at his father's house. He asked them not to kiss him, but before he could say more, his old greyhound jumped up and licked his mouth. After that he forgot the giant's daughter.

She sat beside a well where the Prince had left her, but he did not return. In the mouth of night, she climbed into the fork of an oak tree by the well, and lay there.

Next day, a shoemaker, who lived near by, asked his wife to fetch him a jug of water. At the well she saw, in the water, the reflection of the giant's daughter and thought it was herself. She had not imagined till now that she was so beautiful, so she threw away the jug and went home.

'Where is the water?' said the shoemaker.

'You stupid old man,' said she, 'I've been too long your wood-and-water slave!'

'I'm thinking, wife, that you've gone crazy,' said he. 'Go, daughter, and fetch your father a drink.'

His daughter went, and the same thing happened to her when she saw the reflection in the water. She had not imagined till then that she was so bonny and, without fetching any water, she went home.

'Where's my drink?' said the shoemaker.

'You homespun old man,' said she, 'do you think I'm fit only to be your slave?'

The poor shoemaker thought they had lost their wits, and went to the well himself. There he saw the lass's reflection in the water. Looking up at the tree, he saw the fairest woman he had ever seen.

'You've a bonny face,' said the shoemaker. 'Come down, for I need you at my house.'

The shoemaker knew that this was the reflection that had driven his family crazy. He took her to his house, and gave her a share of everything.

One day, three young men came to have shoes made for the Prince, who was soon to be married. They saw the giant's daughter.

'You've a bonny daughter,' they said.

'She is that,' said he, 'but she's no daughter of mine.'

'By St Crispin,' said one of them, 'I'd give a hundred pounds to marry her.' And his companions said the same.

'It has nothing to do with me,' said the shoemaker.

'Ask her tonight,' they said, 'and tell us tomorrow.'

The giant's daughter heard this.

'Follow them,' she said. 'I'll marry one of them, but tell him to bring his purse with him.'

The first young man returned, giving the shoemaker a hundred pounds for tocher.

When they went to rest, the lass lay down and asked the young man for a drink of water from the jug on the table. But his hands stuck to the jug, and the jug stuck to the table, so that he could not move till daylight. He went away ashamed, and did not tell his friends what had happened to him.

The next evening the second young man came, bringing a hundred pounds as tocher for the shoemaker. When they went to rest, the lass said to the young man:

'See if the latch is fastened.'

But the latch stuck to his hands, and he could not move till daylight.

He too went away, and did not tell the third young man what had happened.

Then the third man came, and the same thing happened to him. His feet stuck to the ground. He could neither come nor go, and there he stayed till daybreak. That morning he went away and did not look behind him.

'Now,' said the giant's daughter, 'the sporran of gold is yours, shoemaker. I don't need it. It'll help you and reward you for your kindness.'

Now the shoemaker had finished the shoes for the Prince's wedding and was making ready to take them to the castle.

'I would like to peep at the King's son,' said the giant's daughter.

'Come with me then,' said the shoemaker. 'I know the servants at the castle and you'll get a peep at the Prince.'

When the people at Court saw this beautiful young woman, they gave her a glass of wine. As she was about to drink, a flame sprang out of the glass, and a golden pigeon and a silver pigeon flew out of the flame. The pigeons were flying about the hall when three grains of barley fell on the floor. The silver pigeon alighted and ate them.

'When I cleaned the byre,' said the golden pigeon, 'you wouldn't have eaten without giving me a share.'

Three other grains of barley fell. The silver pigeon alighted and ate them up.

'When I thatched the byre,' said the golden pigeon, 'you wouldn't have eaten without giving me a share.'

Three other grains of barley fell. The silver pigeon ate them up too.

'When I harried the magpie's nest,' said the golden pigeon, 'I lost my little claw in the tree.'

Then the King's son noticed that the little finger of the young woman's right hand was missing. At last he remembered, and kissed her from hand to mouth.

The Good Housewife

ONE night, long after her husband and family were in bed, a rich farmer's wife was finishing some cloth she was weaving.

'Oh that I had some help with this cloth!' she said aloud.

At once there was a knock on the door.

'Inary, good housewife, open the door and I'll help you!'

A little old woman dressed in green came in, and sat down at the spinning-wheel. There was a second knock at the door.

'Inary, good housewife, open the door and I'll help you!'

And another little woman dressed in green came in, and sat down at the distaff. There was a third knock on the door.

'Inary, good housewife, open the door and I'll help you!'

And the third little woman dressed in green came in, and sat down to card the wool. Then there was a fourth knock at the door.

'Inary, good housewife, open the door, and I'll help you!'

Another little woman in green came in, and sat down to tease the wool. There was a fifth knock on the door.

'Inary, good housewife, open the door and I'll help you!'

And the fifth little woman in green came in and sat down to pull the wool. A sixth and a seventh and an eighth and a ninth and a tenth, and many more weird little women and men came in, and went to work with distaff, cards, spinning-wheel and loom. The house was full of fairies teasing, carding, pulling and rolling. The fulling-water was boiling over, as they were busy with the cloth, fulling and cleansing it with soap and fuller's earth.

Among the whirr and rasp and rustle and thrum, the good housewife prepared a meal for all her busy little helpers. But the more they worked the hungrier they grew, till the sweat poured off the goodwife's face, as she cooked at the fire for them.

At midnight, she tried to waken the goodman, but he slept like a millstone. Then she thought of a wise man who might help her. So, leaving the fairies eating her newly baked loaves, she slipped out of the house.

'As long as you live,' said the wise man, 'don't wish for anything without thinking about it well beforehand, in case your wish is granted and brings bad luck. Your husband is under a spell, and before you can waken him, your visitors must leave the house, and then you must sprinkle some fulling-water over your goodman.'

'How can I rid myself of my strange visitors?' she asked.

'Return home,' said the wise man, 'stand on the knowe beside your door, and shout three times: "Burg Hill's on fire!" The fairies will all rush out to look. As soon as they are all outside, reverse, invert, put everything topsy-turvy and mixter-maxter.'

The goodwife went home and climbed the knowe at her door.

'Burg Hill's on fire! Burg Hill's on fire! Burg Hill's on fire!' she shouted.

The fairy people rushed out of the house, crying for the treasure they had left in the fairy mound, Burg Hill. The good housewife shut her door and fastened it. Then she took the band off the spinning-wheel, spun the distaff the wrong way round, put the wool-cards together, turned the loom mixter-maxter, and took the fulling-water off the fire.

'Inary, good housewife, let us in!' begged the fairies.

'I can't,' said the goodwife, 'I'm baking bread!'

'Spinning-wheel, come and open the door!' they cried.

'I can't,' said the spinning-wheel, 'I have no band.'

'Distaff, come and open the door!' they cried.

'I can't, I'm twisted the wrong way.'

'Wool-cards, come and open the door!'

'We can't move,' said the cards.

'Loom, come and open the door!'

'I can't, I'm all mixter-maxter.'

'Fulling-water, come and open the door!'

'I can't. I'm off the fire.'

Then the fairies remembered the little bannock that was toasting on the hearth,

'Little Bannock,' they cried, 'open the door!'

The little bannock jumped up and ran to the door. But the goodwife was too quick for him. She caught him and he fell on the floor, broken.

Then the goodwife remembered what she had to do with the fulling-water. She threw a cogful over the goodman, who woke up at once. He got out of bed, and opened the door. At once the fairies became quiet and went away.

THE KING OF LOCHLIN'S THREE DAUGHTERS

THERE was a King of Lochlin, who had three daughters. One day when they were out for a walk they were carried off by three giants and no one knew where they had gone. The King consulted a story-teller and this wise man told him that the giants had taken them under the earth.

'The only way to reach them,' said he, 'is to build a ship that will sail on land and sea.'

So the King sent out a proclamation that any man who could make such a ship could marry his eldest daughter.

Now there was a widow who had three sons. The eldest went to his mother and said:

'Bake me a bannock and roast me a cock. I am going to cut wood and build a ship to sail on land and sea.'

'A large bannock with a malison, or a small bannock with a blessing?' asked his mother.

'A large bannock will be small enough before I've built the ship!'

Away he went with his bannock and roasted cock, to a wood by the river. He sat down to eat, when a great Uruisg, or water goblin, came up out of the water.

'Give me a share of your bannock,' said the Uruisg.

'I'll not do that,' said he. 'There's little enough for myself.'

After he had eaten, he began to chop down a tree, but as soon as he felled a tree it was standing again. At night he gave up and went home.

The next day the second son asked his mother to bake him a bannock and roast him a cock.

'A large bannock with a malison, or a small bannock with a blessing?' she asked.

'A large one will be little enough,' said he.

And away he went with the bannock and roasted cock, to the wood by the river. He sat down to eat, when a great Uruisg came up out of the water.

'Give me a share of your bannock,' said she.

'There's less than enough for myself,' he replied.

The same thing happened to him as to his eldest brother. As fast as he cut down a tree, it was standing again. So he gave up and went home.

Next day the youngest son asked his mother to bake him a bannock and roast him a cock. But he chose the wee bannock with a blessing.

Away he went to the wood by the river. There he sat down to eat, when a great Uruisg came up out of the water, and said:

'Give me a share of your bannock.'

'You shall have that,' said the lad, 'and some of the roasted cock too, if you like.'

After the Uruisg had eaten, she said:

'Meet me here at the end of a year and a day, and I shall have a ship ready to sail on land and sea.'

At the end of a year and a day, the youngest son found that the Uruisg had the ship ready. He went aboard, and sailed away.

He had not sailed far when he saw a man drinking up a river.

'Come with me,' said the lad. 'I'll give you meat and wages, and better work than that.'

'Agreed!' said the man.

They had not sailed far when they saw a man eating all the oxen in a field.

'Come with me,' said the lad. 'I'll give you meat and wages, and better work than that.'

'Agreed!' said the man.

They had not sailed much farther when they saw a man with his ear to the ground.

'What are you doing?' asked the lad.

'I'm listening to the grass coming up through the earth,' said the man.

'Come with me,' said the lad. 'I'll give you meat and wages, and better work than that.'

So he went with the lad and the other two men, and they sailed on till the Listener said:

'I hear the giants and the King's three daughters under the earth.'

So they let a creel down the hole, with four of them in it, to the dwelling of the first giant and the King's eldest daughter.

'You've come for the King's daughter,' said the giant, 'but you'll not get her unless you have a man that can drink as much water as I.'

The lad set the Drinker to compete with the giant. Before the Drinker was half full, the giant burst. They freed the eldest daughter, and went to the house of the second giant.

'You've come for the King's daughter,' said he, 'but you'll not get her till you find a man who can eat as much as I.'

So the lad set the Eater to compete with the giant. Before he was half full, the giant burst. They freed the second daughter, and went to the house of the third giant.

'You've come for the King's daughter,' said the giant, 'but you'll not get her unless you are my slave for a year and a day.'

'Agreed!' said the lad.

Then he sent the Listener, the Drinker and the Eater up in the creel, and after them the three Princesses. The three men left the lad at the bottom of the hole and led the Princesses back to their father, the King of Lochlin. They told the King of all the brave deeds they had done to rescue his daughters.

Now, at the end of a year and a day, the lad told the giant he was leaving, and the giant said:

'I've an eagle that will carry you to the top of the hole.'

The lad mounted the eagle's back, taking fifteen oxen to feed the eagle, but the eagle had eaten them before she had flown half way. So the lad had to return.

'You'll be my slave for another year and a day,' said the giant.

At the end of that time the lad mounted the eagle's back, taking thirty oxen to feed the eagle, but the eagle ate them all before she had flown three-quarters of the way. So they returned.

'You must be my slave for another year and a day,' said the giant.

At the end of that time, the lad mounted the eagle's back, taking sixty oxen to feed the eagle on the way, and they had almost reached the top when the meat was finished. Quickly the lad cut a piece from his own thigh and gave it to the eagle. With one breath they were in the open air.

Before leaving him, the eagle gave the lad a whistle.

'If you are in difficulty,' said she, 'whistle, and I'll help you.'

When the lad reached the King of Lochlin's castle, he went to the smith and asked him if he needed a gillie to blow the bellows. The smith agreed to take him.

Shortly after, the King's eldest daughter ordered the smith to make her a golden crown, like the one she had worn under the earth,

'Bring me the gold, and I'll make the crown,' said the new gillie to the smith.

The smith brought the gold. Then the gillie whistled, and the eagle came at once.

'Fetch the gold crown that hangs behind the first giant's door.'

The eagle returned with the crown, which the smith took to the King's eldest daughter.

'This looks like the crown I had before,' said she.

Then the second daughter ordered the smith to make her a silver crown like the one she had worn under the earth.

'Bring me the silver, and I'll make the crown,' said the gillie.

The smith brought the silver. Then the gillie whistled, and the eagle came.

'Fetch the silver crown that hangs behind the second giant's door,' said the lad.

The eagle returned with the crown, which the smith took to the King's second daughter.

'This looks like the crown I had before,' said she.

Then the King's youngest daughter ordered the smith to make her a copper crown like the one she had worn under the earth.

'Bring me the copper, and I'll make the crown,' said the lad.

The smith brought the copper. Then the gillie whistled, and the eagle came at once.

'Fetch the copper crown that hangs behind the third giant's door,' said the gillie.

The eagle returned with the crown, which the smith took to the King's youngest daughter.

'This looks like the crown I had before,' said she.

'Where did you learn to make such fine crowns?' the King asked the smith.

'It was my gillie who made them,' said he.

'I must see him,' said the King. 'I must ask him to make me a crown.'

The King sent a coach-and-four to fetch the gillie from the smiddy, but when the coachmen saw how dirty he looked they threw him into the coach like a dog. So he whistled for the eagle, who came at once.

'Get me out of this,' said the lad, 'and fill the coach with stones.'

The King came to meet the coach, but when the door was opened for the gillie, a great heap of stones tumbled out instead.

Other servants were sent to fetch the gillie, but they treated him just as badly, so he whistled for the eagle.

'Get me out of this,' said he, 'and fill the coach with rubbish from the midden.'

Again the King came to meet the coach, but when the door was opened for the gillie, a great mound of rubbish fell out on to the King.

The King then sent his trusted old servant to fetch the gillie. He went straight to the smiddy, and found the lad blowing the bellows, his face black with soot.

'The King wishes to see you,' said the King's servant, 'but first, clean a little of the soot off your face.'

The lad washed himself and went with the servant to the King. On the way he whistled for the eagle.

'Fetch me the gold and silver clothes belonging to the giants,' said he.

The eagle returned with the clothes, and when the lad put them on he looked like a prince.

The King came to meet him, and took him to the castle, where he told the King the whole story from beginning to end.

The Drinker, the Eater and the Listener were punished. The King gave his eldest daughter to the lad, so they were married, and the wedding lasted twenty days and twenty nights.

THE WIFE AND HER BUSH OF BERRIES

ONCE upon a time there was a wife who lived in a house by herself. As she was sweeping the house one day, she found twelve pennies.

She wondered what she would do with her twelve pennies, and at last thought she couldn't do better than go to market with them. So she went to the market and bought a kid.

As she was going home she spied a bonny bush of berries growing beside a bridge.

'Kid, kid,' said she, 'look after my house till I pull my bonny, bonny bush of berries.'

'Indeed not,' said the kid, 'I'll not look after your house till you pull your bonny bush of berries.'

Then the wife went to the dog, and said:

> 'Dog, dog, bite kid!
> Kid won't look after my house,
> Till I pull my bonny, bonny bush of berries.'

'Indeed,' said the dog, 'I'll not bite the kid, for the kid never did me any harm.'

Then the wife went to the stick, and said:

> 'Stick, stick, beat dog!
> Dog won't bite kid,

Kid won't look after my house,
Till I pull my bonny, bonny bush of berries.'

'Indeed,' said the stick, 'I won't beat the dog, for the dog never did me any harm.'

Then the wife went to the fire, and said:

'Fire, fire, burn stick!
Stick won't beat dog,
Dog won't bite kid,
Kid won't look after my house,
Till I pull my bonny, bonny bush of berries.'

'Indeed,' said the fire, 'I won't burn the stick, for the stick never did me any harm.'

Then the wife went to the water, and said:

'Water, water, quench fire!
Fire won't burn stick,
Stick won't beat dog,
Dog won't bite kid,
Kid won't look after my house,
Till I pull my bonny, bonny bush of berries.'

'Indeed,' said the water, 'I'll not quench the fire, for the fire never did me any harm.'

Then the wife went on to the ox, and said:

'Ox, ox, drink water!
Water won't quench fire,
Fire won't burn stick,
Stick won't beat dog,
Dog won't bite kid,
Kid won't look after my house,
Till I pull my bonny, bonny bush of berries.'

'Indeed,' said the ox, 'I won't drink the water, for the water never did me any harm.'

Then the wife went to the axe, and said:

'Axe, axe, fell ox!
Ox won't drink water,
Water won't quench fire,
Fire won't burn stick,
Stick won't beat dog,
Dog won't bite kid,
Kid won't look after my house,
Till I pull my bonny, bonny bush of berries.'

'Indeed,' said the axe, 'I'll not fell the ox, for the ox never did me any harm.'

Then the wife went to the smith, and said:

'Smith, smith, blunt axe!
Axe won't fell ox,
Ox won't drink water,
Water won't quench fire,
Fire won't burn stick,
Stick won't beat dog,
Dog won't bite kid,

Kid won't look after my house,
Till I pull my bonny, bonny bush of berries.'

'Indeed,' said the smith, 'I won't blunt the axe, for the axe has never done me any harm.'

Then the wife went to the rope, and said:

'Rope, rope, hang smith!
Smith won't blunt axe,
Axe won't fell ox,
Ox won't drink water,
Water won't quench fire,
Fire won't burn stick,
Stick won't beat dog,
Dog won't bite kid,
Kid won't look after my house,
Till I pull my bonny, bonny bush of berries.'

'Indeed,' said the rope, 'I won't hang the smith, for the smith never did me any harm.'

Then the wife went to the mouse, and said:

'Mouse, mouse, nibble rope!
Rope won't hang smith,
Smith won't blunt axe,
Axe won't fell ox,
Ox won't drink water,
Water won't quench fire,
Fire won't burn stick,
Stick won't beat dog,
Dog won't bite kid,
Kid won't look after my house,
Till I pull my bonny, bonny bush of berries.'

'Indeed,' said the mouse, 'I'll not nibble the rope, for the rope never did me any harm.'

Then the wife went to the cat, and said:

'Cat, cat, kill mouse!
Mouse won't nibble rope,
Rope won't hang smith,
Smith won't blunt axe,
Axe won't fell ox,
Ox won't drink water,
Water won't quench fire,
Fire won't burn stick,
Stick won't beat dog,
Dog won't bite kid,
Kid won't look after my house,
Till I pull my bonny, bonny bush of berries.'

'Indeed,' said the cat, 'I'll not kill the mouse, for the mouse never did me any harm.'

'Do it,' said the wife, 'and I'll give you a dish of cream.'

With that,

The cat began to kill the mouse,

The mouse began to nibble the rope,

The rope began to hang the smith,
The smith began to blunt the axe,
The axe began to fell the ox,
The ox began to drink the water,
The water began to quench the fire,
The fire began to burn the stick,
The stick began to beat the dog,
The dog began to bite the kid,
And the kid looked after the house,
Till the wife pulled her bonny, bonny bush of berries.

BROWNIE THE COW

A CROFTER and his wife lived in a lonely croft in the north-west Highlands of Scotland. They had a son called Tam and a cow called Brownie.

One day the goodwife went to the byre and found the cow was not there. She told her husband and son and together they searched far and wide, but they could not find the cow anywhere.

'What shall we do without Brownie—no milk, no butter and no cheese—we'll get thin.'

'I'll go and look for her,' said Tam.

Off he went with a stout stick and a knapsack of food, for his mother said:

'You'll be away long enough if it's a giant that has taken our Brownie!'

Tam walked on and on till he was tired and hungry. As he sat and ate, he called:

'Brownie! Brownie! Moo so that I can hear you!'

Far, far away there was a faint mooing, so Tam went in that direction. Again he called:

'Brownie! Brownie! Moo so that I can hear you!'

This time the mooing was louder, and again Tam went in that direction. When he felt tired he sat down and called:

'Brownie! Brownie! Moo so that I can hear you!'

This time the mooing was so loud it seemed right underneath him. Tam listened carefully, then he climbed down the hillside to a cave. Inside he found Brownie tied fast by a rope. The rope was too thick and tough to cut with his pocket knife, so he had to undo the complicated knot. When she was freed, he led her out of the cave and they set off for home together.

They had not gone far when Tam saw two giants, one even bigger than the other.

'I don't like the look of those giants,' said Tam. 'With those great strides, they'll catch us up in no time. Brownie, whatever shall we do?'

'Take a hair from my tail and lay it across the road.'

Tam did this, then the cow said:

'Hair of my tail, turn into a river so wide that none can cross but a bird on the wing.'

At once the hair changed into a vast river, so wide Tam could barely see the giants on the other side. All the same, the bigger giant of the two shouted across:

'That's not going to stop me from catching you, my lad!' And he said to the smaller giant: 'Go, fetch our biggest bull.'

Soon he was back with the biggest bull Tam had ever seen. The bull drank up the river, every drop.

'Whatever shall we do now, Brownie?' asked Tam.

'Take a hair from my ear and lay it across the road.'

Tam did this and the cow said to the hair:

'Hair of my ear, turn into a fire that nothing can quench, except a wide river that none can cross but a bird on the wing.'

Instantly the hair turned into a fire that blazed as far as the eye could see.

'That'll not help you, my lad,' said the giants and called their bull. The bull spewed up all the river water it had drunk, and put the fire out.

'What shall we do now, Brownie?' asked Tam.

'Take a hair from my back and lay it on the ground.'

Tam did this and the cow said:

'Hair of my back, turn into a mountain range so high that none can cross but a bird on the wing.'

At once the hair turned into a mountain range so high the top of it was out of sight.

'That'll not help you, my lad,' shouted the bigger giant, and he sent the smaller one to fetch their giant drill.

The giants drilled a hole right through the mountain. The bigger giant was very excited when he looked through the hole and saw the boy and his cow. He immediately tried to squeeze through to catch them. This was a great mistake. The giant was much too big. The more he struggled to get through the hole, the faster he stuck. Try as he may, his companion could neither push him forward nor pull him back. Nor could he drill another hole by himself, so he had to stay where he was. As for the bigger giant, he was stuck fast and there he stayed till he turned into stone.

Tam led Brownie safely back to his mother and father. And there she stayed and gave them milk for the rest of her days.

HOW THE COCK GOT THE BETTER OF THE FOX

A Fox came to a farm and caught hold of a cock. Away he went with the Cock in his mouth, and all the farm-hands after him.

'Aren't they silly, running after you,' said the Cock. 'They'll never catch you!'

The Fox nodded with pleasure. He was glad the Cock was so willing to go along with him, but he didn't say a word.

'Oh, clever Fox, won't you say to those farm-hands, "This is my good friend, the Cock"? Then they'll turn back.'

'Fiddlesticks! You stupid fellow!' said the Fox, determined not to be taken in by the Cock's flattery.

But as soon as he opened his mouth, the Cock flew away. It was a long, long time before the Fox had the face to go back to that farm, where everyone was waiting to laugh at him.

The Smith and the Fairies

YEARS ago there lived in Crossbrig a smith called MacEachern. His only child was a strong healthy lad about fourteen years old. Suddenly he fell ill, and nobody knew what was wrong with him. He became thin, old and yellow. His father was afraid he would die, although he had an enormous appetite.

One day an old man, well known for his knowledge of the out-of-the-way things, walked into the smiddy, and MacEachern told him about the lad. The old man looked very grave, and said:

'That is not your son. Your lad has been carried away by the fairies, and they have left a changeling in his place.'

'What am I to do?' asked the smith. 'How am I ever going to see my lad again?'

'I will tell you how,' said the old man. 'But first, make sure it is not your own son. Take as many egg-shells as you can find. Take them into his room, and spread them out carefully where he can see them. Then fetch water in them, carrying them two by two in your hands as if they were very heavy. When they are full, arrange them round the fire as if it were very important.'

The smith did this.

He had not been long at work when there came a shout of crazy laughter from the bed, and a voice said:

'I'm now eight hundred years old, and I've never seen anything like that before!'

The smith told this to the old man, who said:

'Get rid of this changeling as soon as possible, and I think I can promise you your son. First of all, you must light a very big fire by the changeling's bed. Then you must seize him and throw him into the middle of it. Then he'll fly through the roof.'

The smith took the old man's advice. He kindled a big fire, and seizing the changeling, flung him into the fire without hesitation. The changeling gave a terrible yell, and sprang up through the roof, leaving a hole that let out the smoke.

Then the old man told the smith that his son was inside the green hill of the fairies.

'Go there tonight when it is dark,' said the old man, 'and take a sleeping cock with you. You'll find your son.'

So that night the smith, with a sleeping cock in his arms, went out into the darkness. When he got to the hill of the fairies, he saw a light and heard sounds of piping, dancing and other merriment. Boldly he approached the entrance to the fairies' cave and went in. There he saw his son working at a forge. The fairies saw him and asked him what he wanted.

'I want my son,' said he, 'and I'll not go away without him!'

The fairies roared with laughter. This wakened the cock. It leapt up on the smith's shoulder, clapped its wings and crowed loud and long.

Now fairies cannot bear the crowing of a cock, for when they hear it the power of magic leaves them. Mad with anger, these fairies seized the smith and his son and threw them out of the green hill, into the darkness.

For a year and a day the lad did no work and seldom spoke. One day he was sitting by the fire watching the smith finish a sword he was making for a chief. It was to be a very special sword.

'That's not the way to make it,' said the lad.

Taking the tools from his father, he set to work and made a sword, the like of which had never been seen before in the country.

From that day, the lad worked constantly with his father. The fame of the special sword and the skill that had made it, spread far and wide. It kept the smith and his son busy and made them wealthy. They were never again troubled by the fairies.

The Gael and the London Baillie's Daughter

Once a young Gael fell in love with a lady he saw in a dream. He told his father about her.

'I will marry no one else,' said he, 'though I have to search the whole world for her.'

'Go, if you must,' said his father, 'and I'll give you a hundred pounds to take with you. When it is spent, come home, and I'll give you another hundred.'

So the lad took the hundred pounds, and went to France, to Spain, and all over the world, but he could not find her anywhere. By the time he arrived in London, he had spent his money, his clothes were worn, and he did not know what he was going to do for a night's lodging. As he wandered along the streets, he told his story to an old woman, who offered to help him.

'I'm from the Highlands of Scotland, too,' she said, 'and I'd be pleased to give you hospitality.'

She took him to her house, gave him some clean clothes, a good supper and a comfortable bed to lie on.

'Go out into the city,' she said next day, 'and maybe you'll meet the one you're looking for.'

The lad was walking along a city street when he saw a beautiful young woman at a window. He knew at once that she was the one he had seen in his dream, but he was too shabby to approach her. So he went back to the old woman and told her everything.

'That was the London Baillie's daughter. I was her nurse, so perhaps I can help you. I'll give you fine Highland clothes. When you see her walking along the High Street, you must tread on her gown. When she turns round, speak to her.'

The lad thanked her, and did this. He went out, saw the beautiful young woman, and stepped on the edge of her gown. At once she turned round.

'I ask your pardon,' he said, bowing.

'It was not your fault,' she said, 'the gown is too long. You are a stranger here. Will you not come home and dine with us?'

As they dined, he told her his story, and how he had seen her in a dream, and had searched for her ever since.

'I saw you in a dream on the same night,' she said.

'Will you marry me?' said he.

'Come back here in a year and a day. In this city the Baillie, my father, must put my hand in yours before we can marry.'

So the lad returned to Scotland, and told his father all that had happened. When the year was nearly spent, he set off for London. His father had given him another hundred pounds and some good oatmeal bannocks.

On the road he met a Sassenach.

'What's your business in London?' said the Saxon.

'When I was there last I planted a lint-seed in a street, and I'm going back to see how it is growing,' said the lad, 'If it is ripe, I'll take it back with me, if not I'll leave it.'

'Well,' said the Saxon, 'that's a stupid thing to do. As for me, I'm going to marry the London Baillie's only daughter.'

They walked on together. At last the Saxon felt hungry. He had no food with him, and there was no house near. So he turned to the lad:

'Will you give me some of your food?'

'I've only some oatcakes,' said the lad, 'but you're welcome to share them. If I was a gentleman like you, I'd never travel without my mother.'

'What a foolish idea!' said the Saxon, as he took a bannock and ate it. Then they went on their way.

They had not gone far when it began to rain. The Gael had a rough plaid to protect him, but the Saxon had nothing.

'Lend me your plaid!' said he.

'I'll lend you part of it,' said the lad, 'but if I were a gentleman like you, I'd never travel without my house.'

'You are a fool!' laughed the Saxon. 'My house is four storeys high, so how could I bring it with me?'

Then he wrapped one end of the Highlander's plaid about his shoulders, and on they went.

They had not gone far when they came to a river. There was no bridge over it, and the Saxon would not wet his feet.

'Will you carry me over?' he said to the lad.

'I'll do that,' he said, 'but if I were a gentleman like you, I'd never travel without my own bridge.'

'You certainly are a silly fellow,' laughed the Saxon. But he got on to the lad's back for all that, and on they went. At last they came to London town.

The Saxon went to the Baillie's house, and told this story:

'On the way, I met a Gael, a most stupid fellow! He was coming to London for lint he had planted a year ago. He told me I should never travel without my mother, my house and my bridge! However, he was a good-natured fool. He shared his food and his plaid, and carried me over a river.'

'He would appear to be wiser than the man he spoke to,' said the Baillie. 'The lint was the maid he left in London. If her love had grown, he would take her with him. By your mother he meant the food you should have had with you, for she was your first nourishment. By your house he meant a coach, and the bridge was your saddle-horse. A gentleman should not travel without these things and then ask help from others. A smart lad indeed, and I'd like to meet him.'

Next day the Highlander visited the Baillie, and was warmly welcomed.

'I'd like to help a smart lad like you!' said the Baillie.

'I hear it is the custom in this city,' said the lad, 'that no man can marry unless the Baillie gives him the bride by the hand. Will you give me the hand of the lass I've come to marry?'

'I'll do that,' said the Baillie.

Next day the Baillie's daughter went disguised to her old nurse. The Baillie, when he came, did not recognise her.

'It's an honour for you to marry such a fine lad,' said he. 'Put your hand in his, lass!' Then he placed his daughter's hand into the lad's and they were betrothed.

The Baillie went home, feeling well pleased with himself. He remembered that he would be giving his daughter's hand to the Saxon gentleman. But his daughter was nowhere to be found.

'I'll lay a wager that young Gael has got her after all!' he said.

Just then, in came the Gael with his daughter, and they told him all that had happened.

'Well, I've given you my daughter's hand,' said he, 'and I'm glad she has such a smart lad for a husband!'

The London Baillie's daughter and the young Gael were married and had a wedding that lasted a year and a day.

The Wee Bannock

There lived an old man and his old wife at the side of a burn. They had two cows, five hens and a cock, a cat and two kittens. The old man looked after the cows, and the old wife span on the distaff. The kittens often clawed at the old wife's spindle as it danced over the hearth-stone.

'Sho, sho,' she said, 'go away!' And so it danced about.

One day, after porridge time, she thought she would have a bannock. So she baked two oatmeal bannocks, and set them to the fire to toast. After a while, the old man came in, sat beside the fire, took up one of the bannocks and snapped it through the middle. When the other one saw this, it ran off as fast as it could, and the old wife after it, with the spindle in one hand and the distaff in the other.

But the wee bannock went away, out of sight, and ran till it came to a fine large thatched house, and in it ran till it came to the fireside. There were three tailors sitting on a big table. When they saw the wee bannock come in, they jumped up and went behind the goodwife, who was carding flax beside the fire.

'Don't be frightened,' said she. 'It's only a wee bannock. Catch it, and I'll give you a mouthful of milk with it.'

Up she got with the flax-cards, and the tailor with the smoothing-iron, and the two apprentices, the one with the big shears and the other with the lap-board. But it dodged them and ran about the fire. One of the apprentices, thinking to snap it with the shears, fell into the ash-pit.

The tailor threw the smoothing-iron, and the goodwife the flax-cards, but it was no use. The bannock escaped, and ran till it came to a wee house at the roadside, and there was a weaver sitting at the loom, and the wife winding a hank of yarn.

'Tibby,' said he, 'what's that?'

'Oh,' said she, 'it's a wee bannock.'

'It's welcome,' said he, 'for our gruel was but thin today. Catch it, woman, catch it!'

'Ay,' said she, 'if I can. That's a clever bannock. Catch it, Willie! Catch, man!'

'Cast the clew at it!' said Willie.

But the wee bannock ran round about, across the floor and over the hill, like a new-tarred sheep or a mad cow. On it ran to the next house, and in to the fireside, where the goodwife was churning.

'Come away, wee bannock,' said she. 'I'm having cream and bread today.'

But the wee bannock ran round the churn, the wife after it, and in the hurry she nearly overturned the churn. Before she had set it right again, the wee bannock was off, down the hillside to the mill and in it ran.

The miller was sifting meal at the trough but, looking up, he smiled at the wee bannock.

'Ay,' said he, 'it's a sign of plenty when you're running about and no-body to look after you. I like bannock and cheese. Come away in and I'll give you a night's quarters.'

But the wee bannock wouldn't trust itself with the miller and his cheese. It ran out of the mill, and the miller didn't trouble to chase after it.

Well, it ran and it ran, till it came to the smiddy. In it went and up to the anvil. The blacksmith was making his horse-nails.

'I like a cog of good ale, and a well-toasted bannock,' said the smith. 'Come away in here.'

The bannock was frightened when it heard about the ale, and ran off as hard as it could, the smith after it. He threw his hammer at it, but the wee bannock whirled away, and was out of sight in an instant. It ran and ran till it came to a farmhouse with a large peat-stack at the end of it. In it ran to the fireside. The goodman was separating lint, and the goodwife was dressing flax.

'Janet,' said he, 'there's a wee bannock. I'll have the half of it!'

'Well, John, I'll have the other half. Hit it over the back with a clew.'

The bannock played tig. The goodwife threw the heckle at it, but it was too clever for her.

Off it ran up the stream to the next house, and whirled away in to the fireside. The goodwife was stirring gruel and the goodman plaiting rush-ropes for the cattle.

'Hey, Jock,' said the goodwife, 'come here! You are always crying about a bannock. Here's one. Come in, hurry now! I'll help you catch it.'

'Ay, wife, where is it?'

'See, there. Run over to that side.'

But the wee bannock ran in behind the goodman's chair. Jock fell among the rushes. The goodwife threw the porridge-stick and the goodman a rope, but the bannock was too clever for either of them. It was off and out of sight in an instant, through the whins, and down the road to the next house. In it went to the fireside just as the folk were sitting down to their gruel, and the goodwife was scraping the pot.

'Losh,' said she, 'there's a wee bannock come in to warm itself at our fireside!'

'Shut the door,' said the goodman, 'and we'll try to get a grip of it.'

When the wee bannock heard this, it ran into the kitchen, and they after it with their spoons. The goodman threw his bonnet, but the wee bannock ran and ran, and faster ran, till it came to another house. When it went in, the folk were just going to their beds. The goodman was casting off his trousers, and the goodwife was raking the fire.

'What's that?' said he.

'Oh,' said she, 'it's a wee bannock.'

'I could do with the half of it, for all the porridge I supped,' said he.

'Catch it!' said the wife, 'and I'll have a bit too. Throw your trousers at it! Kep! Kep!'

The goodman threw his trousers at it and nearly smothered it. But it wrestled out, and ran, the goodman after it without his trousers. There was a rare chase over the croft field, up the yard, and among the whins. There the goodman lost it, and had to go home half naked. But it had grown dark. The wee bannock couldn't see. He went through a whin bush, and right into a fox's hole. The fox had had no meat for two days.

'Welcome, welcome,' said the fox, and snapped it in two.

And that was the end of the wee bannock.

The Brown Bear of the Green Glen

There was once a King who became blind. One day his two eldest sons came to him and said:

'Father, if you bathe your eyes in water from the Green Glen you'll certainly see. We'll go and look for the Green Glen and if we find it we'll bring three bottles of water for you.'

The King gave them his blessing and off they went in search of the Green Glen. They refused to take their youngest brother, John, who wanted to go with them. They said he was too stupid, but he put three empty bottles in a knapsack and followed them. At the next town he caught up with them.

'So there you are,' said he.

'Take yourself off home,' said his brothers, 'we don't want to be bothered with you.'

'Don't worry,' said John, 'I'll not follow you. I'll go my own way.' And so he did. On and on he went till he came to a dark wood.

'I'm not going through that wood,' said John to himself. 'It's much too dark.' And he climbed to the top of a tree.

Soon he saw Brown Bear carrying a burning stick in his mouth. Brown Bear stopped, dropped the stick on a rock, and looked up at John.

'I see you, Son of the King of Erin,' said he. 'Come down from that tree! I want to talk to you.'

'I will not,' said John. 'I'm safer up here.'

'If you don't come down, I'll climb up to you!'

'Wait,' said John, 'stand two steps away from the tree and I'll come down.'

Brown Bear stepped from the tree, and John climbed down.

'Now we can be friends,' said Brown Bear. 'Are you hungry?'

'I am,' said John.

'Then watch me!' Brown Bear chased a roebuck and caught it. 'We'll have roebuck for supper,' said he. 'Do you like your meat cooked or raw?

'Cooked,' said John.

Brown Bear took the burning stick and made a fire. Then he roasted the roebuck and they ate it between them.

'Lie here, between my paws,' said Brown Bear, 'and you'll have a good night's sleep and not feel cold nor hunger.'

John lay down, his head between Brown Bear's paws, and was soon fast asleep. Early next morning Brown Bear nudged him, and said:

'Are you awake, Son of the King of Erin?'

'I am,' said John.

'Then it's time you were on the soles of your feet. We've a long way to go. Come, jump on my back and we'll go like the wind!'

John jumped on Brown Bear's back, and away they went till they reached a giant's house.

'You must stay here tonight,' said Brown Bear. 'This giant is grumpy but if you tell him Brown Bear of the Green Glen brought you here, he'll give you supper and a comfortable bed.'

John got off Brown Bear's back. He knocked on the door and the giant opened it.

'I've been waiting for you,' said he. 'I'm not sure whether to stamp you into the earth with my foot or blow you into the sky with my breath.'

'You'll do neither,' said John. 'Brown Bear of the Green Glen brought me here.'

'In that case, you'll be well cared for tonight.'

Sure enough, the giant kept his word. John got a good supper and a comfortable bed. Next morning Brown Bear came.

'Are you awake, Son of the King of Erin?' he asked. 'It's time you were on your feet. We've a long way to go. Come, jump on my back.'

John got on Brown Bear's back and did not let go till they reached the second giant's house.

'You'll spend the night here, and you'll find this giant grumpier than the last, but tell him I brought you and you'll be well cared for,' said Brown Bear.

So John knocked on the door, the giant opened it and said:

'So you've come at last! Shall I stamp you into the earth with my foot or blow you away with my breath?'

'You'll do neither,' said John. 'Brown Bear of the Green Glen brought me here.'

'Well, in that case you're welcome to stay the night.'

Again John was given a good supper and a comfortable bed, and the next morning Brown Bear came for him.

'It's time you were up and about,' said he. 'We've a long way to go. Come, get on my back and hold tight.'

John did as the Bear told him. They rode as fast as the wind till they came to the third giant's house.

'This giant is difficult,' said Brown Bear. 'As soon as you're inside his house he'll wrestle with you. He'll be hard on you, and as soon as you need help, tell him I'll get the better of him.'

Sure enough, once John was inside the house, the third giant seized him. They wrestled till they made a bog of the rock. They sank so deep into the ground that spring-water gushed from under their feet. The giant was so hard on John that he called out:

'If Brown Bear of the Green Glen were here, you'd not be so rough!'

Immediately Brown Bear was at John's side, ready to defend him.

He threw the carcass of a stag between John and the giant, and the giant vanished.

'Son of the King of Erin,' said the Brown Bear, 'now I must leave you. An eagle will fly down and settle on the stag's carcass. With this sword, and without shedding a drop of blood, cut off the wart above Eagle's left eye.'

Eagle alighted on the carcass and began to eat. John saw the wart, and with one stroke of the sword, struck off the wart without drawing a drop of blood.

'Come, sit between my wings,' said Eagle.

John did as he was told and away they flew over sea and land till they came to the Green Glen.

'Fill your bottles with the water,' said Eagle. 'Be quick! Fill them before the Black Dogs see you!'

As John filled his bottles, he saw a house at the edge of the water. He found no one there, but on the table were a glass and a bottle of wine. He filled the glass and after he had drunk the wine, the bottle was still full.

'I'll take this bottle with me,' said he.

There was also a loaf of bread on the table. John cut a slice, ate it and still the loaf remained whole.

'I'll not leave you behind,' said John, putting the loaf in his knapsack.

There was also a big round cheese on the table. John cut a wedge of cheese, ate it and still the round cheese was whole, so he put it into his knapsack with the loaf, the bottle of wine, and the three bottles of Green Glen water. Then he returned to Eagle.

'You're lucky the Black Dogs didn't see you,' said Eagle.

Beside him, John suddenly saw the Bonny Lass. She was so lovely he kissed her and he was very sorry to leave her, but he had to climb on the Eagle's back.

Eagle flew back the way they had come. As they passed, the third giant called out:

'Son of the King of Erin, give me a drink.'

Eagle swooped down and John offered the giant the bottle of wine. The giant drained it and still it was full.

'I'll give you a bag of gold for this bottle,' said the giant.

'That's a bargain,' said John, 'but you must promise to give it to the Bonny Lass when she comes this way.'

'She'll get it,' promised the third giant.

John gave him the bottle of wine and put the bag of gold in his own knapsack. On he flew on Eagle's back till they passed over the second giant's house.

'Son of the King of Erin,' called the giant, 'give me a bite of bread.'

Eagle swooped down and John cut a chunk of bread from the loaf. When the giant had eaten it he saw the loaf was still whole.

'I'll give you a bag of silver for that loaf,' said he.

'That's a bargain,' said John, 'but you must promise to give it to the Bonny Lass when she comes this way.'

'She shall have it,' promised the giant.

So John gave him the loaf of bread and put the bag of silver in his knapsack. Away he flew on Eagle's back till they came to the first giant's house. The giant waved to them and shouted:

'Son of the King of Erin, give me a slice of cheese.'

Eagle swooped down and John cut the giant a slice from the big round of cheese. When the giant had eaten it he saw that the round of cheese was still whole.

'I'll give you a bag of precious stones for that cheese,' said he.

'Done,' agreed John, 'but you must promise to give it to the Bonny Lass when she comes this way.'

'I'll do that,' promised the giant.

So John gave him the cheese and put the bag of precious stones in his knapsack. He jumped on Eagle's back and away they flew till they came to his father's palace. Outside the palace walls, he saw his two elder brothers. They were not pleased to see him, but he greeted them.

'Did you have any luck?' he asked. 'Did you find the waters of the Green Glen?'

'We did not,' they replied, 'and nor did you, by the look of you.'

'That's where you're wrong,' said John. 'Look at this.' He opened his knapsack and showed them the three bottles of water from the Green Glen.

'There's a bottle for each of us. Come lads, let's take them to our father. He'll be tired of blindness.'

So the three brothers went off together, but when they were in a quiet place, the two elder lads attacked John. When they thought he was dead they threw him behind a dyke, stole the three bottles of water from his knapsack and took them to the King of Erin, their father.

Meanwhile John lay behind the dyke and did not stir when the smith came and threw some rusty old iron over the dyke, on top of him. He lay there as though he was dead. The rusty iron got into his wounds, and it was a long time before they healed. When they did, they left rough and ugly scars all over his face; no one recognised him as the son of the King. He became known as the Lad with the Rough Skin who helped the smith in his foundry and smiddy.

As for the Bonny Lass John had left in the Green Glen, she grew pale and heavy, and after nine months she had a little son. She looked for John and could not find him, so she went to a spey-wife.

'Can you help me find the father of my little son?'

'All I can do is to give you this bird,' said the spey-wife. 'It will perch on the head of your young son's father and on the head of no one else.'

So the Bonny Lass took her son and the magic bird. They searched the Green Glen from end to end, but the bird did not stir.

'I'll walk the four brown quarters of the earth to find him,' said the Bonny Lass.

At last she came to the third giant's house. There, on a table, was a bottle of wine.

'Who gave you that?' she asked the giant.

'The son of the King of Erin,' he replied. 'He told me to give you the bottle of wine when you came this way.'

So she took the bottle and went on her way till she came to the second giant's house. There, on a table, she saw a loaf of bread.

'Who gave you that?' she asked the giant.

'The son of the King of Erin,' said he. 'He told me to give it to you when you came by.'

She took the loaf and went on and on till she came to the first giant's house, and there, on a board, was a large round cheese.

'Who gave you the cheese?' she asked the giant.

'The son of the King of Erin,' he replied. 'Now I have to give it to you.'

The Bonny Lass took the cheese, along with the bread, the wine, the magic bird and her small son. On and on she went till she came to the palace of the King of Erin. There she stood at the gate, watching the people as they came and went. There were many young men amongst them, but not once did the bird stir. At last it seemed as if everyone in the town had passed through the gate. Bonny Lass was in despair. She thought she would never see the Prince again. She asked the smith if there were any young men in the town who had not passed through the gate that day.

'Well, there's the rough-skinned lad who helps me in the smiddy. He hasn't left his work today,' said the smith. 'But you'll not be meaning him, surely?'

'Rough or not, I'd like to see him,' she said.

'I'll send him here right away,' said the smith.

As soon as the magic bird saw the rough-skinned lad, it perched on his head. When she saw that, Bonny Lass ran to him and kissed him. As soon as she kissed him, the rough skin healed and she knew him without a doubt.

'You're the father of my little son,' said she.

'And you're my Bonny Lass,' said the Prince and kissed her.

The King came to see what was happening. He recognised his long-lost youngest son, for he had recovered the sight of both eyes after bathing them with the water from the Green Glen.

'John,' said he, 'was it you who fetched the water for my eyes?'

'It was, father. My brothers took it from me.'

'What shall be done with your cruel brothers?'

'The same as they did to me.'

Then John took the Bonny Lass by the hand and they were married. There was a magnificent feast and the Brown Bear of the Green Glen came and danced at the wedding.

FATHER WREN AND HIS TWELVE SONS

ONE day, Father Wren and his twelve sons were in the barn threshing corn, when the sly fox, Tod, came by.

'I want one of your sons, old wren,' said he.

'Which of us are you speaking to?' said a wren. 'We know we all look alike and there's nothing to choose between us. If you can point out which is the father, you may have your pick of us.'

The fox looked at the wrens. It was true. They all looked exactly alike, as they carried on with the threshing. He could not tell one from another. Then he said:

'It's easy to tell the old hero from the rest of you, by the skilful way he works!'

'Ah, you should have seen me when I was a young wren,' said the old one, giving himself away without thinking, for he could not resist the flattery of the sly fox, Tod.

After that the fox took away one of his sons without any argument.

❧ ❧ ❧

There was another old wren who, with his twelve sons, was by the peat-bog, when he saw a plant he wanted. He tried to pull it up by the root, but he was not strong enough, so he called to one of his twelve sons to help him. They both pulled this way and that way, till they were white in the face and red in the cheeks, but they could not pull the root out of the ground.

'Come and give us a hand!' called the old wren to another son.

But the three of them were no better than two. Although they pulled this way and that with all their strength, they could not move the root.

One after another of the sons came to help. They all pulled together but it was no use till the twelfth son came. Then the thirteen wrens pulled, pulled with all their might and were white in the face and red in the cheeks, when all of a sudden, the plant came out of the ground, root and all. The old wren fell back on his first son, the first fell back on the second son, the second fell back on the third son, the third fell on the fourth son, the fourth fell on the fifth son, the fifth fell on the sixth son, the sixth fell on the seventh son, the seventh fell on the eighth son, the eighth fell on the ninth son, the ninth fell on the tenth son, the tenth fell on the eleventh son, and the eleventh fell on the twelfth son, who fell back into the peat-bog, taking all the others with him.

MALLY WHUPPIE

ONCE upon a time a man and a woman had so many children they could not get enough food to feed them all. So they took the three youngest lasses and left them in a wood.

The three children walked and walked, without seeing a house. It began to grow dark and they were hungry. At last they saw a light, and made for it. They found it was a house.

They knocked at the door. A woman opened it and asked them what they wanted. They begged her to let them in and give them a bite of bread. The woman said she could not do that, as her husband was a giant and he would kill them if he came home and found them there.

'Let us stay just for a while,' they begged. 'We'll go away before your husband returns.'

So the woman took them in and set them down by the fire, and gave them bread and milk. But just as they had begun to eat, there was the sound of heavy footsteps and in came the giant, and bellowed:

'Fee, fa, fo, fum!
I smell the blood of some earthly one!'

'What have you there, wife, what have you there?' he said.

'Three poor lasses cold and hungry. They'll go away as soon as they've had a bite of food,' said she. 'You'll not touch them, husband?'

The giant said nothing, but ate his supper. Then he ordered the three lasses to stay the night, and share a bed with his own three daughters.

Before they went to bed, the giant put straw ropes round the necks of the strangers, while round the necks of his three daughters he put chains of gold. Now, the youngest of the three strangers was called Mally Whuppie. She was very clever, and noticed what the giant had done. She took good care not to fall asleep, but waited till she was sure all the others were sound asleep.

Then she slipped out of bed and exchanged the necklaces. The giant's daughters now wore straw necklaces, while Mally Whuppie and her two sisters wore necklaces of gold. Then she lay down again, pretending to be asleep.

In the middle of the night, the giant got up, armed with a heavy club, and in the dark he felt for the girls with the straw necklaces. He took his own three daughters out of the bed and beat them. Then he lay down again.

Mally Whuppie thought it was time she and her sisters were away, so she wakened them and told them to be very quiet. They slipped out of the house and ran, and ran, till morning when they came to a King's house. Mally told their story to the King.

'Well, Mally, you're a clever lass,' said he, 'and you've done well. But if you'd do better, go back and take the giant's sword that hangs at the back of his bed. Bring it to me and I'll marry your eldest sister to my eldest son.'

Mally said she would try. So she went back, slipped into the giant's house and crept below the bed.

The giant came home, ate a big supper, hung up his sword and went to bed. Mally Whuppie waited until he was snoring, then she crept out, stretched over the giant and took down the sword. But as she did so, it gave a rattle. Up jumped the giant, but Mally Whuppie dodged out of the door with the sword.

Mally ran, and the giant ran, till they came to the Bridge of One Hair. She won over, but he could not.

'Woe be to you, Mally Whuppie!' cried the giant. 'May you never come here again!'

'Twice yet, carle!' said she.

Mally Whuppie took the sword to the King, and her eldest sister was married to his eldest son.

'You've done well, Mally Whuppie!' cried the King, 'but if you would do better, bring me the purse under the giant's pillow, and I'll marry your second sister to my second son.'

Mally said she would try. She set out for the giant's house, slipped in below the bed, and waited till the giant had eaten his supper and was snoring.

Then she crept out, slipped her hand under the pillow and took the purse. But just as she was going out the coins clinked in the purse. The giant woke up, and was after her in no time.

She ran, and he ran, till they came to the Bridge of One Hair. She won over, but he could not.

'Woe to you, Mally Whuppie,' said he. 'May you never come here again!'

'Once more, carle!' said she.

Mally took the purse to the King, and her second sister was married to his second son.

'Mally, you're a clever lass,' said the King, 'but if you would do better still, bring me the giant's ring he wears on his finger, and I'll give you my youngest son.'

Mally said she would try. Back she went to the giant's house, crept in, hid below the bed and waited till the giant came in and had eaten his supper. Soon he was snoring.

Then Mally crept out, reached over the bed and took hold of the giant's hand. She twisted and twisted till the ring came off. But at that very moment the giant rose and gripped her by the hand.

'Now, I have caught you, Mally Whuppie,' said he, 'and if I had done as much ill to you as you have done to me, what would you do?'

'I'd put you in a bag,' said she, 'and I'd put a cat and a dog beside you, and a needle, thread and scissors. Then I'd hang you on the wall. I'd go into the wood for a thick stick, and I'd come home and take the bag down, with you still inside. Then I'd beat it with the stick.'

'Well, Mally, I'll do just that to you,' said the giant.

So he put Mally into a large bag, and the cat and dog in beside her, and a needle, thread and scissors. Then he hung the bag up on the wall, and went to the wood to find a heavy stick.

'Oh, if you saw what I see!' sang Mally, inside the bag.

'What do you see?' asked the giant's wife.

But Mally only went on singing: 'Oh if you saw what I see!'

The giant's wife begged Mally to take her up into the bag so that she might see what Mally saw. So Mally took the scissors and cut a hole in the bag, and jumped out, taking the needle and thread with her. She helped the giant's wife up into the bag, and sewed up the hole.

'I see nothing!' cried the giant's wife. 'Let me out!'

But Mally took no notice, and hid herself at the back of the door.

Home came the giant, a great stick in his hand. He took down the bag, and began to beat it.

'Stop! It's me, husband!' cried his wife. 'It's me!'

But the dog barked and the cat mewed inside the bag, and he did not hear his wife's voice. Now, Mally did not want the wife to be killed, so she ran out by the back door. The giant saw her and was after her.

He ran, and she ran, till they came to the Bridge of One Hair, and she won over, but he could not.

'Woe be to you, Mally Whuppie,' he cried. 'May you never return here again!'

'Never more, carle!' said she.

Mally Whuppie took the ring to the King, and married his youngest son.

THE WHITE PET

THERE was once a farmer who had a sheep he called his White Pet. One day before Christmas, he decided to kill this animal. The White Pet heard this and ran away. He had not gone far when he met a Bull.

'Hullo, White Pet,' said the Bull. 'Where are you going?'

'I'm going to seek my fortune,' said White Pet. 'They were going to kill me for Christmas, so I thought I'd better run away.'

'I'll go with you,' said the Bull. 'They were going to do the same with me.'

'The bigger the party, the better the fun,' said White Pet.

So they went on together till they met a Dog.

'Hullo, White Pet,' said the Dog.

'Hullo, Dog!'

'Where are you going?' said the Dog.

'I'm running away. I heard they were going to kill me for Christmas.'

'They were going to shoot me,' said the Dog, 'so I'll go along with you and the Bull!'

'Come on then,' said the White Pet.

So on they went, all three, till a Cat joined them.

'Hullo, White Pet,' said the Cat.

'Hullo, Cat,' said White Pet.

'Where are you going?' said the Cat.

'I'm going to seek my fortune,' said the White Pet. 'They were going to kill me for Christmas.'

'They were talking of drowning me,' said the Cat, 'so I'll go along with you, the Bull and the Dog.'

'Come on then!' said the White Pet, and away they went, all four, till they met a Cock.

'Hullo, White Pet,' said the Cock.

'Hullo to yourself, Cock,' said the White Pet.

'Where are you going?' said the Cock.

'I'm running away,' said the White Pet. 'They were going to kill me for Christmas.'

'They were going to kill me too,' said the Cock, 'so I'll go along with you.'

'Come on then,' said the White Pet, and away they went all five, till they met a Goose.

'Hullo, White Pet!' said the Goose.

'Hullo yourself, Goose,' said the White Pet.

'Where are you going?' said the Goose.

'Oh,' said the White Pet, 'I'm running away. They were going to kill me for Christmas.'

'They were going to kill me too,' said the Goose. 'So I'll go along with you.'

'Come on then,' said the White Pet, and on they went all six, till it was dark. They saw a light far away. It came from a house, and though it was far away, they were not long getting there. They looked in at the window, and there they saw thieves counting money.

'Let each one of us call his own call,' said the White Pet. 'I'll call my own call. Let the Bull call his own call, the Dog his own call, the Cat her own call, the Cock his own call and the Goose her own call.'

With that they gave one LOUD SHOUT:

'GAIRE! GAIRE!'

When the thieves heard the noise, they fled into the wood near by. When the White Pet and his companions saw the house was empty, they went in. They divided the money among themselves, and then decided to go to sleep.

'Where will you sleep tonight, Bull?' said the White Pet.

'I'll sleep behind the door,' said the Bull. 'Where will you sleep yourself, White Pet?'

'I'll sleep in the middle of the floor,' said the White Pet.

'I'll sleep beside the fire,' said the Dog. 'Where will you sleep, Cat?'

'I'll sleep in the candle-cupboard,' said the Cat.

'Where will you sleep, Cock?' said the White Pet.

'I'll sleep on the rafters,' said the Cock. 'Where will you sleep, Goose?'

'I'll sleep in the midden,' said the Goose.

After they had all gone to rest, one of the thieves returned to the house and looked in. Everything was dark and still. He went to the candle-cupboard for a candle, but when he put his hand in the box, the Cat scratched him. He tried to light the candle, but the Dog, dipping his tail in water, shook it and put out the flame. The thief fled. As he passed, the White Pet butted him with his horns, the Bull knocked him down and the Cock began to crow. Outside the Goose beat her wings about his legs. So he ran into the wood as fast as his legs would carry him.

'What happened?' asked his companions.

'Well, when I went into the candle-press, there was a man in it, and he thrust knives into my hand. When I went to the fire to light the candle, there was a big man in the middle of the floor who gave me a shove. Another man behind the door pushed me out. There was a little fellow on the left, calling: "*Cuir-anees-an-shaw-ay-s-foni-mi-hayn-da! Send him up here and I'll do for him!*' And there was a shoemaker out on the midden, hitting me about the legs with his apron.'

When the thieves heard that, they didn't go back to look for their money. The White Pet and his companions kept it, and lived happily ever after.

BIG FOX AND LITTLE FOX

THERE were once two foxes who hunted together for food. Although they shared the hunt, one of them always managed to get twice as much food as the other. So one got bigger and bigger, while the other got smaller and smaller.

One day, Big Fox and Little Fox saw a man walking along carrying a creel full of herring.

'I'd like herring for my supper,' said Big Fox.

'So would I,' said Little Fox.

'Well, I know what we must do,' said Big Fox. 'You follow this man while I run ahead. Further up the road I'll lie down and pretend to be dead.'

'All right, I'll do that,' said Little Fox.

So Big Fox ran ahead by a short cut, lay down in the middle of the road, and pretended to be dead.

When the man with the creel came along, he was pleased to find a fine fox lying dead on the road.

'This fox's skin will bring me more money than twenty creels of herring,' said he, as he flung Big Fox across his back.

That was not Big Fox's idea at all. He settled himself comfortably on the man's back, and then began to throw the herring out of the creel to Little Fox, who picked them up and followed on behind.

When the creel was half empty, Little Fox stopped and cried:

'Thank you, Big Fox! Now I'll leave you the rest of the herring, for it's time I was off home.'

'You can't do that,' cried Big Fox. 'It isn't fair!'

'Fairer than the shares you've always given me,' called Little Fox, as he ran through a hedge and off to the woods.

The man felt Big Fox moving on his back, and was about to tighten his grip, when Big Fox jumped down leaving his share of the herring in the creel, for he knew he'd be lucky to get away with his skin.

Away he ran, as fast as he could, through the hedge and off to the woods. But he never found Little Fox, who shared his herring with a fox more his own size.

The Tale of the Hoodie

NCE upon a time there was a farmer who had three daughters. One day they were waulking clothes by a river, when a hoodie came and said to the eldest:

'Will you wed me, farmer's daughter?'

'I'll not wed you,' said she. 'The hoodie is an ugly creature.'

The next day he came to the second daughter, and said:

'Will you wed me, farmer's daughter?'

'I'll not wed you,' said she. 'The hoodie is a horrid creature!'

The third day he came to the youngest daughter, and said:

'Will you wed me, farmer's daughter?'

'Yes, I'll marry you,' said she. 'The hoodie is a bonny bird.'

So next day they were married.

'Would you prefer me to be a hoodie by day, and a man by night, or a hoodie by night and man by day?' he asked.

'I'd rather you were a man by day and a hoodie by night,' said she.

After that he was a handsome young man by day, and a hoodie at night. Soon after their marriage he took her to his house.

At the end of nine months they had a little son. One night, when everyone was in bed, there came the most beautiful music ever heard, but everyone slept and the child was taken away by the hoodie.

The young mother wept. Her husband returned in the morning, but he did not seem to know what to do when he heard that his child had been taken away.

At the end of nine months, another little son was born. Everyone kept watch. But one night the music came as before, and while everyone slept, the second child was taken away by the hoodie.

The young mother wept. And when her husband returned home and found that his son had been taken away, he did not seem to know what to do.

At the end of nine months, yet another son was born. Watch was kept, but one night the music came as before, and while everyone slept, the child was taken away by the hoodie.

In the morning the husband returned, and took the young mother away in a coach. On the way, he said to her:

'See if you've forgotten anything.'

'I've forgotten my comb,' she said. And at that instant the coach in which they were travelling became a withered stick, and the husband flew away as a hoodie.

His young wife followed him. When he was on a hilltop, she would climb the hill to catch him; but when she reached the top of the hill, he'd be down in the valley. And when she was down in the valley, the hoodie was on another hill. Night came and she was tired. She had nowhere to

sleep. Then she saw a light in a house far away, so she went on toward the house and was there in no time.

Looking in through the window, she saw a wee lad in the house, and her heart went out to him. The woman of the house asked her to come in and rest. So the hoodie's wife lay down, and slept till dawn.

She left the house, and went from hill to hill looking for the hoodie. She saw him on a hill, but when she reached the top of the hill he was down in the valley. And when she went down into the valley, the hoodie was on another hill. When night came she had no place to sleep. She saw a light in a house in the distance and she got there in no time.

She went to the door and, peeping in, she saw a wee lad on the floor, and her heart went out to him. The woman of the house made up a bed for her, so she lay down and slept till dawn.

Next day she left and walked on searching for the hoodie, and when night came she reached another house. The woman of the house welcomed her, and told her that the hoodie had just left.

'He will return here tonight,' said the woman. 'If you want to catch him you must be clever and not fall asleep.'

The hoodie's young wife tried to keep awake, but when he came she was fast asleep. He dropped a ring on her right hand and this woke her. She tried to catch him, but all she caught was a feather from his wing. He left the feather and flew away, and in the morning she did not know what to do.

'He has gone over the hill of poison,' said the woman. 'But no one can climb that hill without a horseshoe on each hand and foot.'

The woman dressed the hoodie's wife up as a man and told her to go to the smith where she would learn to make horseshoes for herself. The smith taught her and soon she made horseshoes for both her hands and both her feet.

Then she went over the hill of poison, and on to the town, only to hear that her husband was about to marry the Laird's daughter.

Now, there were races in the town that day, and everyone was to be at the races, except the stranger who had come over the hill of poison. The Laird's cook came to her and said:

'As you're not going to the races, will you take my place, and make the meal for the Laird's family? I'd be grateful if you'll do this, otherwise I'll not be able to go to the races.'

'I'll make the meal,' said she. 'I can do that.'

So the hoodie's wife prepared the meal and watched carefully to see where the bridegroom was sitting. Then she let the ring and the feather drop into the bowl of broth that was set before him. With the first spoonful he took up the ring, and with the second he took up the feather.

'Bring me the cook who prepared this broth,' said he.

They fetched the usual cook, but the bridegroom shook his head when he saw him.

'This is not the one who cooked that broth,' said he, 'and I'll not marry until she is brought to me.'

So they fetched the one who had indeed prepared the broth, and she was his own true wife, who he had thought was lost to him for ever.

He recognised her and the spell was broken. Together they returned over the hill of poison. She threw the horseshoes behind her, and he followed her. As they went home, they took with them their three young sons from each of the three houses where she had slept on the three nights of her search. And from that day they lived happily ever after.

THE STOOR WORM

HE length of the Master Stoor Worm was beyond telling, and reached out thousands and thousands of miles in the sea.

His tongue itself was hundreds and hundreds of miles long, and with it he would sweep away whole towns, trees and hills into the sea. It was forked, and the prongs he used to seize his prey. With it he would crush the largest ship like an egg-shell. With it he would crack the walls of the biggest castle like a nut and suck every living thing out of it.

One time the Master Stoor Worm laid his head near the shore. Every Saturday morning the people had to feed him with seven young maidens.

The people went to a wise old man for advice. He said that, if the King's daughter was given to the Stoor Worm, the monster would leave and trouble them no more. The King was very sad, for the Princess was his only child and heir. Nevertheless he had to agree. But first he insisted on having ten weeks' grace. He used the time to send messengers to the countries near by, offering his daughter and his kingdom to any man who would destroy the Stoor Worm.

On the last day of the ten weeks the Master Assipattle made his appearance. In his boat he entered the Stoor Worm's mouth, rowed down its gullet, set fire to the monster's liver, rowed out of its mouth and returned to land.

The Stoor Worm's liver, being full of oil, blazed into a terrible fire. The heat caused the monster great pain; he almost capsized the world by his struggles.

He flung out his tongue and raised it far into the heavens. By chance he caught hold of the moon, and they say he shifted it in the sky. He took hold of one of the moon's horns, but by good fortune his tongue slipped over the horn. Down fell the tongue and caused a great earthquake.

Where it fell, the tongue formed a channel in the face of the earth, now filled with sea, dividing Denmark from Norway and Sweden. At the inner end of the sea, they say, two bays were made by the fork of the Stoor Worm's tongue.

As the serpent lay struggling in great agony, he lifted up his head to the sky and let it fall violently. As he did so, he shed some of his great teeth, and they became the Orkney Isles.

The second time he did this, more teeth fell out, and they became the Shetland Isles.

While in his death throes, he threw up his head, and again it fell, striking, as it always did, the bottom of the sea. This time the teeth that were knocked out became the Faroe Isles.

Then the Stoor Worm rolled himself up, and his huge body, when he died, became the large island of Iceland. But his liver still burns, and the flames of its fire are sometimes seen rising from the mountains of that cold land.

The Mermaid

ONE day a mermaid rose at the side of a poor fisherman's boat. 'Are you catching many fish?' she asked.

'I am not,' said he.

'What will you give me for sending you plenty of fish?'

'Ach,' said the old man, 'I haven't much to spare.'

'Give me your first son,' said she.

'I'll give my son if I have one, but I'll not have one now,' said he, 'my wife is too old.'

'What do you have?'

'I have an old mare, an old dog, myself and my old wife. These are all I have in the world.'

'Here are twelve grains,' said the mermaid. 'Give three to your wife, three to your dog, three to your mare, and three you must plant behind your house. In time your wife will have three sons, the mare three foals, and the dog three pups. Three trees will grow behind your house, and when one of your sons dies, one of the trees will wither. Now go home, and remember me when your eldest son is three years of age. You will catch plenty of fish from now on.'

Everything happened as the mermaid had said.

At the end of three years the old fisherman went to fish as usual, but he did not take his eldest son with him. The mermaid rose at the side of his boat, and said:

'Have you brought your son to me?'

'I did not bring him. I forgot that this was the day,' said he.

'Very well, you may have four more years of him,' said the mermaid, and she lifted up her child. 'Here is a lad of the same age. Is your son as fine as this one?'

The fisherman did not answer but he went home very happy, for he had four more years. He kept on catching plenty of fish, but at the end of four years he grew sad. He went on fishing as before, and the mermaid rose at the side of his boat.

'Have you brought your son to me?' she said.

'I forgot him this time too,' said the old man.

'Go home then,' said the mermaid, 'and seven years from now you are sure to remember me. You'll still catch plenty of fish.'

At the end of seven years the old man could rest neither day nor night.

'What is worrying you, Father?' asked his eldest son.

'That is my affair,' said the old man.

The lad said he must know, and at last his father told him about the mermaid.

'You shall not go, my son,' said he, 'though I never catch another fish.'

'Then go to the smiddy,' said his son, 'and tell the smith to make me a strong sword, and I'll go seek my fortune.'

His father went to the smiddy, and the smith made him a sword. The lad grasped it, and shook it once or twice, and it broke into a thousand pieces. So he asked his father to go to the smiddy and order another sword, twice as heavy. His father did so, and the same thing happened to the second sword.

Back went the old man to the smith, who then made the strongest sword, the like of which he had never made before.

'There's a sword for you,' said the smith. 'The hand must be good that plays this blade.'

The old man gave it to his son, who shook it once or twice.

'This will do,' said he. 'It's high time I was on my way.'

The next morning he put a saddle on the black horse, son of the old mare. Away he went, his black dog with him. When he had gone some way, he saw the carcass of a sheep beside the road. By the carrion sat a dog, a falcon and an otter. He got down off his horse and divided the carcass among the three.

'If swift foot or sharp tooth will help you, remember me, and I'll be by your side,' said the dog.

'If swimming foot at the bottom of a pool will help you, remember me, and I'll be by your side,' said the otter.

'If swift wing or crooked claw will help you, remember me, and I'll be by your side,' said the falcon.

The lad went on till he reached a King's house, where he took service as a cowherd. He went out with the cattle, but the grass was poor. When evening came, he took them home, but the cows gave little milk, and the lad had little to eat and drink that night.

Next day he took the cows to a grassy place in a green glen. When he was due to take the cattle home, he saw a giant with a sword in his hand.

'Hiu! Hiu! Hogaraich!' shouted the giant. 'My teeth have rotted a long time waiting for you. The cattle are now mine. They are on my land, and you're a dead man!'

'There's no knowing,' said the cowherd. 'It's easier to say than to do.' Then he called his black dog. With one spring it caught the giant by the neck, and the cowherd struck off his head.

He mounted his black horse, rode to the giant's house, and went in. There was plenty of money, and clothes of silver and gold, but he took nothing.

At the mouth of the night he returned to the King's castle. When the cows were milked there was plenty, so he ate well that night. The King was pleased to have such a cowherd. This went on for some time, but at last all the grass in the glen was eaten. So he took the cattle further on till they came to a great park, where he put them to graze. A giant came running.

'Hiu! Hiu! Hogaraich!' shouted the giant. 'Your blood shall quench my thirst this night!'

'There's no knowing,' said the cowherd.

Then he called his dog. With one spring it caught the giant by the neck, and the cowherd struck off his head.

That night he went home tired, but the cows gave plenty of milk. The King and his family were delighted to have such a cowherd.

One night the dairymaid was weeping. The cowherd asked her what was the matter. She said a great beast with three heads was in the loch. Each year it had been given a victim, and this year it was the turn of the King's daughter. At midday, next day, the Princess was to meet the monster at the loch. But a mighty suitor was going to rescue her.

'What suitor will that be?' said the cowherd.

'He is a great General,' said she, 'and the King has said that the man who rescues her will marry her.'

Next day, near the time, the King's daughter and the General went to meet the beast. They reached the black corrie at the top of the loch. Shortly after, the beast moved in the middle of the loch. But when the General saw the beast with three heads, he hid himself. Then the King's daughter saw a handsome youth, on a black horse, riding toward her. His black dog followed him. He sat down beside her, and told her he had come to rescue her.

'Now I must rest,' said he, 'and if I fall asleep, you must waken me as soon as you see the beast.'

'How am I to wake you?'

'Put the gold ring from your finger on my little finger.'

Not long after she saw the monster coming. She took off her ring and put it on the young man's little finger. He awoke, and went to meet the monster. His black dog sprang on the monster, and the youth was able to cut off one of its heads.

'You have won,' said the King's daughter. 'I am safe tonight but the monster will come again and again, until its other two heads are cut off.'

He put a willow branch through the monster's head, and told the King's daughter to bring it back with her next day. She went home with the head slung over her shoulder, and the cowherd returned to his herding. The General came out of his hiding place and caught up with her. He threatened to kill her if she told anyone who had cut off the monster's head.

When they reached the castle, the head was slung over the General's shoulder. Everyone was very happy that the King's daughter had come home alive.

Next day the General and the King's daughter went back to the loch. When the monster moved in the middle of the loch, the General again hid himself, and along came the young man on the black horse with his dog following.

'I'm glad to see you,' the Princess said. 'Come and rest beside me.'

'If I sleep before the beast comes, wake me up,' said he.

'How shall I wake you?'

'Take the earring out of your ear, and put it in mine!'

He had just fallen asleep when the King's daughter cried:

'Wake up! Wake up!' but wake he would not. When she took the earring out of her ear, and put it in his, he awoke at once and went to meet the beast. About the mouth of night he cut another head off the monster. He put the second head on the willow branch, and gave it to the King's daughter. Then he leaped on his black horse and returned to his herding.

The King's daughter went home with the second head on the willow branch. The General met her as before, and took it from her.

Everyone was delighted to see her return home alive, and the King was sure the General would save his daughter.

Next day they returned to the loch, and when the monster stirred in the loch, the General hid himself. Along came the lad on the black horse, and lay down beside the Princess.

'If I sleep before the monster comes, wake me,' said he.

'How shall I wake you?'

'Take the earring off your other ear and put it in mine,' he said.

No sooner was he asleep than the King's daughter saw the monster.

'Wake up! Wake up!' she cried, but wake he would not.

So she took the earring from her other ear, and put it in his. At once he awoke, attacked the beast, and cut off its third head. He put the third head on the willow branch and handed it to the King's daughter. Then he leapt on his horse, and returned to the herding.

The King's daughter went home with the third head on the willow branch, but the General took it from her.

Everyone was delighted that she was safe and well and the monster dead. The King arranged that the General should marry her the next day. But when the priest came, the Princess said she would only marry the man who could take the monster's three heads off the willow Branch without breaking the branches.

'Who should take the heads off the willow branch but the man who put them there,' said the King.

The General tried, but he could not loose them. Then every man in the castle tried, but they could not. There was one other man who had not tried, the cowherd, so he was sent for. He took them off at once.

'The man who cut off the monster's heads has my ring and my earrings,' said the King's daughter.

The cowherd put his hand in his pocket, and drew out the ring and the earrings.

'You are my man,' said the Princess.

So they were married that very night.

One day while the Princess and her husband were walking by the side of the loch, there came a monster more terrible than the first, and carried the husband off into the loch.

The Princess met an old smith, and she told him what had happened. The smith told her to spread out all her treasures at the edge of the loch. She did so, and the monster put its head up out of the water.

'Your jewellery is very fine, Princess,' it said.

'Not as fine as the jewel you took from me,' said she. 'Let me see my husband once, and you shall have one of these jewels.'

The monster brought him to her.

'Give him to me and you shall have all you see,' said she.

The monster did so, threw her husband alive on the shore, and then went off with her jewels.

Soon after this, they were walking beside the loch, when the monster came and took away the Princess. Her husband met the smith, who told him there was only one way to kill the beast.

'On the island in the middle of the loch is the white-footed hind. Catch her, and out of her will spring a hoodie. Catch the hoodie, and out of her will spring a trout. Catch the trout, and out of it will fall an egg. In the egg is the soul of the monster. Break the egg and the monster will die.'

Now the monster sank any boat going to the island, so the cowherd leaped across to the island on his black horse, his black dog after him.

He saw the hind, and the black dog chased her. But when the black dog was on one side of the island, the hind was on the other.

'Oh, that the hound that I once saw by the carcass of sheep were here to help me!'

At once the hound was chasing the hind. The two dogs soon brought her to earth. She was no sooner caught than a hoodie sprang out of her.

'Oh, that the grey falcon with the sharp eye and swift wing were here to help me!' cried the young man.

At once the grey falcon was after the hoodie, and brought her down. She was no sooner caught than a trout sprang out of her into the loch.

'Oh, that the otter, the swift swimmer, were here to help me!'

At once the otter was there and leapt into the loch. No sooner was the otter back on the shore with the trout, than an egg fell from its mouth.

'Don't break that egg,' screamed the monster, and I'll give all you ask.'

'Give me back my wife!' cried the young man.

At once she was by his side. He took her hand in his, but he crushed the egg under his foot, and the monster died.

The Prince, who had once been a cowherd, was walking with his Princess one day, when he saw a little castle beside the loch, in a wood. He asked his wife who lived there. She told him that no one had come back alive who had gone near that castle.

'Things can't be left like that,' said he. 'I'll find out who lives there.'

'Please don't go,' she begged him.

But he went to the castle, and a little old woman met him at the door.

'Welcome, fisherman's son,' said she. 'I'm pleased to see you. Come in and rest.'

He went, but she struck him on the back, and he fell dead.

Now, far away in the fisherman's house, they had seen the first tree planted from the mermaid's grains withering. The second son said that his elder brother must be dead. He swore he would go and find out where his brother lay. He mounted his black horse and, with his black dog by his side, followed his brother's footsteps to the King's castle.

He was so like his elder brother that the King at first thought he was the Princess's husband. When he was told what had happened to his brother, he went to the little castle by the loch and, just as it had happened to his elder brother, so it happened to him. With one blow the old woman stretched him out dead.

When the youngest brother saw the second tree behind the house begin to wither, he decided to find out how death had come to his two brothers. He mounted his black horse and followed his black dog to the King's castle.

The King was pleased to see him and told him all that had happened to his two brothers. At first he was not allowed to go to the castle by the loch. At last he went, and was met by the old woman.

'Welcome, fisherman's son,' said she. 'I'm pleased to see you. Come in and rest.'

'Go in before me, old woman,' said he. 'Go in, and let me hear what you have to say.'

The old woman went on. He drew his sword and cut off her head. But the sword flew out of his hand. The old woman caught her head with both hands, and stuck it on again. The black dog sprang at her, but she struck the dog a blow with her magic club, and there he lay.

The youngest brother caught the old carlin, seized her magic club, and struck her one blow on the top of her head. She fell down dead.

He saw his brothers lying side by side. He touched each of them with the magic club, and they sprang to their feet, alive and well. Then he touched the black dog with the magic club, and up he jumped. They found gold and silver in the old witch's castle, and returned to the Princess and the King with the treasure. There was enough for them all, including their mother and their father, the old fisherman.

When the King grew old, the fisherman's eldest son and his wife were crowned King and Queen. They all lived happily ever after.

The Winning of Hyn-Hallow

THERE was once a goodman of Thorodale, in the Orkney Isles. He had three sons, who helped him with the fishing, and a bonny wife whom he loved dearly.

One day the goodman and his bonny wife were down on the beach, at the water's edge. The goodman bent down to tie his boot-lace, turning his back to his bonny wife. Suddenly she screamed, as a dark Fin-man dragged her to his boat and pushed out to sea before the goodman could reach them. Thorodale never saw his bonny wife again.

He pulled up his breeches, rolled down his stockings, and went on his knees below the flood-mark. There he swore that, living or dead, he would be revenged on the Fin-folk for stealing his bonny wife.

One day he was out fishing on the sound that lies between Rousay and Evie, when he heard a woman's voice singing. He knew it was his wife, although he could not see her, for she sang:

> 'Goodman, weep no more for me,
> For me again you'll never see.
> If you would have of vengeance joy,
> Go speir the wise spey-wife of Hoy.'

Thorodale went ashore, took his staff in his hand, his silver in a stocking, and set off for the island of Hoy. There the spey-wife told him how he might get the power of seeing Hilda-land, and what he was to do when he saw it.

Thorodale returned home and for nine months at midnight, when the moon was full, he went nine times on his knees round the Odin Stone of Stainess. For nine months, at full moon, he looked through the hole in the Odin Stone, and wished that he might have the power of seeing Hilda-land. He filled a girnal with salt, and set three baskets beside it; he then told his three sons what they must do when he gave them the word.

One summer morning, just after sunrise, the goodman of Thorodale saw a little island in the middle of the sound where he had never seen land before. He could not turn his head, nor wink his eye, for if he once lost sight of that land he knew he would never see it again. So he shouted to his three sons in the house:

'Fill the baskets with salt, and hold for the boat!'

The sons came, each carrying a basket of salt. The four men jumped into the boat, and rowed for the new land, although nobody could see it except the goodman.

In a moment, the boat was surrounded by whales. The three sons wanted to drive the whales away, but their father cried:

'Pull for dear life!'

A great whale lay right in the boat's course, and opened up a mouth big enough to swallow both boat and men. Thorodale, standing in the bow of his boat, flung two handfuls of salt into its mouth, and the whale vanished.

As the boat neared the shore of Hilda-land, two mermaids stood on the rocks and sang. The lads began to row slowly, listening to the song, but Thorodale gave them a kick, without turning his head, and cried out to the mermaids:

'Begone, you unholy creatures! Here's your warning!'

He threw a cross of twisted seaweed on the mermaids, and they dived screaming into the sea.

When the boat touched land, they saw a great monster with long tusks, and feet as broad as millstones. Its eyes blazed and its mouth spat fire. Thorodale flung a handful of salt between the monster's eyes, and it disappeared with a roar. In its place stood a tall Fin-man, with a drawn sword, who cried:

'Go back, you human thieves! or I'll defile Hilda-land with your blood!'

The three sons began to tremble.

'Come home, Father, come home!' they cried.

The tall Fin-man thrust at Thorodale with his sword, but the goodman flung a cross of cloggirs, or goose-grass, on the Fin-man's face, and he turned and fled in pain and anger.

'Come out of that,' cried Thorodale to his sons, 'and take salt ashore!'

He made them walk abreast round the island, each of them scattering salt as he went.

There arose a terrible rumpus among the Fin-folk and their kye. They ran helter-skelter into the sea, like a flock of sheep, and never set foot on Hyn-hallow again.

The goodman of Thorodale cut nine crosses on the turf, and his three sons went three times round the island, scattering their salt. But the youngest son had a large hand, and scattered and sowed the salt too fast. Not one particle would his brothers spare him, so the ninth circle of salt was never completed. That is why cats, rats and mice cannot live on Hyn-hallow,

In the Orkneys they still sing:

> 'Hyn-hallow frank, Hyn-hallow free!
> Hyn-hallow lies in the middle of the sea;
> Wi' a rampan rost on ilka side,
> Hyn-hallow lies in the middle of the tide!'

THE GOODMAN OF WASTNESS

NE day, when the goodman of Wastness was down on the beach and the tide was out, he saw a number of Selkie folk on a flat rock. They had taken off their seal-skins, and had skin as white as his own.

The goodman crept forward and waded swiftly to the rock. The Selkie folk saw him and seized their seal-skins and jumped into the sea. But the goodman took one of the seal-skins, belonging to a Selkie lass. The Selkie folk swam out a little distance, put their heads up out of the sea and gazed at the goodman. One of them did not look like a seal.

The goodman put the seal-skin under his arm, and made for home. Before he left the beach, he heard a sound of weeping behind him. The lass whose seal-skin he had taken was following him.

'If there is any mercy in you, give me back my skin!' she cried. 'I cannot live in the sea, among my own folk, without it. Pity me, if you ever have hope for mercy yourself.'

'It would be better if you came to live with me,' said the goodman.

After a lot of persuasion, the sea-lass agreed to be his wife.

She stayed with him many years, bore him seven children, four boys and three girls. But although the goodman's wife looked happy, and was often merry, her heart was heavy. Many times she looked out at the sea. She taught her bairns many a strange song that had never been heard before.

One day, the goodman of Wastness and his three eldest sons went off in his boat to the fishing. The goodwife sent three of the children to the beach to gather limpets and whelks, but the youngest, having hurt her foot, had to stay at home.

The goodwife began to search for her long-lost skin. She searched up, and she searched down. She searched but, and she searched ben. Never a seal-skin could she find. The youngest lass sat on a stool resting her foot.

'What are you looking for, mother?' she said.

'I'm looking for a bonny seal-skin, to make a shoe to cure your sore foot.'

'Maybe I know where it is,' sasid the little lass. 'One day, when you were all out, and father thought I was sleeping, he took the bonny seal-skin down. He glowered at it a peerie minute, then folded it and laid it up there between the wall and the roof.'

When her mother heard this, she hurried to the place and pulled out her long-lost skin.

'Farewell, wee buddo!' she cried, and ran out of the house. She ran to the shore, put on her seal-skin, and plunged into the sea.

There a Selkie man met her and they swam away together. The goodman, rowing home, saw them both from his boat. His lost wife uncovered her face, and cried:

> 'Goodman of Wastness, farewell to ye!
> I liked ye well, ye were good to me!
> But I love better my man of the sea!'

And that was the last the goodman of Wastness ever saw or heard of his Selkie wife.

TAM SCOTT AND THE FIN-MAN

AM Scott was at the Lammas Fair in Kirkwall, where he had taken a number of folk from Sanday in his parley boat. He was going up and down through the Fair when he met a tall, dark-faced man.

'The top of the day to you,' says the stranger.

'As much to you,' says Tam, 'but who are you?'

'Never heed,' says the man. 'Will you take a cow of mine to one of the north isles? I'll pay you double freight for taking you so soon from the Fair.'

'I'll do it,' says Tam, for he was not the boy to stick at a bargain when he thought the butter was on his side of the bread.

By the time he had got the boat ready, he saw the dark-faced man leading his cow. When he came to the edge of the water, the stranger lifted the cow in his arms, as if she'd been a sheep, and set her down in the boat.

'Where are we to steer for?' said Tam when they got under way.

'East of Shapinshay,' said the man.

'Where now?' said Tam when they reached Shapinshay.

'East of Stronsay,' said the man.

Then they reached the Mill Bay of Stronsay.

'You'll be for landing here?' asked Tam.

'No, east of Sanday,' said the man.

Now, Tam liked a gossip, and as they sailed along he tried to chat to his passenger in a friendly way, but at every remark the stranger only replied gruffly:

'A close tongue keeps a safe head.'

At last it began to dawn on Tam's mind that he had an uncanny passenger on board. As they sailed on through the east sea, Tam saw, rising ahead, a dense bank of mist. Soon the bank of mist began to shine like a cloud lit by the setting sun. Then the mist began to rise, and Tam saw lying under it a most beautiful island. On it men and women were walking, cattle were feeding and yellow cornfields were ripe for the harvest. While Tam was staring with wide open eyes at this braw land, the stranger sprang aft.

'I must blindfold you now for a while. If you do what you are told, no ill shall befall you,' he said.

Tam thought it would only end badly for him if he refused, so he allowed himself to be blindfolded with his own handkerchief. In a few minutes Tam felt the boat grind on a pebbly beach. He heard voices of many men speaking to his passenger, and he also heard the loveliest sound he had ever heard in his life. It was the sweet voices of mermaids singing on the shore. Tam saw them through one corner of his right eye that came below the handkerchief. The braw sight and the bonny sound nearly put him out of his wits for joy. Then he heard a man's voice call:

'You idle creatures, don't think you'll win this man with your singing! He has a wife and bairns of his own on Sanday Isle.'

And with that the music changed to a most mournful song. The sound of it made Tam's heart sad indeed.

Well, the cow was soon lifted out of the boat, a bag of money was laid at Tam's feet in the stern sheets, and the boat shoved off. And what do you think? Those graceless wretches of Fin-men turned his boat against the sun! As they pushed off the boat, one of them cried:

'Keep the starboard end of the fore thraft bearing on the braes of Warsater, and you'll soon make land.'

When Tam felt his boat under way, he tore off the handkerchief which blindfolded him. He could see nothing save a thick mist. But he soon sailed out of the mist, and saw it lying astern like a great cloud. Then he saw what pleased him better, the Braes of Warsater bearing on his starboard bow. As he sailed home, he opened his bag of money. He had been well paid, but all in coppers. The Fin-folk like the white money too well to part with silver.

Well, in a year Tam went to the Lammas Fair as usual. Many a time afterwards he wished he had lain in his bed that day, but what is to be must be, and cannot be helped.

It happened on the third day of the market, as Tam was walking up and down, speaking to his friends. Whom should he see but the same dark-faced stranger who had given him the freight the year before. In his friendly way Tam went up to the man and said:

'How is it with you, good man? I'm glad to see you this day! Come and take a cog of ale with me.'

'Did you ever see me before?' said the man with an ugly look on his face.

'I took you and your cow to east of Sanday,' said Tam.

'Is that so,' said the man. As he spoke, he took out of his pocket what Tam thought was a snuff-box. Then he blew some powder from it into Tam's eyes, and said:

'Now you'll never be able to say you saw me before!'

And from that minute, poor Tam never saw again a blink of sweet light in his two eyes.

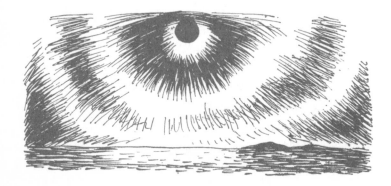

Farquhar the Healer

N the Reay country there was once a drover called Farquhar. He went to England from Glen Gollich to sell cattle, with a hazel staff in his hand. One day he met a doctor, who said:

'What's that in your hand?'

'A hazel branch,' replied Farquhar.

'Where did you cut it?'

'In Glen Gollich, north in Lord Reay's country.'

'Do you remember the exact place?'

'I do.'

'Could you find the tree again?' asked the doctor.

'I could,' replied Farquhar.

'Well, I'll give you more gold than you can lift if you'll go back there and bring me a branch from that very tree.'

'I'll do that,' said Farquhar.

'I want you to bring me something more,' said the doctor. 'Take this bottle. Watch at the hole at the foot of the tree, with the bottle ready. Let go the first six serpents that come out of the hole, but put the seventh into the bottle. Tell no one what you've done, but come back here with the hazel branch and the serpent in the bottle, and I'll give you as much gold again.'

So Farquhar returned to Scotland and Glen Gollich, the hazel glen. When he had cut some branches, he looked for the hole at the foot of the hazel tree. He found it, and, sure enough, out came six serpents, brown and barred like adders. He let them go. Then he put the bottle to the hole. By and by a white snake came crawling through. Farquhar caught it in the bottle, and hurried back to England with it.

The doctor gave him enough gold to buy the Reay country, but he said:

'Before you return to Scotland, you must stay and help me prepare the white snake.'

'I'll do that,' said Farquhar.

Then they lit a fire with the hazel sticks, and put the white snake in a pot to boil. The doctor had to leave, so he asked Farquhar to watch the pot. He was not to allow the snake to escape, and he was not to let anyone near the pot, for fear it might be known what they were doing.

Farquhar promised to be careful. He wrapped paper round the pot lid, but before he had finished doing this, the water began to boil, and steam came out at one place. He pushed the paper down, and put his finger to the place to stem the steam. Then he put his finger, wet with snake bree, into his mouth.

At once a strange thing happened. Farquhar knew all things. Like a blind man suddenly able to see, Farquhar suddenly knew and understood everything. But he decided to tell no one about this new knowledge.

When the doctor returned, he took the pot from the fire, lifted the lid, dipped his finger into the bree, and sucked it. But it was no more than water to him.

'Who has done this?' he cried. And he knew by the look on Farquhar's face, that it was he.

'You've taken the magic from the bree!' cried the doctor in anger. And, throwing the pot at Farquhar, he turned and left.

And this is how Farquhar became all-wise. He returned to Scotland and set up as a physician. There was nothing he did not know, and no disease he could not cure. He went from place to place, healing the sick, and soon he was known far and wide as Farquhar the Healer. One day Farquhar heard that the King was sick, and he went to find out what was wrong with him.

'It is his knee,' he was told. 'He has had many doctors, he pays them well, and sometimes they give him relief, but not for long. You can hear him cry out with the pain in his leg.'

Farquhar walked up and down before the King's house, crying:

'The black beetle to the white bone!'

The people stared at him. They said the strange man from Reay must be daft, but this did not stop Farquhar, and next day, he stood at the castle gate and cried:

'The black beetle to the white bone!'

The King asked who was crying outside and what it was he wanted. He was told it was a stranger from the Reay country, called Farquhar the Healer.

'Then bring him here,' ordered the King. 'Perhaps he can heal me.'

So Farquhar was brought and he stood before the King, and said:

'The black beetle to the white bone!'

And so it was. When Farquhar examined the King's knee, he found a small black beetle deep in a wound, close to the knee-cap. Farquhar removed the beetle and put a dressing on the wound. The doctors, in order to keep the King ill and to get their fees, had at times put a beetle in his wound, making him cry out in agony. All this Farquhar knew by his serpent's wisdom when he put his finger under his wisdom tooth, and under his care the King was soon cured, and the doctors were punished.

The King offered Farquhar whatever he asked, be it land or gold. Farquhar asked for the King's daughter, and all the Isles that the sea runs round, from the point of Stoer to Stromness in the Orkneys. So the King gave him his daughter, and a grant of all the Isles.

JOHNNIE CROY AND THE MERMAID

ONE day, Johnnie Croy went to the shore to look for driftwood. The tide was out, and he walked under the crags on the west side of Sanday. From the boulders there came the sound of singing. He peeped over the rocks. A mermaid was sitting on a rock, combing her hair.

Johnnie swore by the moonstone to court her, though the wooing cost him his life. He crept behind her, sprang forward and kissed her.

She flung Johnnie on the rocks with a blow of her tail that made his spine smart. Then she dived into the sea. Johnnie stood up. It was the first time anyone had laid his back to the ground. Then he found the mermaid's comb at his feet.

'Give me my comb!' she cried.

'Nay, my buddo,' said Johnnie. 'You'll come and bide on land first.'

'I couldn't bear your black rain and white snow,' she said. 'Your sun and smoky fires would wizen me up. Come with me, and I'll make you chief of the Fin-folk.'

'You can't entice me,' said Johnnie. 'I've a house at Volya with plenty of gear, cows and sheep, and you shall be mistress of it all if you come and stay with me.'

But the mermaid saw the Fin-folk coming, and swam out to sea.

Johnnie went home and told the whole story to his mother who was a wise woman.

'You're a fool to fall in love with a sea-lass,' said she, 'but if you want her, you must keep her comb.'

One morning, Johnnie was wakened by music in his room. He sat up and saw the mermaid near his bed.

'I've come for my comb,' said she.

'I'll not give it to you, my bonny lass,' said he. 'But will you not stay with me and be my wife?'

'I'll make you a fair offer,' she said. 'I'll live with you here for seven years, if you'll swear to come with me, and all that's mine, to see my own folk at the end of that time.'

Johnnie swore by the moonstone to keep the bargain. So they were married, and as the priest prayed the mermaid stuffed her hair in her ears.

The mermaid baked the best bread and brewed the strongest ale in all the island. She kept everything in good order, and was the best spinner in the countryside. Indeed she made the best wife and the best mother too. At their house everything went as merry as a Yuletide.

As seven years drew near their end, the family made ready for a long voyage. Johnnie was very thoughtful and said little. His wife had a faraway look on her face.

Now, on the eve of the last day of the seven years the youngest of their seven bairns was sleeping at his grandmother's house. Before midnight came, the grandmother made a wire cross, which she heated on the fire. Then she laid it on the bairn's bare behind, he screaming like a little demon.

When morning came and they were all ready, Johnnie's wife walked down to the boat. When she came to the beach, her goodman and six only of her seven bairns were in the boat. She sent fishermen friends back for the youngest bairn. But they returned and told her that four of them had tried to lift the cradle where the bairn lay, and they could not budge it one inch.

Johnnie Croy's wife ran up to the house and tried to lift the cradle, but she could not move it. She flung back the blanket and tried to lift the bairn out of the cradle. The moment she touched him a terrible burning sensation went through her arms, making her draw back and scream. She went back to the boat, her head hanging and the salt tears streaming from her eyes. As the boat sailed away, the folk on the shore heard her lamenting:

'Aloor, aloor, for my bonny bairn! Aloor, for my bonny boy! Aloor, that I must leave him to live and die on dry land!'

Away, far away, sailed the boat, no one knows where. Johnnie Croy, his bonny young wife and their six bairns were never seen again by mortal eye.

THE WIDOW'S SON

HERE was once a poor widow who had a son called Iain. They lived in a small cottage and all they had were a few hens and a horse. One day, Iain was riding through the forest when he met a man with a gun, a dog, and a falcon. They greeted each other and the man said:

'Will you sell your horse to me?'

'I'll exchange her for your gun, your dog and your falcon,' said Iain.

'Done,' said the man, and rode away on the horse, while Iain returned home to his mother.

'Where's our horse?' said she.

'I exchanged her for this gun, dog and falcon,' said Iain. 'Look at them. Wasn't that a good bargain?'

'It was not,' said his mother. 'What are we going to do without a horse, you stupid lad?' And she beat him and sent him to bed without any supper.

Now, Iain wanted to be a hunter, so in the middle of the night, he left home with the gun, the dog and the falcon. On and on he walked till he came to a farm. The farmer and his wife were up and starting the day's work.

'Good day,' said Iain.

'Good day,' said the farmer. 'I see you're carrying a gun. This must be my lucky day. I've been looking out for a hunter. Every night a deer comes and eats my corn. Soon there'll be none left. Stay with us a while, and we'll give you bed and board if you promise to shoot the deer.'

Iain promised, ate a good meal and slept in a soft bed.

Just before dawn, he got up, dressed and went out with his gun. As the sun rose, he saw the deer and took aim, but he saw that the deer had a woman's head and shoulders.

'Don't shoot me!' she said. Iain could not shoot a woman, so he lowered his gun and went back to the farm.

'I didn't hear your gun,' said the farmer.

'No,' said Iain, 'but I'll try again tomorrow morning.'

He had three good meals that day, and slept in a soft bed all night. Just before dawn, he got up, dressed, and went out with his gun. As before, he saw the deer just as the sun rose, and took aim. But the deer was a lovely woman down to the waist.

'Don't shoot me!' she cried. Iain could not shoot her, so he lowered his gun and went back to the farm.

'I didn't hear your gun,' said the farmer.

'No,' said Iain, 'but I'll try again tomorrow morning.'

He had three good meals that day, and slept in a soft bed all night. But before he went to bed, the farmer told him this was his last chance. They were not going to give him bed and board any longer, unless he killed the deer. So, just before dawn, Iain got up, dressed, and went out with his gun. He saw the deer just as the sun rose, and took aim. But the deer was a lovely woman from head to toe.

'Don't shoot me!' she said, and Iain lowered his gun.

'I'm the King of Lochlin's daughter,' she said. 'I was enchanted, but you have broken the spell. As your reward, I'll marry you if you follow me.'

Iain followed her till they came to a house thatched with heather.

'Go in,' said she, 'and eat your fill.'

Iain opened the door and went in. The table was laid with a meal but there was no one else to eat it, so Iain ate and drank till he was satisfied. Then he heard many feet approaching the door. Afraid he would be blamed for eating the food, he hid under an empty barrel, just as twenty-four robbers entered. They were very angry that someone had been eating their meal. They searched the house, and found Iain under the barrel. The leader ordered four of his men to take Iain outside and cut off his head. This they did, and soon after the twenty-four robbers ate the food that was left and went to sleep. In the morning they went off on a raid, after one of them had laid the table with food and drink for their supper.

While they were away, the deer came running to where the dead Iain was lying near the house. She shook her head over Iain, and out of her left ear some wax fell on him, and he jumped to his feet, alive again.

'Trust me,' said the deer. 'Go in again and eat your fill!'

Iain went into the house, and saw the table laid with food and drink. He ate and drank till he was satisfied. When he heard the robbers approaching the door, he hid under the empty barrel. When the robbers saw that their supper had been eaten again, they searched the house and found Iain under the barrel. The robbers' leader ordered his men to execute the four who had been told to kill Iain the night before. The four men were executed, and another four ordered to cut off Iain's head. This they did. Then, twenty robbers sat down to table, ate and drank, and went to bed.

In the morning, after breakfast, the robbers went off on a raid. The deer came running. She shook her head and out of her right ear some wax fell on the dead Iain, who immediately jumped to his feet, alive.

That night, when twenty robbers came home, they again found some of their food eaten, and Iain alive, hiding under the barrel. The four who had killed Iain the night before were executed for disobedience, and only sixteen robbers were left. They were terrified at what had happened and became mutinous. They rebelled against their leader, began to quarrel, and then to fight. They killed each other and their leader.

Not one of them was left alive. Then the deer came and led Iain to the white house of the Old Carlin and her son, the Black Lad.

'Meet me here tomorrow at eleven,' said the deer to Iain, and told him to spend the night at the Old Carlin's house.

But next day, just before eleven, the Old Carlin gave him a pin to stick in his coat. This put Iain to sleep.

Beautiful music came out of the air, and the deer came, changed back into a lovely woman dressed in white, riding a white horse. She dismounted, sat beside Iain, and laid his head in her lap. She combed his hair but could not waken him. Under his arm she wrote her name, 'Daughter of the King of the Kingdom under the Waves.'

'I'll come again, tomorrow at eleven,' she said to the Black Lad, and rode away on her white horse.

When Iain woke, the Black Lad told him what had happened, but said nothing about the name the White Lady had written under his arm.

Next day, just before dawn, the Black Lad stuck a pin in Iain's coat and he fell asleep. Music came out of the air as the Lady, dressed in grey, rode up on a grey horse. She laid Iain's head on her lap, combed his hair, and tried to waken him. She put a snuff-box in his pocket, and rode away weeping. She told the Black Lad she would return the next day at eleven, for the last time.

Next day, just before eleven, the Old Carlin offered Iain the pin but he refused to take it. Instead she gave the Black Lad an apple, which he did not eat.

'I'm thirsty,' said Iain. 'Give me the apple if you don't want it!'

The Black Lad gave him the apple, and when he ate it he fell asleep. The Lady came dressed in black, riding a black horse. She laid Iain's head on her lap, combed his hair, but still he did not wake. So she put a ring on his finger, and told the Black Lad:

'He'll not see me again. I must go home.'

Next day, at eleven, the Lady did not come, though Iain was awake. So he set off to look for her. On and on he went, with dusty shoes, till he wore holes in the soles. The birds were going to roost in the trees when he came to a house. A woman opened the door and invited him in.

'I'll make supper for you, and a soft bed,' she said. 'I know why you've come this way, and I'll help you.'

Next morning, after breakfast, she gave him a pair of old shoes.

'I've a sister,' she said, 'who may be able to help you. She has a house by the roadside, a year and a day from here, but if you wear these old shoes, you'll be there in no time. When you arrive, turn their toes to the known and their heels to the unknown, and they'll come back here to me.'

Sure enough, Iain arrived at the sister's house in no time, Iain told her his story, and she gave him another pair of old shoes.

'I've another sister,' she said, 'who lives a year and a day from here. She may help you. If you wear these old shoes, you'll be there in no time. When you arrive, turn their toes to the known and their heels to the unknown, and they'll come back to me.'

Iain arrived at the third sister's house in no time.

'I don't know how to help you,' she said, 'but maybe my son will know. He's herd to the birds of the air.'

Her son came and he knew what to do. He killed a cow, cooked the meat, turned the hide inside out, and made a bag into which Iain was able to crawl.

Soon an eagle flew down, and carried the bag, with Iain in it, out to sea. When she was tired, the eagle dropped it in the water. Another eagle came, lifted the bag out of the sea, and carried it in her claws to an island where she slept with all the birds of the air. Iain crawled out of the bag and searched for food. He finished all he could find on the island, then he searched his pockets for scraps or a crust. All he found was the snuff-box the Grey Lady had put there. He opened the box, and out jumped three wee men.

'What can we do for you?' they all said together.

'Take me to the Kingdom of the King under the Waves!'

At once he was there. He found board and lodgings in the house of a weaver. The weaver told him there was to be a horse-race in the town, and the winner would marry the King's daughter. Iain took out his snuff-box and opened it. Out jumped the three wee men.

'What can we do for you?' they all said together.

'Bring me the fastest horse ever seen, and the finest clothes and a pair of glass shoes.'

The first wee man appeared leading the horse Iain had bartered for the gun, the dog and the falcon. The second wee man appeared carrying a very fine suit of clothes over his arm; while the third wee man brought a beautiful pair of glass shoes.

Iain put on the fine suit of clothes and the glass shoes and rode off to the races on his mother's horse. He had never thought much of it, but it came in first and won the first prize, and the first prize was a bag of gold.

Iain was amazed to hear the people talking about his beautiful racehorse. It surprised him, for the horse had never looked out of the ordinary. He recognised the Princess, but she didn't know him.

He changed into his old clothes and shoes and rode to the weaver's house on his mother's horse. He went into the weaver's house and threw a handful of gold into the weaver's apron, then broke his loom and tore his cloth. The weaver thought he was mad, but did not mind as the gold was worth more to him than the loom.

Next day, there was a dog-race. In the morning, Iain took out his snuff-box, opened it and out jumped the three wee men.

'What can we do for you?' they said.

'Fetch me the fastest dog in the world, a suit of silver, and silver shoes!'

The wee men went away, and brought back Iain's own dog from nowhere, as well as a silver suit and silver shoes, Iain put on the silver clothes and rode, with his dog trotting by his side, to the dog-races. But when the race started, Iain's dog, running like a greyhound, led all the other dogs round the course, came in first and won the first prize. The crowd admired his beautiful dog, but the Princess did not know him.

When he returned to the weaver's house, he gave the weaver a handful of gold, then smashed up his furniture. He looked at his horse, it looked like any ordinary horse, and his dog looked like an ordinary dog.

Next day was the falcon race. Again he asked the three wee men to help him, and this time the first wee man brought him his own falcon. The second wee man brought him a suit of gold, and the third wee man brought him a pair of gold shoes. Iain's falcon won the first prize. He took the bag of gold from the King's daughter, but still she did not recognise him. After the race, he slipped away quietly, put on his old suit and his old shoes and rode back to the weaver's house on his mother's old horse, his dog trotting beside him like any ordinary dog. No one they passed looked at them twice. The horse did not look like a horse that could win a race, nor did the dog and nor did the falcon. As for Iain, he looked so ordinary, no one could imagine that he might marry the King's daughter. Even the house he was living in was a ruin, for after he had given the weaver another handful of gold, Iain had knocked in the windows and pulled half the thatch off the roof.

When the King's men came to the weaver's house, looking for the winner of the horse race, the dog race, and the falcon race, Iain said that he was the man they were looking for. The King's men looked at the horse, then at the dog and the falcon, and then at Iain in his tattered clothes and old shoes, standing outside the broken-down house. They laughed. They laughed at the old horse, the mangey dog and moulting falcon, but they laughed loudest of all at Iain.

'Take me to the King,' said Iain in a firm voice.

So they took him to the King's court, where a crowd was waiting outside the palace, and into the palace where the courtiers waited for the man who had won the horse race, the dog race and the falcon race. When the crowd heard that Iain was the man who had won the races, and that *he* was the man who should marry the King's daughter, they laughed and laughed so loudly that all the windows of the palace were cracked. Inside the palace, the courtiers laughed, but when the King looked at the horse, the dog and the falcon, he turned and looked at Iain, and he was very angry indeed.

'You're insulting my daughter, the Princess,' he said. 'How dare you come to my palace in those rags, with that old horse, that mangey dog and that moulting falcon? You're just a common swindler, and you'll hang for this!'

The King ordered his executioner to take Iain away to the gallows and hang him. So Iain was led to the gallows, up the steps, and a noose was put round his neck.

'Have you anything to say before you die?' asked the executioner; for it was an old custom to ask the criminal who was about to be hanged this question.

Iain raised his arm to address the King, the Princess and the courtiers, who were all there looking at him. They were wondering what he would say before he was hanged. Just then, the Princess saw her name written under his upraised arm, 'Daughter of the King of the Kingdom under the Waves.'

'Stop! stop!' cried the Princess. 'This is the man I am destined to marry!'

The executioner was ordered to take the noose off Iain's neck and lead him from the gallows.

Then Iain turned to the King and said:

'Allow me to go home first, so that I may dress correctly for the court.'

The King gave his permission and Iain returned to the weaver's house. He changed into his suit of gold and the golden shoes. Even his horse, his dog and his falcon looked like the creatures that had won the races. As for the weaver, he was already building himself a better loom and house with the gold Iain had given him.

Meanwhile, the Princess told the King, her father, how Iain had lifted the spell from her when she had been turned into a deer, and how he had faced death at the robbers' hands, three times, for her sake, and how she had written her name under his arm while he slept. The King agreed that such a young man deserved to win her.

So, when Iain returned to the palace, the crowds outside cheered him. Inside he was given a royal welcome by the courtiers, for he looked a fine young prince in his gold clothes.

The King greeted him warmly, while the Princess took both his hands in hers. Soon after, they had a magnificent wedding, with feasting and dancing and merry music.

OSCAR AND THE GIANT

OSCAR used to play shinty with his school-fellows on the sea-shore. By the time he was sixteen his side always won, for he had grown very big, twice as big as any lad his own age. Twice as many lads played against him as for him. At last he played alone against the rest.

One day, when they were playing shinty, they saw a boat coming in. There was a giant in it like nothing they'd seen before. All the lads were afraid of the giant and gathered round Oscar for protection.

The giant came towards them. Only his eyes could be seen, for he was covered with green scales. Every lad he struck with his enormous hand lay dead on the shore. Then he struck Oscar and made him dizzy. He could just rise, but he thought it best to lie still, for if he got up he would surely be slain.

The giant seized Oscar and put him, like a trout, on the end of a branch, with sixteen of his school-fellows on top of him. Then the giant slung the branch over his shoulder and threw it, lads and all, into his boat, with Oscar underneath.

On sailed the boat till it came to a shore, with a castle on the edge of it. The giant went inside, put down the boys, and called for his house-keeper. A fine big woman appeared at the door.

'I'm going to rest now, goodwife,' said the giant. 'Cook me the biggest lad for my supper!' Then he fell asleep.

The woman went over to the branch, and felt all the lads. Oscar was the biggest, but he caught her by the hand and begged her to let him be for the present. So she took the best of the others. This one was no sooner cooked than the giant awoke.

'Is my supper ready?' he roared.

'It is,' said the goodwife, setting the dish before him.

'There was a bigger lad than this,' said the giant. 'I'll go to sleep again, and unless you have that big lad cooked when I wake, I'll have you instead!'

So the goodwife went to Oscar, and said:

'I must take you now.'

'That's not the best thing for you,' said he. 'Let me live, and I'll think of a better idea. You're not his wife, are you?'

'Not I. He stole me seven years ago, and I dread each day that he will kill me.'

'Help me,' said Oscar, 'and I'll help you. First put the poker in the fire, and then free me from this branch.'

The woman did this, and freed him. When the poker was red hot, Oscar took it and drove it through the green scales of the monster's head to the ground, and the woman took the giant-monster's sword and struck off his head. The monster was dead, the spell broken, and all the boys lifted themselves up off the branch.

When Oscar and his fifteen school-fellows left the castle, they took the woman with them, and as much of the giant's gold and silver as they could carry. Then they found his boat and rowed back to the shore.

FINN AND THE YOUNG HERO'S CHILDREN

ONE day Finn and his men were hunting on the hill. They had killed many deer and sat in the sun out of the wind. They could see everyone, but nobody could see them.

Finn saw a ship sailing straight for the haven beneath them. A young Hero leaped out of her, and pulled the ship on to the green grass. Then he climbed the hill to Finn and his men.

Finn and he greeted each other, and Finn asked where he had come from and what he wanted. He answered that he had come through the night watches and the storms of the sea, because he was losing his children, and only one man could help him. That man was Finn, King of the Feinne.

'I'll lay a spell on you,' said he to Finn, 'to be with me before you eat, drink or sleep.'

Having said this, he left them. When he reached the ship, he pushed her with his shoulder into the water. Then he leaped into her, and sailed away over the horizon.

Finn said goodbye to his men, and went down to the shore. He walked along it, and saw seven men coming to meet him.

'What are you good at?' Finn asked the first man.

'I'm a good carpenter.'

'How good are you at carpentry?'

'With three strokes of my axe I can make a ship of the alder tree yonder.'

'What are you good at?' Finn asked the second man.

'I'm a good tracker.'

'How good are you?'

'I can track wild duck over the nine waves within nine days.'

'What are you good at?' Finn asked the third man.

'I am a good gripper.'

'How good are you?'

'I will not let go till my two arms part from my shoulders, or till what I hold comes with me.'

'What are you good at?' Finn asked the fourth man.

'I am a good climber. I can climb a thread of silk to the stars if you tie it there.'

'What are you good at?' Finn asked the fifth man.

'I am a good thief. I can steal the heron's egg while she is watching me.'

'What are you good at?' Finn asked the sixth man.

'I am a good listener. I can hear what people are saying at the end of the world.'

'What are you good at?' Finn asked the seventh man.

'I am a good marksman. I can hit an egg in the sky as far away as bowstring can carry the arrow.'

The Carpenter went to the alder tree, and with three strokes of his axe the ship was ready. Finn ordered his men to push her into the water, and they went on board.

The Tracker went to the bow. Finn told him how the Young Hero had left the haven in his ship, and Finn wanted to follow him to the place where he now was. The Tracker told him to keep the ship that way or to keep her this way. They sailed a long time without seeing land, till evening. In the gloaming they saw land ahead, and made straight for it. They leaped ashore and drew up the ship.

They walked toward a large house in the glen above the beach. As they came near it the Young Hero came to meet them.

'Dearest of all men in the world, have you come?' he said, and threw his arms about Finn's neck.

In the house, after their hunger and thirst were satisfied, the Young Hero told them his story:

'Six years ago, my wife had a baby. But a large hand came down the chimney and took the child away. Three years ago, the same thing happened. Tonight my wife is going to have another baby, and I have been told you are the only man in the world who can keep my children for me.'

Finn told his men to stretch themselves on the floor, and he would keep watch. He sat by the fire. He had an iron bar in the fire, and when his eyes began to close he pushed the bar against his palms to keep himself awake.

About midnight the baby was born, and immediately the Hand came down the chimney. Finn called the Gripper, who sprang to his feet and grasped the Hand, pulling the Giant in as far as the eyebrows. The Hand pulled the Gripper out as far as the top of his shoulders. The Gripper pulled the Hand out again, and brought it in as far as the neck. The Hand pulled the Gripper, and brought him out as far as his waist. The Gripper pulled the Hand, and brought it in as far as the two armpits. The Hand pulled the Gripper, and brought him out as far as the soles of his two feet. Then the Gripper gave a great pull on the Hand and it came out of the shoulder. When it fell on the floor the pull of seven horses was in it. But the big Giant put his other hand down the chimney, and took the child away.

They were all very sorry for the loss of the child. But Finn said:

'We will not give in. I and my men will go after the Hand before sunrise.'

At dawn, Finn and his men launched the ship. The Tracker went to the bow, and Finn steered. The Tracker told Finn to keep her in that direction, or keep her in this direction. They sailed without seeing anything but the ocean. At sunset there was a black spot in the sea ahead.

Finn thought it was too small for an island and too big for a bird, but he steered toward it. At dusk they reached it, and it was a rock. On top of it was a castle thatched with eelskins.

They landed on the rock, but the castle had neither window nor door, except on the roof, and the thatch was slippery.

'I'll not be long in climbing it,' cried the Climber.

He sprang toward the castle, and in a moment was on the roof. He looked in, took note of everything he saw, and slid down where the others were waiting.

'What did you see?' Finn asked.

'I saw a big Giant lying on a bed, a silk covering over him, and a satin sheet under him. An infant slept in his out-stretched hand. Two boys were playing shinty on the floor with sticks of gold and a silver ball. A very large deer-hound was lying beside the fire nursing her two pups.'

'I don't know how we'll bring the children out,' said Finn.

'I'll not be long fetching them out,' said the Thief.

'Come on to my back and I'll take you to the door,' said the Climber. The Thief did so, and went into the castle.

He fetched the child from the Giant's hand, the two boys who were playing, the silk cover from over the Giant, and the satin sheet from under him. Then he fetched the sticks of gold and the silver ball, and the two pups from their mother. There was nothing else of value, so he left the Giant sleeping and came away.

They put everything into the ship and sailed away. Soon after that the Listener stood up.

'I hear him,' said he.

'What do you hear?' said Finn.

'The Giant has just wakened,' said the Listener, 'and missed everything we stole. He is very angry. He's sending the deer-hound. He's telling her that if she won't go he'll go himself. It's the hound that's coming.'

Soon behind them they saw the hound coming. She was swimming so fast, red sparks were coming from her. They were afraid.

'Throw out one of the pups,' said Finn. 'Maybe when she sees the pup drowning, she'll go back with it.' They threw out the pup, and she went back with it.

Soon after the Listener stood up, trembling.

'I hear him,' he said.

'What do you hear?' said Finn.

'The Giant is sending the hound again. But she won't go, so he's coming himself.'

After they heard this, their eyes were always behind them. At last they saw him coming, and the ocean rose no farther than his thighs. They were terribly afraid, and didn't know what to do. But Finn remembered his wisdom tooth, and put his finger under it. He learned that the Giant was immortal, except for a mole on the palm of his right hand.

'If I catch one glimpse of the mole, I'll have him,' said the Marksman.

The Giant waded through the sea to the side of the ship. He put up his right hand to seize the top of the mast, to sink the ship. But when his hand was up, the Marksman saw the mole and shot an arrow which hit the spot, and the Giant fell dead into the sea.

They turned about, and sailed back to the castle. The Thief again stole the pup, and they took it along with the one they had. They returned to the Young Hero. In the haven they leaped ashore, and pulled the ship to dry land.

Then Finn went to the Young Hero's house, taking with him the Young Hero's sons and everything he and his men had taken out of the Giant's castle.

'What reward do you want?' asked the Young Hero.

'I ask for nothing but my choice of the two pups we took from the castle,' said Finn.

The pup was Bran, and his brother, which the Young Hero kept, was the Grey Dog.

The Young Hero took Finn and his men into his house, and made a merry feast which lasted a year and a day, and if the last day was not the best, it was not the worst.

FINN AND THE GREY DOG

ONE day Finn and his men were hunting on the hill. They had killed many deer, and when they were preparing to go home, they saw a tall lad coming. He greeted Finn, and Finn returned his greeting. Finn asked him where he came from and what he wanted.

'I have come from the east and from the west, seeking a master,' he said.

'I need a lad,' said Finn, 'and if we can agree, I'll employ you. What reward do you want at the end of a year and a day?'

'Not much,' said the lad, 'only that you go with me, at the end of the year and the day, to feast at the palace of the King of Lochlan.'

Finn engaged the lad, and the lad served him faithfully to the end of a year and a day.

On the morning of the last day, the Tall Lad asked Finn if he was satisfied with him. Finn said he was perfectly satisfied.

'Well,' said the lad, 'I hope I shall have my reward, and that you'll go with me as you promised.'

'You'll have your reward,' said Finn, 'and I'll go with you.'

'It is the day I have to keep my promise to the lad,' Finn told his men, 'and I don't know when I shall return. But if I am not back within a year and a day, let the man who is not whetting his sword be bending his bow to revenge me on the shore of Lochlan.'

When he had said this, he bade them farewell and went into his house. His Fool was sitting by the fire.

'Are you sorry I am going away?' Finn asked.

'I am sorry you are going that way,' said the Fool, weeping, 'but I'll give you advice if you'll take it.'

'Yes,' said Finn, 'for often the King's wisdom comes from the Fool's head. What is your advice?'

'It is to take Bran's chain in your pocket,' said the Fool.

Finn did so, said goodbye to him and went away. He found the Tall Lad waiting for him at the door.

'Are you ready to go?' asked the lad.

'I am ready,' said Finn. 'Lead the way, you know the road better than I do.'

The Tall Lad set off, and Finn followed. Yet, though Finn was swift, he could not touch the Tall Lad with a stick all the way. When the Tall Lad was disappearing through a gap in the mountains, Finn would be appearing on the ridge behind him. They kept that distance between them till their journey's end.

They entered the palace of the King of Lochlan, and Finn sat down wearily. But instead of a feast, the lords of the King of Lochlan were considering how to bring about his death.

'Hang him!' said one. 'Burn him!' said another. 'Drown him!' said a third. 'Send him to Glenmore!' said another. 'He'll not go far there before he's killed by the Grey Dog. There would be no death more disgraceful, in the opinion of the Feinne, than the death of their King by a cur.'

They all clapped their hands and agreed with this suggestion.

At once they took Finn to the glen where the Grey Dog was. They had not gone far up the glen before they heard the Dog howling. When the men of Lochlan saw the Dog, they said it was time to run. So they ran and left Finn at the Dog's mercy.

If Finn ran away, the men of Lochlan would kill him, if he stayed the Dog would kill him. He decided it would be better to be killed by the Dog than by his enemies. So he stayed.

The Grey Dog came with his mouth open and his tongue hanging to one side. Every breath from his nostrils burned everything three miles in front of him and on both sides of him. Finn was tortured by the heat, and knew he could not stand it long. If Bran's chain was going to be of any use, now was the time to take it out. He put his hand in his pocket, and when the Dog was near him he took the chain and shook it. The Grey Dog stopped at once, and wagged his tail. He came to Finn, and licked all his wounds from head to foot, healing with his tongue what he had burned with his breath. At length, Finn put Bran's chain round the Grey Dog's neck and he went down the glen with the Dog on a leash.

An old man and woman, who had fed the Grey Dog, lived at the foot of the glen. The old woman was at the door, and when she saw Finn coming with the Dog she went into the house, calling to her husband.

'What have you seen?' said the old man.

'I saw the tallest and most handsome man I've ever seen, coming down the glen with the Grey Dog on a leash.'

'If all the people of Lochlan and Ireland were together,' said the old man, 'not one man of them could do that, but Finn, King of the Feinne, with Bran's golden chain.'

'Whether it's he or not, he's coming,' replied the old woman.

'We'll soon know,' said the old man, going out.

He met Finn, and they greeted each other. Finn told him why he was there, and the old man invited him into the house for a rest and a meal. The old woman told Finn he was very welcome to stay for a year and a day, and Finn accepted the invitation.

At the end of the year and a day, the old woman was standing on a knowe near the house. She looked toward the shore and saw a great army of men on the beach of Lochlan. She ran into the house, her eyes big with fear.

'What did you see?' asked the old man.

'I saw something I have never seen before. There's a great army of men on the beach, and among them a red-haired man with a squint. I don't think there's his equal, as a fighter, this night under the stars.'

'They are my companions, the Feinne,' said Finn. 'Let me go to meet them.'

Finn and the Grey Dog went down to the shore. When his men saw him coming they shouted, so that it was heard in the four corners of Lochlan. The Feinne and Finn, their King, greeted each other, and no less friendly was the greeting between Bran and the Grey Dog, for they were brothers, taken together from the same castle by Finn when he had rescued the Young Hero's children from the giant.

The Feinne took vengeance on the men of Lochlan for their treatment of Finn. They began at one end of Lochlan and did not stop till they were out at the other end.

After they had conquered Lochlan they went home, and in the Hall of Finn they made a great feast that lasted a year and a day.

FINN IN THE HOUSE OF THE YELLOW FIELD

FINN and his men had been hunting deer all day. They had killed many. Now they sat and rested on the hillside, and discussed where they should hunt next day. As they talked, Finn looked down the glen and saw a big lad coming towards them.

'There's a stranger coming this way,' he said.

The stranger greeted Finn and Finn greeted the stranger.

'Who are you,' asked Finn, 'and what do you want?'

'I'm seeking a master,' said the big lad.

'I need a servant,' said Finn. 'If we can agree on your wages, I'll engage you.'

'I'd not do that if I were you, Finn,' said Conan, one of the Feinne. 'I thought you were tired of these wandering lads.'

'Never mind that, Conan,' said Finn, and he turned to the big lad. 'I like the look of you. What wage do you want?'

'I want you to promise that, after a year and a day's service, you and your men will go with me to a great feast.'

'There's no reason why I shouldn't agree to that,' said Finn. 'We'll be together, all the Feinne. There should be no danger in it.'

So the big lad became Finn's servant. At the end of a year and a day, Finn and his men discussed how they should follow the big lad to the feast, as they promised.

'He looks a swift mover,' said Finn, 'so Caoilte shall follow him and keep him in sight. Cuchulainn shall go next, and the rest of us will follow.' And so they did.

The big lad set off, bare-headed, bare-footed and unprepared for battle. Swiftly he went from hilltop to glen, from glen to strath, and Caoilte had to move fast to keep him in sight. Cuchulainn followed at the same distance, then Finn and his men. They went in that order until they reached the Yellow Field.

The big lad waited for them at the house where the feast was to be. He opened the door and invited them in. Finn went in first and his men followed.

'Be seated,' said the big lad before he left them.

They all got seats against the wall except Conan. He was the last to go in and, because all the places were filled, he had no choice but to stretch out on the hearthstone.

Finn and his men were so tired after their long journey, they were content to sit and rest, but after a while they grew impatient. They were hungry and still there was no sign of the feast.

'Go and see if anyone is coming with the food,' said Finn.

One of his men tried to get up out of his seat, but he could not. He was stuck fast. So were all the others.

'Didn't I warn you about wandering lads?' cried Conan, whose back and hair were stuck fast to the hearthstone.

Finn did not reply, he was too worried about the plight they were in. He remembered his wisdom tooth, so he put his finger under it. Then he understood that only the blood of the King of Insh Tilly's three sons, filtered through silver rings into gold cups, could release them. He wondered who would be able to fetch the blood, then he remembered that two of his men, Lohary and Oscar, were not with him that day, but they would come if he called them.

Now, Finn had a wooden whistle, which he never used unless he was in great trouble. It was a magic whistle, and when he blew it, the sound travelled the seven borders of the earth to the Uttermost World. He knew that Oscar and Lohary would hear it, so he blew the wooden whistle, and before the sun had set, they were outside. But they were unable to get in.

'Are you there?' cried Oscar. 'Tell us what you want us to do.'

'We're prisoner!' said Finn. 'We're unable to move from the place where we're sitting. Our backs and legs are stuck fast, and only the blood of the King of Insh Tilly's three sons, filtered through silver rings into gold cups, can save us.'

'Where can we find these three princes?' asked Oscar.

'At sunset, they'll be by the ford of the river,' said Finn. 'But first, you must find food for us. We're very hungry.' And he added: 'Oscar, remember to take your dart!'

So Lohary and Oscar went in search of food. At last they came to a house. They looked in through a window and saw a fierce hero lifting venison out of a pot. But when they went into the kitchen, the fierce hero had gone. In his place was a buzzard with outstretched wings, ready to pounce on them. Oscar aimed his dart and the buzzard fell to the ground, dead.

There was no one to stop them, so they carried off the venison and took it to Finn.

They returned to the house where the Feinne were imprisoned. As they could not enter, they made a hole in the stone wall, and passed the food through to Finn and his men. They all had a share except Conan. He lay on the hearthstone, stuck fast to it by his back and hair. So they made a hole in the roof and dropped food down to him that way.

Before the sun set, Oscar asked Finn how they should approach the three princes when they met at the ford of the river.

'They'll be surrounded by an army of soldiers,' said Finn, 'but they will be dressed in green, that's how you'll know them.'

Oscar and Lohary went to the ford. They saw an army of soldiers coming towards them. Although they were only two against many, they defeated the soldiers, and no one was left to tell the tale. But there was no sign of the three sons of the King of Insh Tilly.

'They'll come in good time,' said Finn when he was told. 'Rest now, and in the morning you must both go and find food for us. We've eaten all you brought us.'

Next morning they set out and Finn told Oscar to take his two-edged sword and shield. He took them and they reached the house. Through a window they saw a man with four hands lifting venison out of a pot. They went into the kitchen but the man had gone. In his place was an eagle ready for attack. Before Oscar could draw his sword, Lohary lifted the pot and poured the boiling broth over the eagle. She let out a terrible shriek and vanished.

Then they took the venison to Finn and his men and gave each of them a share.

At sunset they went to the ford. They saw an army of soldiers there and, although they were only two against many, they defeated the soldiers and not one of them was left to tell the tale. But there was no sign of the three sons of the King of Insh Tilly.

'They'll come in the end,' said Finn, 'but now you must rest. In the morning you shall go and fetch food for us.'

Next day they set out, and as they left, Finn reminded Oscar to take his long spear.

'When your spear is tipped with the blood of the Winged Dragon of Shiel,' said Finn, 'the King of Insh Tilly will surely lose his three sons.'

Again they reached the house and there, through a window, they saw a huge man with two heads and four hands lifting venison out of a pot. They went into the kitchen but the man was not there. In his place was the Winged Dragon of Shiel with two serpent heads.

'You take care of the venison, while I tackle the dragon,' said Oscar.

He raised his long spear and drove it into one of the dragon's heads, and half-way into its second head. The Winged Dragon fought hard but it was badly wounded, and when Oscar drew out his spear to make another thrust, the dragon vanished completely.

Then they took the venison to Finn and his men.

'Is your spear tipped with the Winged Dragon's blood?' asked Finn.

'It is,' said Oscar.

'Then it is now time to take the silver filter rings and the gold cups and fetch the blood that will release us,' said Finn.

As soon as the sun had set, they went to the ford, but this time they went farther across the river than they had ever been before. They saw the army of soldiers coming and there, in their midst, were the three sons of the King of Insh Tilly dressed in green.

'You fight the three princes, while I tackle the soldiers,' said Oscar, and although he was only one against so many, he defeated them, and there was not one left to tell the tale.

Meanwhile Lohary had the three princes on their knees, and as soon as Oscar saw their blood flowing, he took the silver rings, filtered it into the gold cups, and took it to Finn.

'Rub it into the soles of your feet and into every part of you that will touch this house. Only then can you cross the threshold.'

They did this and passed easily into the enchanted house of the Yellow Field. They rubbed every part of Finn and his men that was stuck to the walls, the seats and the floor, until they were all released except Conan. He was the last to be rubbed with the blood from the gold cups, and because there was not enough left to be rubbed into every hair at the back of his head, some of it remained stuck to the hearthstone. But when he saw his companions leaving, he pulled his head up with all his strength, leaving some of his hair stuck fast to the stone. It never grew again, and he became known as Bald Conan because of it.

The Feinne returned home and Finn never again engaged a wandering lad to work for them.

GREEN KIRTLE

ONE day, the son of the King of Erin met a bonny lass called Green Kirtle. No one knew where she had come from nor where she was going.

'Let's play a game of cards,' she said to the Prince.

So they sat, facing each other, played a game and the Prince won.

'As I lost that game,' said Green Kirtle, 'what forfeit must I pay you?'

'You've nothing I want,' said the Prince.

'Let us meet here tomorrow,' said Green Kirtle.

'I'll be here,' said the Prince.

Next day they met at the same place. Again they played a game of cards but, this time, Green Kirtle won.

'As I lost this game,' said the Prince, 'what forfeit must I pay you?'

'I lay a spell on you,' said Green Kirtle. 'You'll not rest till you find me again under the four brown quarters of the earth.'

The Prince went home, put his elbows on the table, his hand under his cheek, and sighed.

'Whatever is the matter with you?' asked the King. 'Are you under a spell? If so, I can remove it. I've a smiddy for making swords, spears and arrow-heads. I've ships too. As long as I've gold and silver, I'll pay your debts.'

'None of these will help me to lift the spell,' said the Prince. 'I must do that myself.'

So, next day, the Prince set off without servant or dog.

He walked on and on till his shoes burned his feet and the soles were worn through. For days he saw neither cottage nor house. For days he had nothing to eat or drink. At last he saw a castle. He found it had no doors nor windows, not even a little hole in the walls to peep through. So he turned away.

'Come back, Son of the King of Erin!' called a girl from the castle. 'There's a feast waiting for you.'

The Prince turned and went back. He found the castle had a door for each day of the year, and a window for each day of the year, where none had been before. Inside the castle, music played and there was a table laden with food. He sat down at the table with the girl and a fine company of men and women.

That night, a servant bathed his feet in warm water and prepared a soft bed for him. The day that followed was as delightful as the night before, and so it was, day after day, till one morning the girl of the castle said:

'Son of Erin's King, how long is it since you came here?'

'A week, I should think,' said the Prince.

'It is exactly a quarter of a year,' said the girl, 'but you may stay as long as you like.'

So the Prince stayed and time passed so happily he forgot about it until the girl asked him again:

'Son of Erin's King, how long have you been here?'

'About a month,' said the Prince.

'Today,' she said, 'you have been here for two years.'

But this did not worry the Prince, he felt so well he began to boast:

'I feel strong,' said he, 'and if my arms were long enough I'd lift the peak of that mountain and put it on top of this one. I don't believe there's a man on earth as strong as I am.'

'Don't be daft,' said the girl. 'There's a little band of men called the Feinne. No man can beat them.'

'I'll not eat nor drink nor sleep till I find these men and know them,' said the Prince.

'I'll tell you where you can find them,' said the girl. 'The Feinne are by the river with a net, fishing for trout. Alone, on the other side of the river, is Finn. Go to him and bless him. In return he will bless you. But when you ask him for work, he'll say there's no place for you. He'll ask your name, and you must tell him you are the son of the King of Erin. Then Finn will reply: "Though I don't need a man, there is surely a place for the son of your father." And take this cloth. Give it to Finn and tell him to wrap you in it, alive or dead, if ever it is necessary.'

The Prince set off and soon reached the place where the Feinne were fishing for trout, and Finn sitting on the other side of the river. The Prince went to Finn and blessed him, and Finn blessed the Prince.

'I heard there were such men as you, and I came to offer my service to you,' said the Prince.

'Just now I've no need of a man,' said Finn. 'What is your name?'

'I'm the son of the King of Erin.'

'To whom should I give service but to the son of your father?' said Finn. 'Come, catch the end of this net and drag it along with us.'

So the Prince dragged the net along with Finn and the Feinne. Then he looked up and saw a stag run past.

'Wouldn't young men, strong and swift as you are, rather hunt the stag, than fish for trout in this river?' said he. 'A mouthful of trout won't satisfy your hunger as well as a meal of venison, surely.'

'Even if the stag is better than the trout, we're seven times tired of it,' said Finn.

'I've heard there's a member of the Feinne called the Swift One, who can catch the March wind,' said the Prince. 'I'd like to meet him.'

'We'll send for him,' said Finn.

The Swift One came, and Finn shouted to him across the river:

'We've a job for you! Will you catch the stag?'

'I've wasted days, chasing that beast,' said the Swift One. 'I've not been able to catch it but I'll try again.' And off he ran, after the stag.

'What will the Swift One look like at top speed?' asked the Prince.

'He'll have three heads at top speed,' said Finn.

'How many heads will the stag have at top speed?'

'There'll be seven heads on the stag at top speed.'

'How far has he to go before he reaches the end of his journey?' asked the Prince.

'Seven hills and seven glens.'

'Let's go on fishing,' said the Prince. But, after a while he said:

'Put your finger under your wisdom tooth, Finn, and see how far they are from each other.'

Finn put his finger under his wisdom tooth and said:

'The Swift One has two heads and the stag has two heads.'

'How far have they gone?'

'Over two hills and two glens, and they've five more to go.'

'Let's go on fishing,' said the Prince. Then after a while he said:

'Put your finger under your wisdom tooth and see how far they are from each other.'

'There are three heads on the Swift One and four heads on the stag,' said Finn.

'How many hills and glens have they still to go?'

'There are four behind them and three in front of them.'

'Let's go on fishing,' said the Prince, but after a while he said:

'Finn, what distance has the stag to go before he reaches the end of his journey?'

'One glen and one hill,' said Finn.

The Prince threw the net from him, and set off at top speed.

He caught the March wind, and he caught up with the Swift One, and left him a blessing as he passed. Going over the ford of Struth

Ruadh, the stag gave a spring. The Prince made the next spring and caught the stag by the hind leg. The stag roared. Then the Old Carlin appeared.

'Who has caught the beast I love best?' she cried.

'I, the son of the King of Erin,' said the Prince. 'I did.'

'Son of the King of Erin, let my stag go!'

'I will not,' said the Prince. 'He is my beast now.'

'Then you must give me a fistful of his bristles or a piece of his flesh,' said the Old Carlin.

'Not one scrap shall you get,' said the Prince.

'The Feinne are coming,' she cried, 'with Finn at their head. I'll bind them back to back!'

'Do as you like,' said the Prince, 'I'll not be here.'

And away he went, taking the dead stag with him, till he met Finn and the Feinne. And he gave the stag to Finn.

'Finn MacCoull, keep this stag for me while I go to the smiddy.'

From the smiddy, the Prince took a number of iron hoops and a hammer. He returned to the Feinne, fixed three hoops round the head of each man of the Feinne, except Finn, and then he tightened the hoops with the hammer.

Out came the Old Carlin, and screamed:

'Finn MacCoull, let me have my stag!'

Her screams were so terrible that the first hoop round each head of the Feinne burst. She screamed again and the second hoop round each head of the Feinne burst. Then she screamed a third time, and the third hoop burst. She was indeed a terrible Old Carlin. She tore off the green branches of willow trees and with these withies, she bound the men of the Feinne back to back, all except Finn MacCoull.

Meanwhile, the Prince had skinned the stag's carcass and prepared it for the pot, which he filled with water. He put the meat into the cauldron and lit a fire under it. Then he turned to Finn.

'Finn MacCoull,' said he. 'Would you rather fight the Carlin or mind the cauldron?'

'Well, if one little bit of the stag's flesh is uncooked,' said Finn, 'the stag will jump out of the pot alive, so it is better that I should stay and mind the cauldron, and see that the meat is properly cooked.'

So the Prince fought the Carlin alone. They fought so furiously that they sank into the ground up to their knees when they fought least and when they fought hardest they sank into the ground up to their eyes.

Then the Prince seized the Carlin and threw her from him.

'Finn MacCoull,' she cried, as she lay on the ground, 'I'll lay you under a spell. Three hours before dawn you will be with the Green Griffin's wife!'

'Old Carlin,' said the Prince, 'I'll lay you under a spell. You shall lie with one foot on one side of the ford at Struth Ruadh and one foot on the other side, with the waters of the river running over you.'

'Take your spell off me and I'll take mine off Finn.'

'I will not,' said the Prince. And they left the Old Carlin lying in the ford, the river running over her.

When the Prince took the cauldron off the fire, he cut a piece of venison and ate it. He then cut a dry turf from the ground and laid it on top of the cauldron.

'Finn MacCoull,' said he, 'it's time for us to go. The sooner we reach the Green Griffin's castle, the sooner you'll be free of the Carlin's spell. Take this rod and strike me with it, then I'll take you there in no time.'

Finn struck the Prince with the rod and the Prince changed into a horse. Finn mounted the horse and away they galloped. With the first leap, the horse jumped over nine mountains. With the second leap, he jumped over nine more mountains, and Finn did not fall off. At last they reached a town and in the distance they could see the Green Griffin's castle.

'Dismount,' said the horse to Finn. 'Take a comb, three stoups of wine, and three wheaten loaves from the store. When we get to the castle, I'll tell you what to do with them.'

Finn did as the horse told him, and on they rode till they came to the high castle walls. Finn took the comb, the wine and the loaves, and got down off the horse.

'Give me a stoup of wine, a loaf of bread, and comb me from head to tail and from tail to head,' said the horse.

Finn did this. The horse sprang at the wall but got only a third of the way up, so Finn gave him a second stoup of wine and a loaf of bread and combed him from head to tail and from tail to head. Again the horse missed the top of the wall, but this time sprang up it two thirds of the way. When Finn gave him the third stoup of wine, and the third loaf and combed him as before, the horse sprang to the top of the wall. He looked over it into the Green Griffin's castle.

'You're in luck, Finn MacCoull,' he cried. 'The Griffin's not at home, but his wife is!'

The horse sprang back down from the wall, and Finn climbed over it, into the castle. The Griffin's wife welcomed him, gave him food and a soft bed. By the time it was three hours before dawn, there was Finn with the Griffin's wife. The Carlin's spell was broken.

In the mouth of morning, Finn left the castle, climbed over the wall and found that the horse had changed back to the Prince. Away they went, but not before the Griffin saw them and chased after them. He would have caught them if he had had his magic book with him, but he had not: so instead he changed himself into a bull.

'Take this cloth,' said the Prince to Finn when he saw the Griffin-bull, 'I'll tell you what to do with it when the time comes.'

Then the son of the King of Erin shape-shifted himself into a bull and attacked the Griffin-bull, who roared with pain and changed into an ass. So the Prince also changed into an ass and bit the Griffin-ass, who changed into a hawk. At once, the Prince changed himself into a hawk. He caught the Griffin-hawk, who fell like a stone, quite dead.

The Prince-hawk flew down, and perched on Finn's wrist.

'Wrap me in the cloth I gave you,' he commanded. 'Cut a turf from the ground and bury me wrapped in the cloth. Cover me with the turf, then stand on it.'

Finn had no sooner done all that the Prince had told him than along came the Griffin's wife, weeping.

'Finn MacCoull,' said she, 'you're one who never tells a lie. Tell me who killed my husband.'

'I know no one on earth who killed your husband,' said Finn, standing on the turf and telling the truth.

When she had gone, Finn stepped off the turf, lifted it and removed the cloth-wrapped hawk from the hole in the earth. He carried the bird carefully to the castle, as the Prince had instructed him.

Now who should open the castle door but Green Kirtle herself! Finn handed her the hawk wrapped in the cloth and waited while she went into the castle with it.

Soon she returned, smiled at Finn and said:

'Come with me. The son of the King of Erin is here!'

Finn followed her and there, in the great hall, stood the Prince, looking as though nothing unusual had happened to him. Green Kirtle had prepared a fine meal for them, but the Prince looked at Finn, and Finn looked at the Prince. They thanked her, but refused to eat. They explained that there was a task they must do before they were free to eat with her.

'We must free the Feinne from their bonds,' they said, 'and we must make sure every scrap of venison we left in the cauldron is eaten up.'

They went to the place where the Feinne lay, still bound back to back by the Carlin's bonds. After their release, the Feinne, who were very hungry, ate the venison that had been cooked in the cauldron and there was not a scrap left. Then they all returned to the castle with Finn and the Prince.

Green Kirtle welcomed them and they all sat down to the feast she had prepared for them. After the feast, they rose to leave. The Prince thanked her, then he turned to Finn.

'My blessings on you, Finn MacCoull,' said he. 'Thanks to you I've found what I was looking for. Now I must return to my father, the King of Erin.'

'Son of the King of Erin,' said Green Kirtle, 'will you go without me?'

'I will not,' said the Prince. 'You are the one I looked for under the four brown quarters of the earth. Now I've found you I cannot leave you.'

So Green Kirtle went with the Prince to Erin. There they were married, and Finn and the Feinne were at the wedding. It is said that the feasting and the merriment, the music and the dancing lasted a year and a day without stopping.

THE LAST OF THE PICTS

LONG, long ago, there were folk in this country called the Picts. Wee short men they were, with red hair, long arms, and feet so broad that when it rained they could turn them up over their heads for umbrellas.

The Picts were great folk for the ale they brewed from the heather. Many wanted to know how they made it, but the Picts would not give away the secret, handing it down from one to the other.

Then the Picts were at war with the rest of the country, and many of them were killed. Soon only a handful of them were left, and they fought a great battle with the Scots. They lost the battle, and all but two of them were killed. These two were father and son.

The King of the Scots had these men brought before him, to frighten them into telling him the secret of the heather ale. He told them that if they did not reveal the secret, he must torture them.

'Well,' said the older man to the King, 'I see it is useless to resist. But one condition you must agree to before you learn the secret.'

'What is that?' said the King.

'Will you fulfil it if it does not harm you?'

'I will,' said the King, 'and promise to do so.'

'Then,' said the Pict,

> 'My son you must kill
> Ere I will you tell

How we brew the yill
From the heather bell!'

The King was astonished, but he ordered the lad to be put to death immediately.

When the Pict saw his son was dead, he stood up before the King, and cried:

'Now do what you like with me. You might have forced my son, for he's but a weak lad, but you'll not force me.

'*And though you may me kill,*
I'll not you tell
How we brew yill
From the heather bell.'

The King was very angry. He had been outwitted by a wild man of the hills. It was useless to kill the Pict, so he was thrown into prison.

And there he lived until he was an old, old man, bedridden and blind. Everyone had forgotten him, then one night some lads sharing his prison cell boasted about their feats of strength. The old Pict leaned out of bed and stretched out his hand.

'Let me feel your wrists,' he said. 'I want to compare them with the arms of the Picts.'

Just for fun, the lads held out a thick iron bar for him to feel. The old Pict grasped the bar between his fingers and thumb, gave it a twist and snapped it in two, as though it was the stem of a clay-pipe.

'It's rather gristly,' said he, 'but the wrists of the Picts were much harder and stronger.'

MURCHAG AND MIONACHAG

MURCHAG and Mionachag went to gather fruit, and as Murchag gathered Mionachag ate. Murcehag went to find a stick to beat Mionachag as she was eating his share of the fruit.

'What's the news today?' said the stick to Murchag.

'I'm looking for a stick to beat Mionachag, for she's eating my share of the fruit.'

'You'll not get me,' said the stick, 'until you find an axe to cut me down.'

So Murchag went on till he met an axe.

'What's the news today?' said the axe.

'I'm looking for an axe to cut the stick to beat Mionachag, who is eating my share of the fruit.'

'You'll not get me,' said the axe, 'till you find a whetting stone to sharpen me.'

So Murchag went on till he found a stone.

'What's your news today?' said the stone.

'I'm looking for a stone to sharpen the axe, that will cut down the stick I need to beat Mionachag, for she's eating my share of the fruit.'

'You'll not get me,' said the stone, 'till you get water to wet me.' So Murchag went to the water.

'What's your news today?' said the water.

'I'm looking for water that will wet the stone, that will sharpen the axe, that will cut down the stick that I need to beat Mionachag, who is eating my share of the fruit.'

'You'll not get me,' said the water, 'till you find a deer to swim me.' So Murchag caught a deer.

'What's your news today?' said the deer.

'I'm looking for a deer to swim the water, that will wet the stone, that will sharpen the axe, that will cut down the stick to beat Mionachag, who is eating my share of the fruit.'

'Then you'll not get me,' said the deer, 'till you find a dog to chase me.' So Murchag found a dog.

'What's your news today?' said the dog.

'I'm looking for a dog that will chase the deer, that will swim the water, that will wet the stone, that will sharpen the axe that will cut down the stick to beat Mionachag, who is eating my share of the fruit.'

'You'll not get me,' said the dog, 'till you get butter to rub on my paws.' So Murchag got some butter.

'What's your news today?' said the butter.

'I need butter to rub on the paws of the dog so that he'll chase after the deer, that will swim the water, that will wet the stone, that will sharpen the axe, that will cut down the stick to beat Mionachag, who is eating my share of the fruit.'

'You'll not get me,' said the butter, 'till you find a mouse to nibble me.' So Murchag found a mouse.

'What's your news today?' said the mouse.

'I'm looking for a mouse to nibble the butter, that will be rubbed on to the paws of the dog, that will chase the deer, that will swim the water, that will wet the stone, that will sharpen the axe, that will cut the stick to beat Mionachag, who is eating my share of the fruit.'

'You'll not get me,' said the mouse, 'till you find a cat to hunt me.' So Murchag found a cat.

'What's the news today?' said the cat.

'I'm looking for a cat to hunt the mouse, that will nibble the butter, that will be rubbed on the paws of the dog, that will chase the deer, that will swim the water, that will wet the stone, that will sharpen the axe, that will cut the stick to beat Mionachag, who is eating my share of the fruit.'

'You'll not get me,' said the cat, 'till you get me some milk.' So Murchag went on till he met a cow.

'What's your news today?' said the cow.

'I need milk to give to the cat, so that she'll hunt the mouse that will nibble the butter, to be rubbed into the paws of the dog, that will chase the deer, that will swim the water, that will wet the stone, that will sharpen the axe, to cut the stick to beat Mionachag, who is eating my share of the fruit.'

'You'll not get milk from me,' said the cow, 'unless you fetch me hay from the gillie in the byre.' So Murchag went to the cowherd.

'What's your news today?' said the cowherd.

'I've come for hay to give the cow, so that she'll give milk for the cat, that'll hunt the mouse, that'll nibble the butter, that'll be rubbed on the paws of the dog, that'll chase the deer, that'll swim the water, that'll wet the stone, that'll sharpen the axe, that'll cut the stick, that will beat Mionachag, who is eating my share of the fruit.'

'You'll not get hay from me,' said the cowherd, 'till you fetch me a bannock from the farmer's wife.' So Murchag went to the farmer's wife, who was kneading oatmeal bannocks in the kitchen.

'What's the news today, Murchag?' said she.

'I'm wanting a bannock for the cowherd, so that he'll give me hay for the cow, so that she'll give me milk for the cat, that'll hunt the mouse, that'll nibble the butter, that'll grease the paws of the dog, that'll chase the deer, that'll swim the water, that'll wet the stone, that'll sharpen the axe, that'll cut the stick, that'll beat Mionachag, who is eating my share of the fruit.'

'You'll not get a bannock from me,' said the goodwife, 'till you fetch me some water in this sieve to knead the oatmeal.'

So poor Murchag took the sieve to the burn and tried to fill it with water. But as fast as he filled it, out ran the water through the holes.

Just then a hoodie flew over and croaked:

'Gawr-rag, gawr-rag, gawr-rag, little silly!'

'You're right, hoodie, you're right,' sighed Murchag, 'but what can I do?'

'Plug the holes with red clay! Gawr, gawr-rag, gawr-rag!'

So Murchag took some clay from the edge of the burn, and plugged the holes of the sieve with it. Then he filled it with water, the water stayed in the sieve, and he took it to the goodwife. She mixed it with the oatmeal and kneaded it, and baked it into a good oatmeal bannock, which he took to the cowherd.

The cowherd ate the bannock, and gave Murchag the hay, the cow ate the hay and gave him some milk, the cat drank the milk and hunted the mouse, the mouse nibbled the butter, that greased the paws of the dog, the dog chased the deer, that swam the water, that wet the stone, that sharpened the axe, that cut the stick which Murchag took to beat Mionachag for eating his share of the fruit.

But when Murchag found Mionachag, she had BURST!

Peerie Fool

THERE were once a King and Queen in Rousay, who lived in a castle with their three bonny daughters. One day the King died and another King took his place, so that the widow Queen and her daughters had to leave the castle and live in a small cottage. All they had was a field, a cow and a kaleyard full of green cabbages.

All went well until, one day, they noticed that some of the kale had disappeared. Next day more had gone, and on the third day only half was left.

'Someone is stealing our kale,' said the eldest Princess. 'I'm going to keep watch tonight and catch the thief.'

So that night, she wrapped her cloak round her and hid in the garden. The moon rose in the sky and a Giant strode up and leaned over the dry-stone dyke, which just came up to his ankle-bone. He cut some kale and threw it into his large basket. When she saw this, the Princess was very angry. She jumped up and shouted:

'Stop taking our kale!'

'Hold your tongue, lass, or I'll take you too!' cried the Giant.

'You'll do no such thing!' said she.

But, without a word, the Giant picked her up and threw her into the basket, on top of the kale. And away he went, over the hills, till he came to his house. He bumped the basket down on the stone floor.

'Come on, out you get!' he roared. 'It's past sunrise and there's work to be done. I'll not have an idle lass about my house.'

'What will you have me do?' asked the Princess.

'First, you must milk the cow and drive her on to the hill to graze. Then you must work that wool, wash it, comb it, and spin it. When you've spun it, you must weave it into cloth. And mind it's ready when I come back tonight.'

The Princess milked the cow and drove her on to the hill to graze, but when she saw the great heap of wool, she was at her wits' end, and didn't know where to begin. So she made herself a bowl of porridge.

She was sitting supping the porridge, when in ran a crowd of Wee Folk with yellow hair and wee pointed faces. They gathered round singing:

> 'If you're kind, you'll give us a sup,
> A greedy one will send us off!
> Kind or greedy? Kind or greedy?
> Which are you? Which are you?'

The eldest Princess was greedy, so she said:

> 'Little for one, less for two,
> Never a grain have I for you!'

The Wee Folk ran off crying: 'Greedy! Greedy! Greedy!' When the Giant came home that night and found that the Princess had not finished her work, he roared until the roof cracked, seized her by the hair and flung her into the hen-house.

Next night the Giant went to the widow Queen's garden to get a basketful of kale. This time the second Princess was waiting and watching for him, but like her elder sister, she was unlucky. By the following night, she too was locked up in the hen-house, for everything that had happened to her elder sister happened to her.

The widow Queen was worried when her two daughters did not return.

'It's my turn to watch for the thief tonight,' said the youngest Princess, 'and find out what has happened to my sisters.'

'Stay with me,' said her mother. 'I don't want to lose three bonny daughters for the sake of some kale.'

But the youngest Princess refused to listen, and that night, she too was tossed into the Giant's basket and taken to his house. She too was told to milk the cow and drive her on to the hill to graze, and then to wash, comb, spin and weave a heap of wool.

Well, she milked the cow and drove her up the hill to graze, but when she saw the great heap of wool to be worked, she was at her wits' end, and didn't know where to begin.

So she made herself a bowl of porridge. She was sitting, supping it, when in ran a crowd of Wee Folk with yellow hair and wee pointed faces. The Princess was delighted to have someone to talk to.

'Good day to you, Wee Folk,' she said. And they sang:

> 'If you're kind, you'll give its a sup,
> A greedy one will send us off!
> Kind or greedy? Kind or greedy?
> Which are you? Which are you?'

The youngest Princess was kind, so she said:

'Go and get your spoons. There's plenty for us all!'

'Kind, kind, this one is kind!' cried the Wee Folk, taking out their horn spoons.

When the porridge was finished, they thanked the Princess and ran off, all except one wee lad, who stood and bowed.

'Have you any work for me?' he said.

'That I have and more,' said the Princess. She showed him the wool and told him it had to be washed, combed, spun and woven into cloth before the Giant returned that night. 'Even if you can do all that, I've nothing to give you in return.'

'Don't be worrying yourself about that,' said he. 'All I ask is that, when I bring back the wool, woven into cloth, you'll guess my name.'

The Princess agreed, so he took the wool and away he went.

Now, the Princess was not one to meet trouble half-way, so without another thought about the wee lad's name, she set to and prepared the Giant's supper for him. She was busy doing this, when there was a knock on the door. She opened it and there was an old wife begging for a night's shelter.

'Come in, old wife,' said the Princess. 'This is the Giant's house and no place to take shelter, but if you can answer my riddle, there'll be shelter and food for you, right enough.'

'Tell away, bonny lass, tell away,' said the old wife.

'Riddle me ree, riddle me ree!
Riddle me, riddle me, one two three!
Riddle me here, riddle me there,
The name of the lad with the yellow hair!'

'Ah, now, let me see, there was a wee lad with yellow hair on the hillside as I came by,' said the old wife. 'Maybe he can help me.'

So off she went to the hillside. It was growing dark, and she saw a shaft of light shining faintly from behind rocks. The old wife crept up and peered round. There was an entrance to a cave and inside she could see a crowd of Wee Folk busy working with a heap of wool. Some were washing it, some combing and spinning it, while others were weaving it into cloth. Running here and there, among them, was a wee lad with yellow hair, singing:

'Tease, teasers, tease!
Card, carders, card!
Spin, spinners, spin!
Weave, weavers, weave!
For PEERIE FOOL is my name!'

'Well now, there's a good piece of news worth a night's shelter and a bite of food,' said the old wife to herself, as she hurried back to the Giant's house.

When the Princess heard what the old wife had to tell her, she opened the door wide, gave her a large bowl of porridge and a soft bed in a safe place, well out of sight.

When the wee lad arrived with a roll of woollen cloth over his shoulder, he refused to leave it before the Princess guessed his name.

'You can have three guesses,' said he.

'Grey Whaup,' said she.

'It is not,' said he.

'Willie Buck,' said she.

'Willie Buck, me! That's a good one! No, you're wrong, bonny lass, you're wrong, and you've only one guess left!'

And he rocked with laughter.

'Peerie Fool,' said the Princess. 'PEERIE FOOL!'

At this, the wee lad threw down the roll of cloth, and ran off into the darkness.

The Giant was pleased to see his supper ready on the table when he returned that night.

'Have you milked the cow and taken her to graze?' he asked.

'I have,' said the Princess, 'and here's the cloth from the heap of wool you left for me.'

'Well, I *have* found a bonny lass,' said the Giant, and gave her a chuck under the chin with his forefinger that knocked her over, although he meant it kindly enough. 'You must stay with me always and in return, I'll grant you three wishes.'

Next day, while the Giant was away, the Princess looked for her sisters. She searched every room, cupboard and corner but they were nowhere to be found. She was about to give up in despair when she heard a great commotion and clatter coming from the hen-house outside.

She thought a fox must have got in and was worrying the hens, so she ran out and unlocked the hen-house and there she found her two miserable sisters. They were frozen and very, very hungry. The Princess took them into the house, sat them by the fire and gave each of them a bowl of hot porridge. They told her all that had happened to them and begged her to help them escape.

'We'll find a way,' said the youngest Princess.

'The Giant will see us and with two strides, he'll catch us,' said her sisters.

'Then he'll have to carry you home himself!' said the youngest. 'You, elder sister shall go first. You must hide in the bottom of this basket and I'll cover you with grass. This night I'll ask the Giant to take the basket of grass and leave it at our mother's door. He'll do this for me.'

'What shall I do?' asked the second sister.

'I'll hide you in this other basket,' said the Princess, 'and the Giant will carry you home tomorrow night.'

The two sisters curled themselves up in the bottom of the baskets and the Princess covered them with grass. Then she prepared the Giant's supper, but before it was cooked he came in and said:

'Well, bonny lass, what's the first of your three wishes?'

'I wish you would carry this basket over the hills and leave it outside my mother's door. It's grass to feed her cow. But haste you back, for your supper's nearly ready.'

'I'll do that,' said the Giant, and off he went.

Seven strides and he was at the cottage door, where he left the basket. Seven strides more and he was back again, ready for his supper.

Next day, the Princess said that her second wish was the same as her first. So the Giant took the second basket over the hills and left it at the mother's door, and strode seven steps home again, and the supper the Princess had ready for him was tastier than ever.

The following day, before the Giant went off, the Princess told him that she would have another basket full of grass for the cow ready for him to carry to her mother.

'It's my third and last wish, so please take it for me,' she said. 'I'll not be here myself for I'll be gathering fresh herbs for your supper, which will be ready when you return.'

'I'll do that,' said the Giant.

That evening there was a basket ready for the Giant to carry to the cottage door. Seven strides and he put it down beside the door. But this time the widow Queen was at the door waiting for him.

'It's kind of you to bring grass for my cow,' said she, 'but how are my daughters and when shall I see them?'

'Well, that depends! As for your youngest daughter,' said the Giant, 'she's a grand wee cook. I'll not part with her.'

'A grand cook is she,' said the widow Queen. 'She's not as good as I am. Wait till you taste the stew I'm cooking.'

'Let me try it, old wife,' said the Giant. 'I'm hungry enough for two suppers.'

The widow Queen brought out a pot of steaming stew and handed a ladleful to the Giant.

'Taste that,' she said. He tasted it and asked for more.

'You're a good cook,' said the Giant, 'but not as good as your youngest daughter!' And away he went.

He had only taken three strides, when the Giant fell down dead, for the deadly death-cap toadstools had been cooked in that stew. So that was the end of the Giant and the beginning of happiness for the widow Queen and her three bonny daughters.

The Hen

THERE was once a poor woman who gave birth to a hen instead of a baby. The Hen grew big and looked after her mother. Every day she went to the King's house to beg for left-over food. One day the King came to the door, and when he saw the Hen there, he said:

'What do you want, you nasty little creature? Go away!'

'I may be a nasty little creature,' said the Hen, 'but I can do something your wife, the Queen, can't do.'

'And what may that be?' asked the King.

'I can spring from rafter to rafter, with a pot-hook tied to one leg and tongs tied to the other.'

The King fetched the Queen, and when she saw the Hen, she said:

'I'd like to see anything that little creature can do that I can't!'

So the Hen, with a pot-hook tied to one leg and tongs to the other, without any bother sprang from one rafter in the roof to another. Then the Queen with a pot-hook tied to one leg and tongs tied to the other, clambered on to the rafters. She stood there, wobbling, then sprang with all her might. But she slipped. The pot-hook caught on the rafter, the tongs cut her legs, and she fell to the ground, breaking her head.

The King had four more wives and the Hen got rid of them all in this way.

'You'd be better off if you married my mother,' she said to the King. 'She's a very fine woman.'

'Avoid me, you nasty little creature!' said the King. 'You've caused me enough trouble already.'

'You'd better marry her,' insisted the Hen.

'Send your mother here!' said the King.

So the Hen fetched her mother and the King married her.

Now, one day, when the King and the Queen were out, the Hen was left alone in the house with the King's eldest son, who spied on her and saw her remove her hen disguise. He was amazed to see that she was really a beautiful young woman and, when she was out of the room, he took her hen disguise and flung it on the fire. It blazed up and in a few minutes was a little pile of white ashes.

When she saw that her disguise had disappeared, the young woman was furious. She seized a sword and threatened the Prince with it.

'Give me back my hen disguise, or I'll cut off your head,' said she.

The Prince was afraid when he saw the sword, but there was nothing he could do, for he'd burnt the skin. It had gone for ever.

'I don't really want to kill you,' said she, 'but I don't know what will become of me without my hen disguise. If I make another for myself, you'll burn me as a witch, so I must stay as I am.'

When the King came home and saw the fine young woman going about his house, he wanted to know who she was, where she had come from and what sort of woman she was. She told him all that had happened to her and that she was indeed his new Queen's daughter, who had been under a spell from the moment she was born.

'I feel strange as a woman,' she said, 'and I love my mother who did not abandon me.'

The beautiful young woman was welcome in the King's house, and they all were happy together. After a while she married the King's son who had burned her hen disguise. There were great wedding feasts and celebrations that went on for a year and a day in the King's house.

THE YOUNG KING

Soon after the young King of Easaidh Ruadh had ascended the throne, he decided to gamble with the Gruagach, the long-haired, bearded Brownie who lived near by. So he went to the soothsayer.

'I've made up my mind to gamble with the Gruagach,' he said.

'Are you that kind of man?' said the soothsayer. 'Are you rash enough to gamble with the Gruagach? My advice to you is to change your mind, and not go at all.'

'I'll not do that,' said the young King.

'Then my advice to you, if you win against the Gruagach, is to ask as your winnings the maid with the rough skin and the cropped hair who stands behind the door.'

If the sun rose early, the young King rose earlier still to gamble with the Gruagach. When they met, they blessed each other.

'Oh, young King of Easaidh Ruadh, what has brought you here? Do you want to gamble with me?'

'I do,' said the young King.

So they played, and the young King won.

'Name your stake,' said the Gruagach.

'My stake is the girl with the rough skin and the cropped hair who stands behind the door.'

'I've fairer women than she,' said the Gruagach.

'I'll take no other,' said the King.

The Gruagach showed the young King twenty bonny girls.

'Choose one of these,' he said.

And they came out, one after the other, and each one said:

'I am she. You are foolish not to take me with you.'

But the soothsayer had advised him to take none but the last one. When the last girl came, he said:

'That one is mine!'

She went with him, and when they were some distance from the house of the Gruagach, she changed into the most beautiful woman he had ever seen. They went together to the castle, and were married.

If it was early when the sun rose, the King rose earlier still to gamble with the Gruagach.

'I must gamble with the Gruagach today,' he said to his wife.

'He is my father,' said she. 'If you gamble with him, take nothing for your winnings but the shaggy filly with the wooden saddle.'

The young King went to meet the Gruagach.

'Well,' said the Gruagach, 'how did your young bride please you?'

'She pleased me very well.'

'Have you come to gamble with me again today?'

'I have,' said the young King.

They gambled and the King won.

'Name your stake, and be sharp about it!'

'My stake is the shaggy filly with the wooden saddle,' said the young King.

The Gruagach took the shaggy filly out of the stable. The young King mounted her, and how swift she was! His wife welcomed him home, and how merry they were together that night.

'I would rather you did not gamble with the Gruagach any more,' said his young wife, 'for if he wins he will bring you trouble.'

'I'll play with him once more,' said the King.

If the sun rose early, the young King rose earlier still to gamble with the Gruagach, and the Gruagach was pleased to see him. They played, and this time the Gruagach won.

'Name your stake,' said the young King, 'and don't be too hard on me.'

'What you owe me is the Sword of Light that belongs to the King of the Oak Windows, otherwise the girl with the rough skin and the cropped hair will have to kill you.'

The King went home heavy-hearted. The young Queen met him as he came home.

'You've brought nothing with you tonight?'

The King sat down and drew her toward him, and his heart was so heavy that the chair broke under him.

'What is the matter?' said the Queen. The King told her what had happened.

'Don't worry,' she said. 'You have the best wife in Erin, and the second-best horse. You will come out of it well.'

The Queen rose before dawn, and set everything in order. She groomed the shaggy filly with the wooden saddle. The King mounted and the Queen kissed him and wished him luck.

'Take the advice of the filly,' said the Queen. 'She'll tell you what to do, and all will go well.'

The young King set out on his journey. His shaggy filly would overtake the March wind before her, and the wind behind her could not catch her. At the mouth of dusk and lateness they came to the castle of the King of the Oak Windows.

'This is the end of the journey,' said the filly. 'I will take you to the Sword of Light. The King is now at dinner and the Sword of Light is in his room. There is a knob on the end of it, and when you catch the sword, draw it softly out of the oak window. Take it without scrape or creak.'

The young King came to the oak window where the sword was. He took hold of it, and it came softly as far as the point. Then it gave a screech.

'We must go, and hurry now,' said the filly. 'The King has heard us taking the sword.'

When they had gone some distance, the filly said:

'Stop now! Look behind you!'

'I see a herd of brown horses coming,' said the young King.

'So far we are swifter than they,' said the filly, as they rode on.

When they had gone a good distance, she said:

'Look now! Who is coming?'

'A herd of black horses, and one black horse with a white muzzle, galloping madly with a man riding him.'

'That's my brother, the best horse in Erin. Be ready, when he passes me, to take the head off his rider, who will look at you. The sword in your hand is the only sword that can take off his head.'

As the man on the black horse with the white muzzle rode past, he turned to look. The young King drew his sword and cut off his head. Thus died the King of the Oak Windows.

'Leap on the black horse,' said the filly. 'Gallop as fast as he will take you. I will follow!'

The young King leaped on the black horse, and reached his castle before dawn.

'I must see the Gruagach today, to find out if my spells are broken,' he told his Queen.

'The Gruagach will ask you if you have the Sword of Light, and how you got it. Say that if it had not been for the knob on its tip you would not have got it. He will stretch out to see the knob on the sword, and then you will see a mole on the right side of his neck. Stab it with the point of the sword. The King of the Oak Windows was his brother, and the death of the two of them is in that sword.'

The Queen kissed him, and he went to the Gruagach, at the same place as before.

'Did you fetch the sword?' asked the Gruagach.

'I did,' said the young King.

'How did you get it?'

'I wouldn't have got it but for the knob on its tip.'

'Let me see it!'

'It was not part of the bargain to let you see it.'

'How did you win it?'

'By the knob on the tip of it.'

As the Gruagach lifted his head to look at the sword, the King saw the mole on his neck. He was quick and he stabbed the mole with the Sword of Light. The Gruagach fell down dead.

When the young King of Easaidh Ruadh returned home, he found his guards tied back to back. His wife and his horses had vanished.

'A great giant came and took your wife and horses,' said the guards.

'Sleep will not come to my eyes, nor rest to my head, till I have my wife and my horses again.'

Saying this, he followed the track of the horses. Dusk and lateness were coming when, by the side of the green wood, he saw a good place for a campfire, and decided to spend the night there.

There the slim dog of the green wood found him. He blessed the dog, and the dog blessed him.

'Your wife and your horses were here last night with the giant,' said the dog.

'That is why I am here,' said the King.

'You must not be here without meat,' said the dog.

The dog went into the wood, caught and brought a hare and a rabbit, which they cooked on the fire and ate together.

'I've half a mind to return home,' said the King. 'I'm afraid I'll never find that giant.'

'Don't lose heart, you'll succeed,' said the dog. 'But you must not go without sleep.'

So the young King stretched out beside the fire and fell asleep. At the end of his watch, the dog said to him:

'Wake up, young King. Eat some food to keep your strength. Remember, if you are in difficulty, call me.'

They blessed each other, and the King departed. In the time of dusk and lateness he came to a great precipice. He made a fire there, and warmed himself by it. There the falcon of the grey rock found him.

'Your wife and horses were here last night with the giant,' said the falcon.

'That is why I am here,' said the King.

'You must not be without meat,' said the falcon.

Away she flew, and returned with three ducks and eight black cocks. They set out the meat and ate it.

'You must not go without sleep,' said the falcon.

So the King stretched out beside the fire and fell asleep. In the morning the falcon set him on his way.

'Remember, if you are in difficulty, call me!' she said.

At night, the young King came to a river, and a good place for a fire. There the brown otter of the river found him.

'Your wife and horses were here last night with the giant,' said the otter. 'Before midday tomorrow you will see your wife. But you must not be without meat.'

The otter slipped into the river, and came back with three salmon. They prepared the fish and ate it.

'You must not go without sleep,' said the otter.

So the King stretched out beside the fire and fell asleep till morning.

'You'll be with your wife tonight,' said the otter, 'and if you are in difficulty, call me!'

The King went on till he came to a rock. Looking down a cleft, he saw a cave, and in it his wife and two horses. He could not see any way of reaching them, but when he climbed down he found a good path at the foot of the rock, which he followed and soon joined her inside the cave.

After they had greeted each other, his wife made some food for him, and hid him behind the horses.

'I smell a stranger within,' said the giant, when he returned.

'It is nothing but the smell of horse-dung,' said she.

When the giant went to feed the horses, they attacked and nearly killed him. He was just able to crawl away.

'The horses looked like killing you,' said the Queen.

'If I had my soul in my own keeping, they would have killed me,' said the giant.

'Where is your soul, my dear?' asked the Queen. 'I will take care of it.'

'It is in the bonnach stone,' said the giant.

In the morning, after the giant had gone away, she decorated the bonnach stone. In the time of dusk and lateness the giant returned home. He went to feed the horses, and again they attacked him.

'Why did you decorate the bonnach stone like that?' said he.

'Because your soul is in it.'

'I see that if you knew where my soul was you would give it much respect,' said the giant.

'I would,' said the Queen.

'My soul is not in the bonnach stone,' said he, 'it is in the threshold.'

Next day she decorated the threshold. When the giant came home and went to feed the horses they attacked him again.

'Why did you decorate the threshold like that?' said he.

'Because your soul is in it.'

'I see that if you knew where my soul was you would take care of it,' said the giant.

'I would,' said the Queen.

'My soul is not there,' said he. 'There is a great flagstone under the threshold. Under the flagstone there is a ram. In the ram there is a duck. In the duck there is an egg, and in the egg is my soul'.

Next day, while the giant was away, the young King and his Queen raised the flagstone and a ram escaped.

'The slim dog of the green wood could soon bring the ram to me,' said the King. At once the slim dog came with the ram. When they opened the ram, out flew a duck.

'The falcon of the grey rock could soon bring me the duck,' said the King.

At once the falcon of the grey rock came with the duck. When they opened the duck to take out the egg, the egg rolled into the river.

'The brown otter of the river could soon bring me the egg,' said the King.

At once the brown otter came with the egg in her mouth. The Queen crushed the egg, and the giant, coming home late, fell down dead.

On the way home, the young King and his Queen passed a night with the otter of the river, a night with the falcon of the grey rock, and a night with the slim dog of the green wood.

THE RED ETIN

I N Falkland Palace, the young Prince James was tired of his lessons.

'That's enough, for now,' said David Lindsay, his tutor. 'Shut your books and I'll tell you a story about Fife.'

The Prince shut his books, leaned his elbows on the table, rested his chin on the palms of his hands and gazed at his tutor.

'Some say it happened in Ireland but, as I heard it, the story begins in Auchtermuchty, just up the road from here.'

❈ ❈ ❈

Well, just north of here, there were two widows who were having a hard time of it.

'Look here,' said a neighbour to the first widow's son, Andy, as they looked at the thin crop of oats. 'You'll not make much of that poor soil. You should leave home to make your fortune. Then you'll be able to support your mother when she's old.'

So Andy went home and said to his mother:

'I'm tired of scratching that ground of ours. The soil is too poor to feed the oats and kale, so they'll not grow and feed us. I'm off tomorrow to seek my fortune.'

His mother was angry. She thought he was deserting her. However she agreed to bake him a bannock for the journey. She gave him a dish to fetch water from the well. But when he got there he saw that the dish was cracked. He filled it and ran back to the house with it hoping the water would not drip away. All the same, the dish was only half full and the bannock his mother baked was very small.

'Will you take half a bannock with my blessing, or a whole bannock with my malison?' asked his mother.

Andy looked at the small bannock and said:

'The whole bannock, mother.'

This annoyed his mother still more, and she said:

'You've slighted my blessing for a piece of oatcake!

> *May my malison follow wherever you go,*
> *And blast you from top to toe!'*

So the lad went off without his mother's blessing.

Now, before he left Auchtermuchty, he called on the second widow's son, Rab, and left his shining pocket knife with him.

'Keep my knife till I come back. If it stays bright and sharp, I'll be alive and well, but if it turns rusty and blunt you'll know I'm in trouble. Then you'll come and look for me?'

'I'll do that,' said Rab. 'I'll stay at home a while longer to help my mother, but if your knife turns rusty, I'll look for you and try to help you.'

So Andy went on his way. On and on he went till he met a man herding a flock of sheep.

'Whose sheep are these?' asked Andy.

'They belong to the Red Etin of Ireland,' said the shepherd.

'I've heard of him,' said the lad, and went on his way singing a song his mother used to sing as she worked in the kitchen:

> *'The Red Etin of Ireland*
> *Aince lived in Bettigan,*
> *And stole King Malcolm's dochter,*
> *The King of fair Scotland!'*

Then Andy met a man herding swine.

'Whose pigs are these?' he asked.

'They belong to the Red Etin of Ireland,' said the swineherd.

'I've heard of him,' said Andy, and sang his mother's song:

> 'He bends her and he binds her,
> He lays her on a band;
> And ilka day he dings her
> Wi' a bricht siller wand.'

On he went till he met a man herding goats.

'Whose goats are these?' he asked.

'They belong to the Red Etin of Ireland,' said the goatherd, 'but look out if you're going that way, for you'll meet some strange beasts. They're not sheep, they're not swine, and they're not goats. I'm warning you, look out!'

So the lad went on his way, singing his mother's song:

> 'It's said there's ane predestinate
> To be his mortal foe;
> But that man is yet unborn,
> And long may it be so.'

He sang to keep his courage up. Soon he met the strange monsters. They were not sheep with a shepherd, nor swine with a swineherd, nor goats with a goatherd. They were TERRIBLE! Each of them had two heads and each head had four horns, and there was no one herding them. They were so hideous the lad ran for his life. He saw a castle, and ran to it for shelter from the terrible monsters. He knocked on the door and went in. An old wife was sitting by the kitchen fire.

'Where do you come from?' said she.

'From Auchtermuchty,' said the lad. 'I'm a poor widow's son and I left home to seek my fortune.'

'You'll need your mother's blessing for that.'

'I got a malison instead of a blessing,' said Andy.

'That's bad,' said the old wife. 'This castle belongs to the Red Etin of Ireland, and he's a real monster. He has three heads, and he'll be here any minute. But hide in that corner yonder, and I'll not give you away!'

So Andy hid himself in the dark corner of the kitchen. Soon after, the Red Etin came in. One head with its two huge eyes looked into one corner, another head with its two huge eyes looked into another corner. The third head with its two huge eyes looked into the third corner, for the Red Etin knew a stranger was hiding somewhere in the kitchen, and he shouted in a hungry voice:

> 'Be he from Fife
> Or be he from Tweed,
> His heart this night
> Shall kitchen my breid.'

Then one of the heads with its two huge eyes looked into the fourth corner of the kitchen. The Red Etin saw Andy and pulled him out with its two great big hairy hands, and said:

'I'll ask you three questions. If you give me the right answers, I'll not kill you and eat your heart. But if you can't answer them, I'll hit you over the head with this mallet. Now, my first question is: How many ladders do you need to reach the sky?'

'I don't know the answer to that,' said Andy.

'How long would it take to go round the earth?'

'I don't know,' said Andy after a while.

'What wood is neither bent nor straight?'

'I don't know,' said Andy for the third and last time.

So the Red Etin hit him over the head with the mallet and Andy changed into a stone statue, which the Etin lifted and stood up beside the other statues in the castle.

Now, at home in Auchtermuchty, Rab the second widow's son noticed that the knife that Andy had left in his care was dull and beginning to rust. He spoke to his mother about it:

'Mother, our neighbour's son must be in great danger. I'm going to look for him as I promised. Maybe I'll seek my fortune at the same time, for we don't make enough out of this poor soil to pay the rent.'

His mother agreed, although she was sad he was going. She knew it would be hard work, looking after their croft without his help, but she agreed to bake him a bannock for the journey. She handed him a cracked pitcher and said:

'Fetch water from the well and I'll bake you a bannock. If you bring a full pitcher, I'll bake a large bannock, but if there's only a little water I can only bake a small bannock.'

Rab filled the pitcher at the well, and ran back with it. By the time he was half way, the pitcher was empty. All the water had run out through the cracks. As he went back to the well, a black raven flew overhead and croaked:

'Clag it with clay! Clag it with clay!'

Rab did as he was told. He took a handful of clay from beside the well and filled up the cracks in the pitcher. This time no water ran out of it.

So his mother baked him a big bannock. She blessed him from top to toe, and watched him till he was out of sight. She hoped her blessing would protect him from danger. When she went back into her cottage she found that Rab had left her half his bannock for her breakfast.

Rab walked on and on till he met an old woman. She begged him for a bit of his oatmeal bannock. He gave her half of what he had, which left him with a quarter of the bannock his mother had baked for him. In return the old woman gave him the wand she was carrying.

'Take this wand,' said she. 'It is magic. You'll soon learn how to use it in the Etin's castle. I'll get it from you when you come back this way. Till then, it'll keep you safe.'

Rab thanked the old woman and went on his way till he met a man herding sheep.

'Who owns these sheep?' asked Rab.

'The Red Etin of Ireland,' said the shepherd.

'I've heard of him,' said Rab, and he went on his way singing a song he had learned from his mother. On he walked till he met a man herding swine.

'Who owns these pigs?' asked Rab.

'The Red Etin of Ireland,' replied the swineherd,

'I've heard of him,' said Rab, as he went on his way singing his mother's song.

Then he met a man herding goats.

'Whose goats are these?' he asked.

'They belong to the Red Etin of Ireland,' said the goatherd. 'If you're going that way, look out. You'll meet some strange beasts. They're not sheep, they're not swine and they're not goats. I'm warning you, they're terrible.'

Rab thanked the goatherd for his warning and went on his way, singing his mother's song:

> 'It's said there's ane predestinate
> To be his mortal foe;
> But that man is yet unborn,
> And lang may it be so.'

'But I'm that man, and I have been born,' said Rab to himself.

He felt confident. He had his mother's blessing, and the magic wand the old woman had given him. He was not afraid of the Red Etin.

Then he met the monsters. They weren't sheep with a shepherd, nor swine with a swineherd, nor goats with a goatherd. They were TERRIBLE. Each of them had two heads, each head had four horns, and no one was herding them. When one of them put its two heads down and charged with its four horns, Rab ran for his life. He knew he could not run fast enough to escape, so he waited till he felt the monster's breath. He stepped to one side and, as the beast galloped past, he touched it with the magic wand. Immediately the monster fell down dead. The others galloped off out of sight.

Rab walked slowly towards the castle, knocked on the door and went in. There by the fire sat an old, old woman.

'Where have you come from?' said she.

'I'm from Auchtermuchty, and I left home to seek my fortune.'

'Well, you're not the first,' said the old wife. 'Did your mother give you her blessing before you left home?

'She did,' said Rab.

'That's good. You'll need it. This castle belongs to the Red Etin of Ireland and he's a real monster. He'll be here any minute, but hide behind my chair. I'll not give you away.'

Rab hid behind the old wife's chair. Soon the Red Etin came in, and one of his three heads looked in one corner of the room, the second head looked in another corner, and the third looked into the third corner. The Red Etin knew a stranger was somewhere in the room, and he shouted in a loud, hungry voice:

> 'Be he from Fife,
>   Or be he from Tweed,
> His heart this night
>   Shall kitchen my breid.'

Then one head looked over the back of the old wife's chair, and saw the lad. With two great hairy hands, the Red Etin pulled Rab out.

'Ho! ho! ho!' he roared. 'There you are! Now I'll ask you three questions. Give me the right answer and I'll not kill you. If you can't answer them at all, I'll hit you over the head with this mallet! Here's my first question: How many ladders do you need to reach the moon?'

'One,' said Rab, 'if it's long enough.'

'You're the clever one,' said the Red Etin, and two of his six eyes closed as if one of his heads was asleep. 'Now answer my second question: How long would it take to travel round the earth?'

'One day,' said Rab, 'if I travel as fast as the sun and moon.'

The Red Etin looked worried as the two eyes of his second head closed as though he was asleep. Then he asked his last question:

'What kind of wood is neither bent nor straight?'

'Sawdust,' said Rab.

Immediately the eyes of the Red Etin's third head closed. His legs sagged at the knees, he dropped his mallet and fell to the ground, fast asleep.

Swiftly Rab seized a long-handled axe from a corner by the door, and cut off the Red Etin's three heads. Chop! chop! chop! Now the Red Etin lay dead on the kitchen floor.

Rab left the old wife sleeping by the fire and searched the castle for his friend. He found a row of statues, and one of them looked like Andy. He touched it with his wand, and immediately Andy stood beside him alive and well. Then Rab touched all the other statues, and they too came to life again.

Among them was a bonny lass and she, like the others, followed Rab out of the castle. As they went they were attacked by the Red Etin's terrible monsters, but Rab soon drove them off with his wand and killed them one by one.

On the way home, they met the little old woman of the woods.

'I couldn't have managed without it,' said Rab, as he gave her back her magic wand.

There was a great welcome for them in Auchtermuchty. Rab married the bonny lass and everyone came to the wedding. As for Rab's mother, if she blessed him when he went away, she blessed him twice over when he returned.

The Eagle and the Wren

THERE was a time when the birds of the air had a contest to see who could fly the highest. All the birds competed except the Wren, and none could fly as high as the Eagle. So the birds made him King.

'He must be King,' they said. 'He's the biggest and strongest of us all. Not one of us can fly as high as the Eagle.'

'I can,' said the Wren.

'You!' laughed the Hawk. 'Why the Eagle wouldn't waste time competing with a bird as small as you!'

But the Eagle said:

'Come, wee Wren, let's see which of us can fly the higher!'

Off they flew, higher and higher. The Wren was soon out of sight, for she was so small. No one noticed, not even the Eagle, when she hopped on to his back and allowed herself to be carried up by him.

When the Eagle had flown as high as he could, he called out:

'Wee Wren! Where are you?' And the wee Wren slipped off his back and flew above him.

'I'm up here, Eagle,' said she, 'and I'm higher than you are!'

The other birds were very surprised when they heard that the Wren had flown higher than the Eagle.

'The Eagle shall remain our King,' they said, 'for he's still the biggest and strongest of us all, but the wee Wren shall be Queen, and can have twelve eggs.'

And so, as a reward, the Wren was allowed to lay twelve eggs if she wanted to, while the Eagle lays only two.

IAIN THE SOLDIER'S SON

HE Knight of Greenock had three beautiful daughters. One day a beast came from the sea and carried them off, no one knew where.

There was a soldier in the same town who had three sons, and on New Year's Day they were playing at shinty when the youngest son said they should play on the Knight of Greenock's lawn. His brothers said the Knight would not be pleased for their play would remind him of his daughters.

'Let that be as it may,' said Iain the youngest son, 'but we should play there all the same. I don't care whether the Knight is pleased or not.' So they played.

The Knight looked out of a window and saw them playing.

'Bring those lads here,' said he. 'I'll punish them for playing shinty on my lawn and reminding me of my daughters.' So they were brought before him.

'Why did you play shinty on my ground, reminding me of my lost children? You must suffer for this.'

'There's no need to punish us,' said Iain the youngest son. 'Build us a ship, and whether your daughters are leeward or windward, or under the four brown shores of the sea, we'll find them before the end of a year and a day, and we'll bring them back to Greenock.'

'Though you're the youngest, your head holds the best counsel,' said the Knight. 'Let us make the ship!'

So shipwrights were brought and a ship was built in seven days. Food and drink necessary for the journey were put on board. Her bows were turned to the sea, her stern to the land, then they sailed away. In seven days they reached a white sandy beach. They went ashore, and found six men and ten, with a foreman, blasting the face of the cliff.

'What place is this?' asked the captain.

'This is where the three daughters of the Knight of Greenock are to marry three giants,' said the foreman.

'How can we reach them?' asked the three sons.

'There's only one way up the face of the cliff, and that's in a creel.'

The eldest son got into a creel, but when he was half-way up the cliff, a stumpy black raven flew down, clawed at him and beat him with its wings till the lad was almost blind, and he had to come down.

The second son went into the creel, and halfway up the black raven clawed at him and beat him with its wings, till he too had to come down.

Last of all, Iain went into the creel, and half-way up the black raven clawed and beat him about the face. But Iain would not give in.

'Pull me up quickly before I'm blinded,' he shouted. At the top of the cliff he stepped out of the creel.

'Give me a quid of tobacco,' said the raven.

'That's a high price for nothing,' said Iain.

'Never mind that,' said the raven. 'I'll be a good friend to you. Now, go to the big giant's house, and you'll see the Knight's eldest daughter. She'll be sewing, her thimble wet with tears.'

Iain walked on till he came to the giant's house, and he went in. The Knight's daughter was sewing, her thimble wet with tears.

'What brought you here?' said she.

'What brought you here?' said Iain.

'I was brought here against my will,' said she.

'I know that,' said Iain. 'Where is the giant?'

'He's on the hunting hill.'

'How can I bring him home?'

'Shake that chain outside the house. But there's no one to leeward, or to windward, within the four brown shores of the sea, who will fight with him except young Iain the soldier's son, from Albainn. He's only sixteen and too young to fight the giant.'

'There are many in Albainn as strong as Iain the soldier's son,' said Iain.

Then he went outside and hauled at the chain. But he could not move it and fell on his knees. He got up, pulled on the chain a second time and broke a link of it. The giant heard it on the hunting hill.

'Aha!' said he. 'Who could move my chain but young Iain the soldier's son, but he's only sixteen and too young yet.'

The giant strung a dead deer on a willow branch and strode home.

'Are you Iain the soldier's son from Albainn?'

'No!' said Iain. 'There are many as strong in Albainn as Iain the soldier's son.'

'I've heard that,' said the giant. 'How would you like to try your strength?'

'In a wrestle,' said Iain.

Then they seized each other, and hugged each other, and the giant pulled Iain down on his knee. The giant seemed stronger than Iain. But the soldier's son would not give in. They twisted and pulled till Iain kicked the giant's ankle and threw him to the ground on his back.

'Help me, raven!' called Iain. And the stumpy black raven came, clawed the giant's face, and beat his wings on the giant's ears, deafening him.

'Cut off the giant's head!' said the raven.

'I can't,' said Iain. 'I've no sword, not even a knife.'

'Put your hand under my right wing!' said the raven. 'You'll find a sharp little knife I use for gathering rose-buds. Cut his head off with that.'

Iain did as he was told, and cut off the giant's head.

'Now Iain, when you return to the eldest daughter of the Knight, she'll ask you not to go farther. Don't listen to her! Go on till you come to the second giant's house. There you'll find the Knight's middle daughter. Before you go, give me a quid of tobacco!'

'You've earned it,' said Iain. 'I'll give you half of all I have.'

'You will not,' said the raven. 'But wash yourself in warm water. Rub your skin with the balsam you'll find in a dish above the door. Go to bed, and by tomorrow you'll be ready to go to the house where the Knight's second daughter stays.'

'Don't go farther into more danger,' said the eldest daughter when Iain went into the house. 'There's plenty of gold and silver here. We'll take it with us and go home.'

'I'll take the road before me,' said Iain. 'But first I must have a night's rest.'

Early next morning, before the girl woke up, Iain went on his way till he reached the house of the Knight's second daughter. Exactly the same thing happened here, and he killed the second giant.

'Don't go farther into more danger!' said the second daughter. 'There's plenty of gold and silver here. We'll take it with us and go home.'

'I'll take the road before me,' said Iain, and went on till he reached the house of the Knight's youngest daughter.

The same thing happened to him here as before, and he killed the third giant.

'Now,' said the raven, 'rest as you did last night. In the morning you'll find the Knight of Greenock's three daughters waiting for you. They'll have with them the gold and silver from the giants. Your task will be to take them back to the cliff. There you must go down first and let them down in the creel after you. And now you can give me a quid of tobacco.'

'You well deserve it,' said Iain. 'Here, take all of it!'

'I'll only take a quid of your tobacco, but no more!' said the raven. 'It's a long time to May-day!'

'I'll not be here till May-day,' said Iain.

'You know what's behind you, but you don't know what's before you,' said the raven.

In the morning, there were the three daughters waiting for Iain. They fetched donkeys, and loaded the giants' gold and silver on to their backs. At last Iain, the three daughters and the donkeys reached the edge of the cliff. The creel was there, but instead of going first as the raven had told him, Iain lowered the three girls down the cliff, one by one. Each of them was wearing a gold cap, covered in diamonds, and made in Rome, the like of which was not to be found in the whole world. But as he lowered the youngest daughter down in the creel, Iain took her cap and kept it.

When they had all reached the bottom of the cliff, the three girls forgot to help Iain down the cliff, and they hurried on board the ship and sailed home to Greenock. There was no one left to pull the rope and Iain was alone on the cliff top, unable to get down. Then the raven came flying and perched on the ground beside him.

'You didn't take my advice, Iain,' said he. 'But now you must go to the giant's house and sleep there tonight. I can't stay and keep you company, but you can give me a quid of tobacco.'

'I'll do that,' said Iain, and gave him the tobacco.

Next morning the raven came to Iain and told him to go into the giant's stable.

'There's a horse there that can gallop on sea and land. She may help you,' said the raven.

Together they went to the stable, which was chiselled out of rock with a heavy stone door. This door was slamming back and forward, from early morning till night, and from night to day.

'Watch me!' said the raven.

He gave a hop and a jump into the stable, but the swinging door caught his wing and knocked a feather out of it, and he shrieked with pain.

Iain took a run back, and a run forward, and jumped. But the door caught his behind and tore off half his buttocks. Iain cried out and fell senseless on the ground. The raven lifted him and carried him on his wings to the giant's house, and laid him face down on a bench. Then he flew off to fetch herbs. He made an ointment which he rubbed into Iain's wounds, and looked after him. In ten days Iain had recovered and then the raven left him, after asking for a quid of tobacco.

Iain wandered through the hills and in a glen he saw three heroes lying on their backs, each with a spear on his chest, and each of them sound asleep and sweating. Iain lifted the spear off each hero, and they awoke and stood up.

'You are young Iain, the soldier's son from Albainn,' said one of them. 'We now put a spell on you to go with us through the southern end of the island.'

Iain went with the three heroes. A slender smoke was coming from a cave and they went to see what was there. One hero went into the cave, and saw a hag sitting there. Her smallest tooth would have made a knitting needle, a walking stick, or a poker for stirring the embers. Her long finger-nails twisted about her elbows, and her hoary hair tumbled about her toes. She was not very beautiful.

She seized a magic club, struck the hero and turned him to stone. The others wondered why he didn't return, so the second hero went into the cave, and the same thing happened to him. The third hero went in and didn't come out, so Iain went into the cave after them. There a great red-headed cat attacked him with a barrowful of red peat-ash. He kicked her away with the toe of his boot, and again the raven came to help him.

'The heroes are under spells,' said the raven. 'To take the spells off them, you must go to the island of the Big Women of Jura, take a bottle of living water from the island, come back and rub the heroes with it. The spells will then vanish and the heroes will come alive. You see, you did not do as I told you and you've brought more trouble on yourself. After a good night's rest, you'll feed and water the mare. Sea and land are all one to her. When you reach the island of the Big Women, sixteen stable lads will meet you. They'll all be for feeding the mare, and stabling her, but don't let them. Say you'll do that yourself. Every one of the sixteen lads will turn the key in the stable door. But you will put a turn for every turn that they put in the key. And now you'll give me a quid of tobacco.'

'I'll do that,' said Iain.

Next morning, Iain saddled the mare and rode away. He turned her head to the sea and her tail to the shore, and soon they reached the island of the Six Big Women. Everything happened as the raven had said. The mare warned him to drink only water and whey in the house of the Big Women, and not to go to sleep. Iain did as he was told, but the Six Big Women drank till they fell asleep.

When Iain left the room, he heard sweet music. In another room he heard even sweeter music. Beside a stair he heard the sweetest music ever heard, and then he fell asleep. The mare broke out of her stable and kicked him awake.

'You didn't take my advice,' she said, 'and now there's no knowing whether you can straighten things out, or not.'

Iain was very sorry. He seized the Sword of Light in a corner of the room, and cut off the heads of the sixteen grooms. At the well he filled his bottle with living water, and returned. The mare met him, and he turned her head to the sea and her tail to the shore and rode to the other island, where the raven met him.

'Stable the mare, and have a good night's rest,' said the raven. 'To-morrow go, bring the three heroes to life and slay the carlin you'll meet in the cave. Try not to be foolish this time, but do as I tell you!'

In the morning Iain went to the cave, and there he met the carlin.

'Bad health to you!' said Iain. He sprinkled the three heroes with living water from his bottle, and they came to life and stood up. Iain killed the carlin and took the heroes home to the south end of the island. The raven flew to meet him.

'Now you can go home,' said the raven, 'and take with you the mare to whom land and sea are alike. Two of the Knight's daughters are to marry your two brothers. Leave the youngest daughter's cap with me! You've only to think of me when you want it, and I'll bring it to you. If anyone asks you where you come from, say, from behind you; and if anyone asks you where you are going, say you're going forward!'

Iain left the gold cap studded with diamonds with the raven, mounted the mare, turned her head to the sea and her tail to the land. He made no stop nor stay till he reached the old church in Greenock. There was a grass meadow there, a well of water and a rushy knoll. Iain dismounted.

'Now,' said the mare, 'take your sword and cut off my head! In me there's a young girl under a spell, and the spell will not leave me till my head is off. I and the raven were courting, he as a young lad and I as a young girl, when the giants laid spells on us, making a raven of him and a mare of me.'

So Iain drew his Sword of Light, and cut off the mare's head. Then he turned and walked on and another carlin met him. He went into her house and she gave him a drink.

'Where is your man?' asked Iain.

'He's at the Knight of Greenock's house, looking for gold and silver to make a cap for the youngest daughter, just like the caps of her two sisters.'

The carlin's man came home. He was a goldsmith.

'What's your trade, lad?' he asked Iain.

'I'm a smith.'

'That's good,' said the goldsmith. 'You can help me make a cap for the Knight's youngest daughter. She's going to marry.'

'Don't you know how to make it?' said Iain.

'I must try. If I don't make it I'll be hanged tomorrow. Maybe you can make it.'

'Lock me in your workshop,' said Iain. 'Keep your gold and silver, and I'll have the cap ready in the morning.'

The smith locked Iain in, and Iain wished the raven to come to him. The raven came and broke the window of the workshop, and flew in with the cap of gold studded with diamonds.

'Now, cut off my head!' said the raven. 'I'm a young man under a spell and it will not leave me till my head is off.'

So Iain drew his Sword of Light and cut off the raven's head. It was not difficult.

Next morning the smith unlocked the door and came in. Iain gave him the cap and the smith was astonished at its beauty. Then Iain fell asleep. He was wakened by a noble-looking youth with brown hair.

'I was the raven,' said the youth. 'The spell is now off me.'

Meanwhile the smith took the cap to the Knight of Greenock's house. A servant took the cap to the Knight's youngest daughter, and told her that the smith had made it. The youngest daughter looked at the cap.

'That smith did not make that cap,' said the youngest daughter. 'Tell the rogue to bring the man who made it. I want to see him!'

The smith brought Iain to the youngest daughter, and when she saw him, she recognised him as the lad who had saved her from the giant, and she was very happy to see him again. He told her he had kept her cap so that he could find her again. And she told him how she had been hurried to the ship without him.

'You're as brave and strong as Iain the soldier's son, from Albainn,' said she.

'I am Iain the soldier's son from Albainn,' said he.

So they married and lived long in the town of Greenock.

The Legend of Loch Maree

ONCE the King of Denmark sent his son to the Scottish Court. The young Prince took a party of friends with him to hunt, and they landed on the north-west coast of Scotland.

One day, by Loch Maree, the Prince lost his companions, and, feeling tired, he sat down and fell asleep. Awakening, he saw an old man and a young woman coming toward him. Standing in their path, he bowed low.

'Out of my way, stranger!' said the old man.

'I am the Prince of Denmark,' said the young man.

The old man made excuses, saying:

'This is the Princess Tyra of Ireland. She is staying with us at the Monastery on Isle Maree, and I have to protect her from intrusion.'

'This has been our first meeting, and I fear it will be our last,' said the Prince to the Princess.

'That may be,' said the Princess, and went on her way with the old man.

The Prince returned, hoping to see her again, but no one came. The next time he came to this place, hoping to see her, he waited two days and he waited alone. The third time he waited three days, and still no one came. Then he decided to go to Isle Maree.

He found a boatman willing to ferry him across. As they landed on the island, the boatman pointed out a path.

'On your way,' he said, 'you'll come to a Holy Well. You must not pass without drinking from it. Beside the Well is an old oak tree with a hollow side. You should not pass without putting something of value into it.'

But the Prince forgot the Holy Well and the hollow tree. He knocked at the door of the Monastery. He was led to an old monk, who asked him who he was, and what he wanted.

'I am the Prince of Denmark,' said he, 'and I've come to ask the Princess Tyra of Ireland to marry me.'

'The Princess is free to make her own choice,' said the monk.

The Princess was pleased to see him, and they spent the day happily together on the island, but she refused to marry him.

'I saw you only once before,' she said. 'Love that comes as quickly may go as quickly, and I am afraid. Red Hector of the hills wants to marry me, and he would be a dangerous foe.'

'He would meet his match,' said the Prince, and went away, promising to return the next day.

He had not gone far when an arrow passed close to his face. The next one stuck in his bonnet. A tall man was standing beside a rock.

'Why do you make a target of me?' asked the Prince.

'I am Red Hector of the hills,' said the big man. 'We have a matter to settle between us. You must kill me or I must kill you!'

'Surely there's a better way to settle our differences,' said the Prince.

'There is not,' said Red Hector.

So the two men fought. Red Hector struck the Prince with his sword, wounding him deeply.

The Prince lay still and kept his hand on his wound to stop the bleeding. He dragged himself toward a nearby burn, but fainted before he could drink. A monk found him and took him to the Monastery of Isle Maree. There, the Princess Tyra nursed him back to life, and promised to go with him to Denmark.

But a ship sailed into the harbour of Poolewe with bad news. The Princess must return to Ireland where her father was dying.

'Will you return?' asked the Prince.

'Nothing but death shall prevent me,' she replied. And so the Princess Tyra sailed away to Ireland.

The Prince's men looked out for her ship from the highest hills. Each day they returned without news.

One day they saw three ships, and the first one was flying the royal flag of Ireland at its topmast. The Prince took his men to the highest hill to signal a welcome, and on the way they met an old man.

'Wait till I tell you my dream,' said he.

'I care nothing for dreams,' said the Prince.

'I dreamed this dream three nights,' said the old man. 'In my dream, the Princess Tyra of Ireland was dead. But I will go to the ship. If all is well, you'll see a red flag flying. If not, a black one.'

The old man rowed out to the ship. He persuaded the Princess to fly a black flag, saying that the Prince would then get a happy surprise when he saw her alive and well.

But when the Prince saw the black flag, he was so heartbroken, he took out his dirk and killed himself.

The Princess was told what had happened.

'I will go alone to bid him farewell,' she said.

On the way, someone followed her. Turning, she saw it was the old man.

'Wretched old man!' she cried. 'That was evil advice you gave me.'

'Old man, indeed!' said he, tearing off his disguise. 'I am Red Hector of the hills!' And with that, he killed her with his dirk and disappeared into the dark hill.

DIARMID AND GRAINNE

FINN, chief of the Feinne, was to marry Grainne, daughter of the King of Carmaig in Erin. A great feast was made that lasted seven days and seven nights. All the nobles and the men of the Feinne were there, and among them was the handsome young hero, Diarmid. He had a mole on the side of his cheek which, when seen by a woman, made her fall in love with him. Therefore he kept this love-spot hidden by a cap or a helmet.

Now, after the feast was over, the leftover scraps were thrown to the dogs. They were hungry and fought each other for the meat. The heroes of the Feinne went to separate them. As he tried to keep them apart, Diarmid's cap slipped. Grainne saw the fatal love-spot and instantly fell in love with him. As soon as she had a chance to speak with him alone, she said:

'Diarmid, I cannot rest till you take me away!'

'I'll not do that,' said Diarmid. 'I'll not take you on horseback or on foot.' He turned his back on her and went home.

Next morning, Diarmid found Grainne at his door, mounted on a buck-goat.

'Take me away, Diarmid,' she begged. 'I can't live with Finn, and I can't live apart from you.'

'I've told you that I'll not take you on horseback nor on foot,' said Diarmid. 'I can have nothing to do with you.'

'I'm not on horseback and I'm not on my feet,' she said, 'so you must take me with you!'

'There's no place on earth we can go where Finn will not find us. As soon as he puts his finger under his tooth of knowledge, he'll know where we are. He'll come after us and he'll kill me for taking you away!'

'We can go to Carraig,' said Grainne. 'There are many places of that name. He'll not know which one to go to.'

So they went to Carraig am Daimh, which means the Crag of the Stag. They found a place to live and, as Diarmid was a good carpenter, he made wooden bowls, which Grainne sold round the countryside. Diarmid also caught all the fish they needed and Grainne cooked it. But their beds remained apart.

One day, an old carle called Ciofach came their way and stayed with them. Grainne took a great liking for Ciofach, and he for her. Together they planned to kill Diarmid.

While Diarmid was busy making his bowls, Ciofach crept up behind him and attacked him, but Diarmid was too quick for him, and they wrestled on the ground. When Ciofach was nearly defeated, Grainne took a knife and stabbed Diarmid in the thigh.

Weakened by the wound, he crawled away, hid in a fisherman's hut and refused to remove the knife in his thigh. He was given fish and, as he cooked it, he dipped his fingers in a cogie of water to clean them. Now, anything Diarmid touched with his fingers would taste of honey, and he touched the fish which Grainne eventually bought from the fisherman. When she tasted the honey in the fish, she knew that Diarmid must be hiding near by. And this was how she found him.

Grainne told Ciofach where Diarmid was hiding.

'You must kill him,' said she.

Soon Ciofach and Diarmid were wrestling again, but in spite of his wound, Diarmid had the old carle on the ground and this time he killed him.

When Grainne saw that Ciofach was dead, she followed Diarmid to the shores of Loch a Chaisteil, where a heron was screaming and Diarmid was climbing the rock-face of the mountain. So she called to him:

> 'How early the heron cries!
> Oh Diarmid, to whom I gave my love,
> Tell me why the heron cries!'

And Diarmid called back to her:

> 'Oh Grainne, daughter of the King of Carmaig,
> Who never took a right step,
> Her foot stuck to a frozen rock!'

'Oh Diarmid,' she cried, 'here's meat and bread for you if you can find a knife to cut it.'

'You'll find a knife in the sheath where you put it,' said Diarmid, coming to her. And there she saw the knife she had driven into his thigh, still in the place from which he had refused to remove it.

Drawing the knife out of Diarmid was Grainne's greatest shame, and Diarmid's greatest fear was that Finn would now find them together.

They found a place to stay by the side of a burn and their beds were still apart. Again Diarmid made wooden bowls and as he turned them, the shavings floated down the burn.

Meanwhile Finn, filled with rage when he found that Grainne had left him, put his finger under his tooth of knowledge and learned where she was. He and the Feinne searched all the Crags for her.

One day, when they were hunting by the shores of the loch just below the Crag of the Stag, Finn noticed shavings of wood floating down the burn that flowed into the loch.

'These shavings were made by Diarmid,' said he.

'How can that be when he is not alive,' said the Feinne.

'I know the way Diarmid works and they are his shavings,' said Finn. 'We'll shout the FOGHAID. Wherever he is, Diarmid has sworn to answer our hunting call!'

Diarmid heard the hunting call. Grainne begged him not to answer it but he did. He went down to the shores of the loch to meet the Feinne.

Finn gave Diarmid a task. He was to hunt the wild boar. Diarmid hunted the boar and caught up with it. He drew the sword that MacLiobhain had made and killed the boar.

But this was not Finn's revenge against Diarmid. That was to come. Now, Diarmid had a mole on the sole of his foot, and it was known that if the mole was pierced, it would bring death. When Finn told Diarmid to measure the boar he had killed, Diarmid forgot this danger and stepped on one of the boar's bristles. It pierced the mole on his foot and he fell to the ground.

Finn was filled with sorrow as he looked on his fallen friend.

'What can I do to help you, Diarmid?' he said.

'A drink from the palms of Finn's hands will save me,' said Diarmid.

Finn fetched the water, but as he thought about Grainne, he spilled the water. When he thought about Diarmid he was filled with sorrow and carried the water, but by the time he reached him, Diarmid was dead.

Finn and the Feinne walked up the side of the burn till they came to the place where Grainne was, and they went inside. There they saw the two beds set apart and they knew that Diarmid was without guilt. They were all filled with sorrow for all that had happened from beginning to end. And they burned

> Grainne, daughter of the King of Carmaig,
> Who never took a right step,
> Into a heap of grey oak ash.

CHILDE ROWLAND TO THE DARK TOWER CAME

KING Arthur's sons, and their sister, Burd Ellen, were playing at the ball. Childe Rowland kicked it, caught it with his knee, and sent it over the kirk. Burd Ellen went to look for the ball and did not come back. So her eldest brother went to the warlock Merlin.

'Do you know where my sister, Burd Ellen, is?'

'Burd Ellen,' said Merlin, 'was carried away by the fairies. She is now in the King of Elfland's castle.'

'If it is possible to bring her back,' said her brother, 'I'll do it, or die.'

'It is possible,' said Merlin, 'but woe to him who tries it if he is not clear beforehand what to do.'

Burd Ellen's brother made up his mind to try and rescue his sister. Merlin trained him, and he set out. But he failed to carry out Merlin's instructions, and was heard of no more.

The second brother set out in the same way. But he too failed to carry out Merlin's instructions, and was heard of no more.

Childe Rowland, the youngest brother, got the Queen's consent to look for his sister. He took his father's good sword, that never struck in vain, and went to Merlin's cave. The warlock gave him all the necessary instructions for his journey.

'After you have entered Elfland, you must do everything I tell you, or you'll be in trouble,' said Merlin. 'You must strike off the head of everyone you meet with your good sword, whether you want to or not. You'll be offered food and drink, but you must not eat a bite nor drink a drop, no matter how hungry or thirsty you may be, or you'll never again see middle-earth.'

Childe Rowland said that he would be careful to do all that Merlin had told him, then he set out, and travelled on and farther on, till he came to a field where the King of Elfland's horseherd was feeding the King's horses. He knew then that he was in Elfland and that he must be very careful.

'Tell me,' said he, 'where is the King of Elfland's castle?'

'I can't tell you,' said the horseherd, 'but go on a little farther, and you'll come to the cowherd. Maybe he can tell you.'

Then Childe Rowland drew the good sword that never struck in vain and cut off the horseherd's head. He went on a little farther till he met the King of Elfland's cowherd, tending the King's cows.

'Tell me,' said Childe Rowland, 'where is the King of Elfland's castle?'

'I can't tell you,' said the cowherd, 'but go on a little farther, and you'll come to the shepherd. Maybe he can tell you.'

Then Childe Rowland drew the good sword that never struck in vain, and cut off the cowherd's head. He went on a little farther till he met the King of Elfland's shepherd, tending the King's sheep.

'Tell me, where is the King of Elfland's castle?'

'I can't tell you,' said the shepherd, 'but go on a little farther, and you'll come to the goatherd. Maybe he can tell you.'

Then Childe Rowland drew the good sword that never struck in vain, and cut off the shepherd's head. He went on a little farther, till he met the King of Elfland's goatherd, tending the King's goats.

'Tell me, where is the King of Elfland's castle?'

'I can't tell you,' said the goatherd, 'but go on a little farther till you meet the swineherd. Maybe he'll tell you.'

Then Childe Rowland drew the good sword that never struck in vain, and cut off the goatherd's head. And he went on a little farther till he met the King of Elfland's swineherd, feeding the King's swine.

'Tell me, where is the King of Elfland's castle?'

'I can't tell you,' said the swineherd, 'but go on a little farther till you come to the hen-wife. Maybe she'll tell you.'

Then Childe Rowland drew his good sword that never struck in vain, and cut off the swineherd's head. And he went on a little farther till he met the King of Elfland's hen-wife, feeding the King's hens.

'Tell me, where is the King of Elfland's castle?'

'Go on a little farther,' said the hen-wife, 'till you come to a round green hill surrounded by rings from the bottom to the top. Go round it three times widdershins, and every time say, 'Open, door! Open, door! and let me come in!' The third time, the door will open, and you may go in.'

Then Childe Rowland drew the good sword that never struck in vain, and cut off the hen-wife's head.

He went three times widdershins round the green hill, crying, 'Open, door! Open, door! and let me come in!' The third time, the door opened, and he went in. The door closed behind him.

He went through a long passage, where the air was warm. There were neither windows nor candles, and the half-light came from the walls and the ceiling.

He came to two wide and high folding doors, standing ajar. He entered a great hall, rich and brilliant, extending the whole length and height of the hill. From the centre of the ceiling was hung, by a gold chain, an immense lamp of one hollow translucent pearl, in the centre of which was suspended a great carbuncle, that by the power of magic, turned round and shed over the hall a clear and gentle light, like the setting sun.

At the farther end of the hall, under a canopy and seated on a sofa of velvet and silk and gold, combing her yellow hair with a silver comb, sat his sister, Burd Ellen.

Under the power of a magic she could not resist, Burd Ellen brought him a bowl of bread and milk. But he remembered Merlin's warnings.

'I will neither taste nor touch food nor drink, till I have set you free,' said Childe Rowland to his sister.

At that moment, the folding doors opened, and the King of Elfland came in, with

> 'Fe, fi, fo and fum!
> I smell the blood of a Christian man!
> Be he dead, be he living, with my brand
> I'll clash his brains from his brain-pan!'

'Strike then, Bogle, if you dare!' said Childe Rowland. He drew his good sword that never struck in vain.

In the fight that followed, the King of Elfland was struck to the ground. Childe Rowland spared him, but the King of Elfland had to give him back his sister, Burd Ellen, and his two brothers who lay in a trance in a corner of the hall. The King of Elfland brought a small crystal phial holding a bright red liquid. With it he anointed the lips, nostrils, eyelids, ears and finger tips of the two young men, who at once woke up, and the four of them returned home.

CUCHULAINN AND THE TWO GIANTS

ONCE upon a time there was a King in Scotland whose name was Cumhal. He had a great dog that used to watch the herd. When the cattle were sent out, the dog would lead them to good grass. The dog would herd them there for a day, and in the evening would bring them home.

A man and his wife lived near the King's house, and they had one son. Every evening they sent their son on errands to the King's house.

One evening the boy was on his way there. He had a ball and a stick, and was playing shinty on the way. The King's dog met him and began to play with the ball, lifting it in his mouth and running with it.

The boy struck the ball in the dog's mouth, drove it down the dog's throat and choked him. After that the boy had to keep the King's cattle instead of the dog. He drove the cattle to grass in the morning, herded them all day and brought them home in the evening.

So he was called Cuchulainn, which means Cumhal's dog.

One day Cuchulainn was driving the cattle when he saw a giant so big he could see the sky between his legs. The giant came toward him, driving a great ox. The two great horns on the ox had their points backward instead of forward.

'I'm going to sleep here,' said the giant. 'If you see another giant coming, wake me. I'll not be easily wakened.'

'What's the best way to waken you?' said Cuchulainn.

'Take the biggest stone you can find,' said the giant, 'and strike me on the chest. That'll waken me!'

The giant lay and slept. He hadn't slept long when Cuchulainn saw another giant coming. He was so big he could see the sky between his legs.

Cuchulainn tried to waken the first giant, but waken him he could not. At last he lifted a large stone, and struck the giant on the chest. The giant woke up.

'Is there another giant coming?' said he.

'There he comes!' said Cuchulainn, pointing.

'Hi, Crumple Toes, you've stolen my ox!' said the other giant.

'I didn't steal it, Shamble Shanks,' said the first giant.

Shamble Shanks seized one horn of the ox, and Crumple Toes the other. Shamble Shanks broke the horn off at the bone. He threw it away and it fell foremost into the earth.

He seized the head of the ox, and the two giants hauled. They tore the ox apart, through the middle to the root of the tail. Then they began to wrestle.

Cuchulainn started to cut steps up the back of the second giant's leg, to make a stair. Shamble Shanks felt something stinging the back of his leg, so he put his hand down and threw Cuchulainn away.

Cuchulainn went feet first into the ox's horn, and could not climb out. Crumple Toes seized his chance, knocked Shamble Shanks down, and killed him. He looked about for Cuchulainn, but could not see him.

'Where are you, my little hero?' said he.

'I'm here in the horn,' said Cuchulainn.

The giant tried to take him out, but he could not put his hand far enough down. At last he straddled his legs, drove his hand into the horn, got hold of Cuchulainn between his two fingers, and brought him up.

Cuchulainn went home with the cattle at the going down of the sun.

Daughter of the King under the Waves

The Feinne were together on a mountainside. It was a wild night, with pouring rain and snow falling from the north. About midnight, there was a knock at Finn's door. When Finn opened the door he saw a weird woman with long hair down to her heels.

'Let me in out of the storm!' she cried.

'Strange, ugly creature,' said Finn, 'with hair down to your heels. How can you ask *me* to let you in?'

She went away from his door and screamed. She went to Ossian's door, and asked for shelter.

'Strange, ugly creature,' said Ossian, 'with hair down to your heels. How can you ask *me* to let you in?'

She went away from his door and screamed. Then she went to Diarmid's door, and asked for shelter.

'Strange, ugly creature,' said Diarmid, 'with hair down to your heels. But come in!' She came in out of the storm.

'Oh, Diarmid,' she said, 'for seven years I have been wandering over ocean and sea, and in all that time I have not passed a night indoors, till tonight. Let me come in to the warm fire!'

'Come in!' said Diarmid, but when she came in, she was so hideous some people began to leave the room.

'Go to the other side of the fire,' said Diarmid, 'and let the creature warm herself.'

They went to the other side of the fire, to make room for her, but she had not been long by the fire before she tried to creep under Diarmid's blanket.

'You are growing too bold,' said Diarmid. 'First you come in out of the storm, then you warm yourself by the fire. Now you want to come under my blanket, but come!'

She crept under his blanket, but he folded it in the middle to separate them. She had not been long there, till he gave a sudden start and stared at her. He saw the finest woman that ever was, from the beginning of the world to the end of the world. He shouted to the others to come over to his bed.

'Isn't she the most beautiful woman man ever saw?' he asked them.

'She is the most beautiful woman man ever saw,' they said, but Finn and Ossian were jealous of Diarmid, and angry that they had not welcomed the beautiful lady when she first arrived. Now she was asleep, and did not know they were looking at her. Diarmid let her sleep on, and did not wake her. But shortly after she awoke.

'Are you awake, Diarmid?' she asked.

'I am awake,' said Diarmid.

'If you had the finest castle you ever saw,' she said, 'where would you like it to be?'

'If I had my choice,' said Diarmid, 'it would be on this mountain.' They fell asleep again.

Early in the morning, about dawn, a man mounted his horse and, on a hill, saw a castle where no castle had been before. He rubbed his eyes and looked again. The castle was still there. He went back to his house and said nothing. Another man went out, shortly afterwards, saw the castle, although he knew there had been no castle there. He too went back to his house and said nothing. When the day was brighter, two men went out and saw the castle, and when each man knew that the other man saw the castle where no castle should be, they both came back to tell the others.

'Get up, Diarmid!' said the beautiful lady, sitting up in bed. 'Go up to your castle, and don't lie there all morning!'

'If there is a castle I can go to,' said Diarmid, half asleep.

'Look outside, and see if there's a castle there!' said she. He went to the door, and looked out. He looked at the castle, and came back to the lady.

'I'll go up to the castle,' he said, 'if you'll go with me.'

'I'll do that, Diarmid, but don't tell me three times how you found me.'

'I'll never say to you how I found you,' said Diarmid. Both of them went to the castle, and it was very beautiful. There were maidservants and manservants and food on the table. Diarmid was most interested in a greyhound bitch and her three pups. He spent three days with the lady in the castle.

'You are unhappy,' said the lady at the end of the three days, 'because you are not with the rest of the Feinne. Go back to them during the day, but come back at night. Food and drink will always be ready for your return.'

'Who will take care of the greyhound bitch and her three pups?' said Diarmid.

'What is there to fear?' she said. So he returned that day to the Feinne, but though they welcomed him, Finn, his mother's brother, and Ossian were very jealous of Diarmid. The woman had come first to them, and they had turned their backs. However, they were interested in the greyhound bitch and her three pups when Diarmid praised them, while describing his new castle.

After Diarmid had gone, the lady left the castle for a short walk. Soon she saw someone approaching the castle very quickly. She waited for him, and it was Finn. She greeted him, and he caught her by the hand.

'You are not angry with me?' said Finn.

'Not at all!' said the lady. 'Come into the castle for a drink!'

'I'll come if you give me what I ask,' said Finn.

'What is it you want?' said the lady.

'One of the pups of the greyhound bitch,' said Finn.

'Oh, that is not much to ask,' said the lady. 'Take the pup you like best!' So Finn chose the most promising pup, and went away.

Diarmid came at the opening of the night. The greyhound met him outside the castle gate, and howled once. The lady told him about Finn and how she had given him one of the pups. Diarmid was annoyed, remembering how Finn had turned his back on the lady, when she first asked for shelter, how he had seen Finn's jealousy, but he was most angry that Finn should come to his castle when he was not at home, and take away one of his dogs.

'If you had remembered how I gave you shelter when you came in from the storm, with your hair down to your heels, you would not have given the pup to Finn who turned his back on you.'

'What did I ask you not to do? This is the first of three times.'

'I am sorry,' said Diarmid.

'I forgive you this first time,' said the lady. They went into the castle together for food and drink, and Diarmid slept in the castle that night. Next morning he returned to the Feinne.

Ossian, who had admired the pup Finn had brought home, came to the castle and asked the lady for a pup, which she gave him. When Diarmid came home to his castle at the opening of the night, the greyhound bitch met him at the gate and howled twice. Although the lady was beside him, Diarmid spoke to the bitch.

'They've taken another pup from you, my lass. But if she had remembered how I gave her shelter, after Ossian had turned his back on her, with her hair down to her heels, she would not have given the pup to Ossian.'

'This is the second of three times you have said that.'

'I am sorry,' said Diarmid.

'I forgive you this second time,' said the lady. They went into the castle hand in hand for food and drink, and Diarmid slept in the castle that night. Next morning he returned to the Feinne. Next day the third and last pup was taken away, and when Diarmid returned to the castle the greyhound bitch howled three times when she saw him. Although the lady was standing near, Diarmid spoke to the bitch.

'Yes, my lass, you are without any family. If she had remembered how I gave her shelter when she came in from the storm, with her hair down to her heels, she would not have given your third pup away.'

'This is the last of three times,' said the lady sadly.

'I am sorry,' said Diarmid. He slept in the castle that night and, in the morning, woke up on the hillside, in a mossy hollow. He looked round but his castle had vanished. He could not find one stone of it. He decided to look for the lady.

He began to walk across the country. He saw neither house by day nor fire by night. He came on the dead body of the greyhound bitch, lifted her by the tail, and slung her over his shoulder. He loved her so much he could not part from her. He saw a herd on the hillside above him.

'Have you seen a woman, today or yesterday, passing this way?' asked Diarmid.

'I saw a woman early yesterday morning, walking fast,' said the herd.

'Which way was she going?' said Diarmid.

'She went down the headland to the shore, and I did not see her after that.'

Diarmid took the same road till he could go no further. He saw a ship. Using his spear as a vaulting pole, he jumped to the ship, and then to the opposite shore. He lay down on the side of a hill, and went to sleep. When he awoke the ship was gone. He had not long sat on a little hill, when he saw a man rowing a boat in his direction. He went down to the boat, put the greyhound in, and jumped after it. The boat went over the sea, and then under the sea to a land where he could walk. He had gone only a short distance, when he saw a clot of blood on the ground. He lifted it, wrapped it in a handkerchief, and put it in his pouch. He found two more clots of blood, wrapped them up, and put them with the other one. He found only three.

Shortly after, he saw a woman who looked crazy, who was gathering rushes. He asked her what news she had.

'The daughter of the King under the Waves has come home,' said the woman. 'She has been seven years under a spell, and she is ill. The doctors have come to cure her, but none of them know how to do it. A bed of rushes is what she finds most comfortable.'

'I would be very much in your debt, if you could take me where the Princess is.'

'I'll see to that,' said the woman. 'I'll put you into a sheaf of rushes, with rushes under you and over you, and I'll carry you on my back.'

'You couldn't do that. I am too heavy,' said Diarmid.

'Leave that to me!' said the woman. She put Diarmid into a bundle of rushes and slung him on her back. When she reached the Princess's room, she laid the bundle down.

'Oh, hurry up!' said the daughter of the King under the Waves. Diarmid came out of the bundle, and seized the Princess by the hands. They were delighted to meet again.

'Three parts of my illness are gone, but I am still not well. Every time I thought of you on my way here, I lost blood from my heart.'

'I have three clots of your heart's blood in my pouch. Take them in a drink, and you will be well again,' said Diarmid.

'I will not take them,' said the Princess. 'There is one thing missing, which I shall never find in the world.'

'What is that?' asked Diarmid. 'If it's on the surface of the world, I'll find it. Tell me what it is!'

'What I need is three draughts from the cup of the King of the Plain of Wonder.'

'Is he far from here?' said Diarmid.

'He is near my father,' said the Princess, 'but there is a small river before you get there, and a sailing ship with the wind behind her would take a day and a year to cross it.'

Diarmid followed her directions, and reached the small river. He spent a long time walking along the river, and decided that the Princess was right. It could not be crossed. Just as he thought this, he saw a little red man standing in the middle of the river.

'What would you give a man who would help you? Come here, and put your foot on my palm!' said the little red man.

Diarmid put his foot on the little man's palm, and reached the other side.

'I'll come with you to King Mag, whose cup you are looking for,' said the little red man. Outside the palace of the King of the Plain of Wonder, Diarmid shouted for the cup to be sent out, or an army. The King sent out an army of twice four hundred men, and in two hours Diarmid had killed them all.

He shouted again for the cup, or for battle. They sent out twice eight hundred men, and in three hours Diarmid had killed them all.

He shouted again for the cup, or for battle, and they sent out twice nine hundred heroes, and in four hours Diarmid left no man of them alive.

'Where has this man come from?' said the King. 'He has brought my kingdom to ruin. If it is this hero's pleasure, let him tell me where he comes from!'

'It is this hero's pleasure,' shouted Diarmid. 'I am one of the Feinne. I am Diarmid.'

'Why didn't you send a message to say who you were?' said King Mag. 'I would not have spent my realm on you, for you would have killed every one of my men. This was written in the books of prophecy, seven years before you were born. What do you want?'

'The cup of healing from your own hand,' said Diarmid, and the King of the Plain of Wonder gave him the cup, and offered him a ship. But Diarmid said he had a ferry of his own, and departed with the cup. He suddenly realised that he had forgotten the little red man, and had possibly offended him. But the little man again lifted him over the river.

'I know that you are going to cure the daughter of the King under the Waves. She is the girl you love best in the world. You will go to a well you will find in that direction. By the side of the well you will find a bottle. Fill the bottle with water from the well and take it with you. When you have reached the Princess's room, you will put some water in the cup, and a clot of blood in the water, which she will drink. You will do this a second time, and a third time, and she will be well. But when that happens she will be the girl you love least in all the world.

'I am the messenger of the other world. I helped you because your heart is warm to do good to someone else. You will take no reward of gold or silver from the King under the Waves, but the King will send a ship to take you where you came from.'

Diarmid did everything the little red man had said. He cured the Princess with the three clots of blood in the water in the cup given him by the King of the Plain of Wonder. But he lost his love for the Princess. He refused the King's reward for curing the Princess, and he refused to marry the Princess. All he took was a ship to carry him home to the Feinne, who were very pleased that he had returned.

Glossary

AIN own

ALOOR! alas! alack! (Orkney)

ASSIPATTLE one who is loath to leave the fireside to do any work (Orkney)

BAIRN child

BANE bone

BANNOCK oatcake

BARQUE three-masted sailing ship

BEN (1) mountain; (2) the 'front room' of a *but and ben*, a two-roomed cottage

BICKER bowl or dish

BIDE dwell

BOGLE hobgoblin

BONNACH STONE a stone, usually round, on which bannocks were baked before a fire

BRAE hillside

BRAW handsome, beautiful

BREE water in which food has been cooked or preserved

BROSE oatmeal or peasemeal mixed with boiling water

BUDDO (a term of endearment)

BURD (poetic) woman or lady

BURN stream

BUT kitchen or outer room

BYRE cow-house

CANNILY cautiously

CARLE man

CARLIN an old woman

CLEW a ball of yarn

CLOGGIRS goose-grass

COG, COGIE a wooden vessel for milk etc.

COLLOP portion

CORRIE hollow on a mountain side

CREEL basket

CROFT small piece of land adjoining a house

DEIL devil

DIRK dagger

DOO dove, pigeon

ETIN a giant

FIN-FOLK mythical sea-folk

FULLING-WATER water in which cloth is fulled (milled) and cleansed with soap and fuller's earth

GIEN given

GILLIE man-servant, boy

GIRNAL chest for meal, salt etc.

GLOAMING twilight

GRUAGACH a kind of brownie with long hair and beard

HALY WATTER holy water

HECKLE a comb for dressing flax and hemp

HILDA-LAND Fairy-land

HOODIE carrion crow

HYN-HALLOW Holy Island, between Rousay and Orkney mainland

ILKA each

INARY a woman's name

KITCHEN (vb) to season, give a relish to food

KNOCKING STONE stone-mortar, or flat stone

KNOWE knoll, small hill

KYE cattle

LAIRD squire

LAMMAS the beginning of August

LAP-BOARD a board laid across the lap for working on used by tailors, etc.

MALISON curse

MIDDEN dunghill

MIND remember

MIXTER-MAXTER confused, jumbled

MOOR-STONE a granite standing stone

ODIN STONE a stone sacred to the Norse god Odin; there is one in Shapinsay

PARLEY BOAT a small boat of a particular rig

PEAT-HAG a hole from which peat has been cut; a heap of peat

PEERIE small

ST CRISPIN saint of shoemakers

SASSENACH Saxon, foreigner

SELKIE seal

SHINTY game played with stick and ball in the Highlands

SKIRL a shrill cry

SMIDDY smithy, smith's workshop

SPEY-WIFE fortune-teller

SPEIR ask, enquire

SPORRAN purse

STANE stone

STRATH a wide valley

THRAFT OR FORETHRAFT front rowing seat across (athwart) a boat

TOCHER dowry

URUISG water hobgoblin

WARLOCK wizard

WAULKING treading cloth

WHIN gorse

WHUPPITY STOORIE a brownie

WIDDERSHINS anti-clockwise

WITHIES willow branches

YILL ale

STORY SOURCES

THE WELL AT THE WORLD'S END *Popular Tales of the West Highlands,* orally collected with a translation by J. F. Campbell (3 vols., Alexander Gardner, Paisley and London, 1890-93), II, xxxiii, p. 140.

RASHIE COAT *Popular Rhymes of Scotland,* collected from tradition by Robert Chambers (2nd ed., Chambers, Edinburgh and London, 1870), p. 66.

PRINCE IAIN 'Mac Iain Direach' in Campbell, II, xlvi, p. 344.

THE FLEA AND THE LOUSE *County Folklore,* III, printed extract no. 5 (Orkney and Shetland Islands), collected by G. F. Black (Folklore Society Publications 49, London, 1903, reprinted 1967), p, 226.

WHUPPITY STOORIE Chambers, p. 72.

THE FAIRY-WIFE AND THE COOKING-POT Campbell, II, xxvi, p. 52.

THE MAIDEN FAIR AND THE FOUNTAIN FAIRY 'The Paddo' in Chambers, p. 57.

THE TALE OF THE SOLDIER Campbell, II, xlii, p. 290.

THE FECKLESS ONES Campbell, II, xlviii, p. 388.

PIPPETY PEW 'The Milk-White Doo' in Chambers, p. 49.

THE BLACK BULL OF NORROWAY Chambers, p. 95.

ROBIN REIDBREIST AND THE WRAN Oral source: from the recitation of Mrs Begg, youngest sister of Robert Burns. She believed her brother made it.

THE BATTLE OF THE BIRDS Campbell, I, ii, p.25.

THE GOOD HOUSEWIFE *Waifs and Strays of Celtic Tradition, Argyllshire series*, edited by Lord Archibald Campbell (5 vols., David Nutt, London, 1889-95); V, *Clan Traditional and Popular Tales*, collected from oral sources by the Rev. J. G. Campbell, p. 83.

THE KING OF LOCHLIN'S THREE DAUGHTERS Campbell, I, xvi, p. 344.

THE WIFE AND HER BUSH OF BERRIES Chambers, p.57.

BROWNIE THE COW Oral source.

HOW THE COCK GOT THE BETTER OF HER FOX Campbell, III, lxiii, p. 105.

THE SMITH AND THE FAIRIES Campbell, II, xxvill, p. 57.

THE GAEL AND THE LONDON BAILLIE'S DAUGHTER Campbell, I, xvii, p. 289.

THE WEE BANNOCK Chambers, p. 82.

THE BROWN BEAR OF THE GREEN GLEN Campbell, I, ix, p. 168.

FATHER WREN AND HIS TWELVE SONS *Waifs and Strays*, V, p. 120.

MALLY WHUPPIE Campbell, I, xvii, p, 259.

THE WHITE PET Campbell, I, xl, p. 199

BIG FOX AND LITTLE FOX Oral source.

THE TALE OF THE HOODIE Campbell, I, iii, p. 64.

THE STOOR WORM W. Traill Dennison in *Scottish Antiquary*, V (1891), p. 130.

THE MERMAID 'The Sea Maiden' in Campbell, I, iv, p. 72.

THE WINNING OF HYN-HALLOW W. Traill Dennison in *Scottish Antiquary*, VII (1892), p. 117.

THE GOODMAN OF WASTNESS W. Traill Dennison in *ibid.*, p. 173,

TAM SCOTT AND THE FIN-MAN W. Traill Dennison in *op. cit.*, VIII (1893), p. 51.

FARQUHAR THE HEALER Campbell, II, xlvii, p. 377.

JOHNNIE CROY AND THE MERMAID W. Traill Dennison in *Scottish Antiquary*, VI (1892), p. 118.

THE WIDOW'S SON Campbell, II, xliv, p. 307.

OSCAR AND THE GIANT Campbell, I, lxxx, p. 311

FINN AND THE YOUNG HERO'S CHILDREN *Waifs and Strays of Celtic Tradition*, III: *Folk and Hero Tales*, edited, translated and annotated by the Rev. J. MacDougall, p. 1.

FINN AND THE GREY DOG *ibid.*, p. 17.

FINN IN THE HOUSE OF THE YELLOW FIELD *ibid.*, p. 56.

GREEN KIRTLE 'The Fair Gruagach' in Campbell, II, li, p. 424.

THE LAST OF THE PICTS Chambers, p. 80.

MURCHAG AND MIONACHAG Campbell, I, viii, p. 161.

PEERIE FOOL *County Folklore*, III, p. 222

THE HEN Campbell, III, lxiv, p. 106.

THE YOUNG KING 'The Young King of Easaidh Ruadh' in Campbell, I, i, p. 1.

THE RED ETIN Chambers, p. 87.

THE EAGLE AND THE WREN *Waifs and Strays*, V, p. 120.

IAIN THE SOLDIER'S SON Campbell, III, i, p. 9.

THE LEGEND OF LOCH MAREE *Waifs and Strays*, V, p. 74.

DIARMID AND GRAINNE Campbell, III, lx, p. 49.

CHILDE ROWLAND TO THE DARK TOWER CAME *Illustrations of Northern Antiquities*, with contributions from R. Jamieson, H. Weber, and Sir Walter Scott (James Ballantyne, Edinburgh, 1814), p. 398.

CUCHULAINN AND THE TWO GIANTS Oral source.

DAUGHTER OF THE KING UNDER THE WAVES Campbell, III, lxxxvi, p. 421.

INDEX